HEART OF THE HEALER

PART 2

Anatomy of Deception

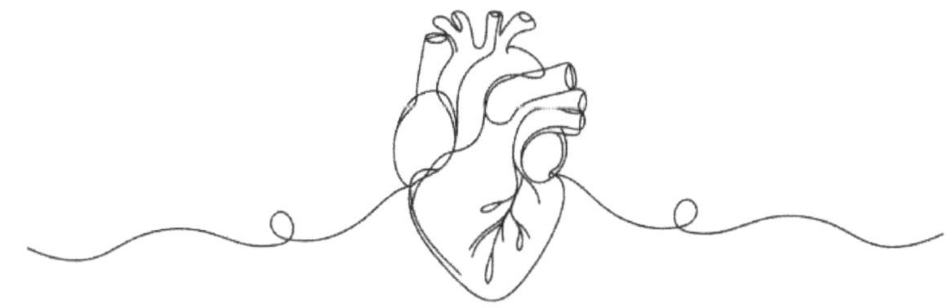

By

MJ Politis, PHD., D.V.M

276 5th Avenue Suite 704 #944
New York, NY 10001

ISBN (978-1-80704-265-3) Paperback

ISBN (978-1-80704-266-0) Hardback

ISBN (978-1-80704-264-6) eBook

Cover Design by Woodbridge Publishers.

Find out more about our upcoming releases and authors at
www.woodbridgepublishers.com and sign up for our
newsletter to stay updated!

Dedicated to you…the reader. With appreciation for your being open to this offering. And all those I have known who made this offering possible.

TABLE OF CONTENTS

I

The gravestone inscribed featured one line bolder than the name or the faith of the departed. "The only Real rest is in motion Itself."

"Fly in peace, John Baldino," the mourner said softly, his voice muffled by the winter wind that echoed more silence than gust, more future than past. "See you later, Doc." He kept a watchful eye out for the procession behind him. Such consisted of 'commoners' who were there for more legitimate purposes.

Jack caught a glimpse of himself in the reflection on the freshly polished stone. "John, are you still in there?" he said. "I know the ER surgeon after the 'accident' that killed me. He did a good job on my face, or, more accurately, my nose, but I'm still uncomfortable with it. By accident or 'coincidence,' I may look like this 'Jack McFarland' guy on my new driver's license, but even I can see that it's still…me."

The procession approached, closer and closer; they wore black suits to honor death. White shirts and blouses to show off the black. Far more than Jack McFarland expected came to mourn the death of the honorable, likable, and even respected medico John Baldino, M.D., Ph.D., his now buried identity. The procession included Baldino's patients, students, nurses, and fellow docs. Then there were the strangers, who didn't look like lawyers but something more insidiously powerful.

"Movie producers," John told himself whimsically. "Or literary agents. My death was the story of the year. I entered a burning building after that terrorist attack and saved ten trapped people, twenty-five according to the News magazines," he pondered, hoping no one was listening to the conversation with himself between his ears. "Who would have thought that a suburban doc with twenty-five years of experience in a Lower Westchester kvetch clinic would spend his last hour on earth stitching up wounds, arteries, and bones with nothing more than an emergency medical bag and a head full of smarts? It would be nice if all of it were true. The plan was to find an accident and be its victim, not its hero. A man who knows too much about life on this side of the rainbow, and Oz, is too dangerous to be allowed to live. John Baldino had to die, but..."

John felt the wind interrupting the dialogue between his mind and soul through the bottom of his kilt. The traditional pattern and length date back to before the Industrial Revolution invaded the Highlands, complemented by a walrus Mustache on his upper lip. "I better keep my mouth shut if I'm going to pull this Scotsman thing off," he thought. "Facejob or no facejob, someone in that crowd is going to see John Baldino's eyes in Jack McFarland's face. Maybe McFarland, the trauma patient who DIDN'T make it, can look into the world of Doctor John Baldino's legacy and not be stared back at. But sometimes, it DOESN'T pay to be too careful. And it was my choice to come here, I think."

The instructions from John's underground contact were explicit. Erica Fisher-Burger, MD, PhD, arranged for John's reconstructive facial surgery, found the accident site, and even ghost-wrote the obituary. John's former fellow resident, friend, and one-time lover knew how organized international terrorism worked and how organized anti-terrorists had to fight it. Only she knew where John's 'superspy even without a cape' brother Vincent was. Only she knew that Vincent was between wars that were not reportable to the standard news outlets. And was not the deceased victim of the one that had just ended. For the moment, all John was told about his brother's whereabouts was that he was on the way to foiling another plot to destroy the world by forces Jack McFarland, Ian Fleming, or even Oliver Stone on a paranoid brand of Ganja could only imagine. The orders as to what John Baldino would do next, as he had risen from the grave or was Jack McFarland, ultimately came from Vincent but reached him through Erica now. A woman who was now also officially dead but very much alive, big A, in John's distant and recent past.

As for the distant past, Erica had been a fellow brilliant-beyond-measure medical student who rose the medical ranks after graduation with John, who, for better or worse, was already married to a woman whom he loved nearly as much as his work. Erica was married to a man who not only loved but understood her. The Platonic relationship between John and Erica ended when 'Don't make me tell you about my undercover work as a Cop' husband was reported missing in action. She faked her own death so she could go underground to find him, disallowing John, for his own good, to follow her into 'the places of change' he was not equipped to handle. Not a day had passed since she kissed John a fond farewell two decades ago, and he hadn't thought of her.

Erica had never lied to John Baldino, in the past or the present...or so it seemed. Her actions, as a live doctor and a nameless anti-terrorist operative, were innovative and heroic.

A few months ago, John had experienced debilitating headaches, tremors, and hallucinations due to, so he was told, a brain tumor that would kill him in a fortnight. The ever-ready workaholic genius doctor-researcher took his first vacation in twenty-five years at an off-season resort. His last act of effective compassion was to write memoirs about the people and patients who made him, rightly or wrongly, the so-called 'brilliant doctor of the mind, body, and soul' others claimed he was. While knowing all along that he had been sheltered from the suffering and death afflicting others, both in his comfortable practice in Westchester County and in 'the places of change and turmoil' overseas. Such places included where his brother Vincent was continuing the family tradition of fighting against evil men and women. On occasion, Vincent asked John to provide medical intel about bioweapons which were supposed to not exist. On other occasions, John was asked to provide his brother, and 'superspy' parents, with antidotes to save the innocent. And, on still other occasions, the Pacifist doctor whose fist punched into only himself and no one else, was asked to provide bioweapons that could 'inactivate' (though not officially kill) the most horrible terrorists and dictators on the planet.

After writing poetic and accurate memoirs about key people in his past, John would go out to his peers to do some fishing at the resort where he was the only occupant. There, he visited the people he wrote about, some from the land of the living and some from the land of the dead, unable to tell the difference. His ability to function deteriorated daily. But with sheer persistence, the anti-military doctor soldiered on to complete writing his last textbook about the human condition as it was and as it should be. From the perspective of an overeducated and over-sheltered doctor who had promoted himself to being a Spiritually awakened 'mister.'

In reality, John did not have a brain tumor but was being given mind-altering drugs by a sophisticated organization of White supremacists who made the Illuminati look like an international chapter of the Elks. Video cameras and hidden mics watched him, as well as the ears of the very single and love-starved landlady of the resort, who were waiting for him to reveal to the 'ghosts' he saw his clandestine biomedical discoveries as well as the whereabouts of his brother, and Erica, made possible by specially formulated medication. Cathy was the prime operative putting 'A-137', a state-beyond-the-art mind-altering and brain-destroying elixir, into John's food and drink, causing John to go mad. The landlady of the off-season resort, who fell in love with him. It was a relationship that was mutual. Till John put all the pieces together and abandoned his 'above all, not harm' policy, he determined to get Cathy to spill the beans about what she and her cohorts were doing, no matter how much harm he had to exert on her.

But Cathy had fled the coup, leaving John with Erica, who came along just in time to give him the antidote to 'A 137'. She invited him to finally join her as an officially dead scientist who knew what science could do for humanity. But John did come out of the experimental cage the terrorists put him in. He could cross the life-death line, conversing with the dead with more ease than those on top of the grass could. And because of his brilliantly artistic rather than logically impersonal medical mind, he found humanistic solutions to biological problems. And be a mighty warrior for Good against the organization known as BITE (Brotherhood of international terrorists elite) and other groups of 'elite' people who wanted to annihilate or enslave other populations of 'insignificant' humans.

John's recollection of discovering Cathy's treasury, exiting his 'above all do not harm' mandate, and Erica's enlisting him into Common Cause was awakened by solid colored sedans screeching their way to the gravesite from all sides. "Feds," John muttered with a Scottish roll to the tongue. "Or worse," he continued in his own Westchester County-altered Bronx diction as one of the G-men and/or hit-men gave him a ten-second stare at the exposed legs under his kilt.

"He likes my legs, I hope," John thought, thankful that the head Fed didn't recognize his face. "At least I hope he's not gay...Hell, I hope I'm not. I haven't been anyone but John Baldino, M.D., Ph.D., for..."

John caught another glance at himself in the reflection of another tombstone, a black laminated slab that served more as a mirror to the mourner than a marker for the deceased. Through the overgrown dark brown mustache on his upper lip, rouge on the sunken cheeks, and rather handsome and shapely bare legs under the wind-blown kilt, there were still wrinkles around the eyes and chin lines that said 'face over fifty.' Yet John's eyes were still that of a child, pure in spirit, not hardened by pain or hardship.

The primary emotion that hit John as the procession approached, then surrounded, his grave was vulnerability. "Maybe it's the clothes," he thought as he felt the emotions, accusations, and threats from everywhere and everyone, even though no one seemed to notice his presence. "Kilts are so...open," he noted with the writer's pen in his head, jotting it down as fast as his eye scanned the group of friends, colleagues, and strangers that seemed like a crowd now.

"We are gathered here to pay tribute to John Baldino, M.D.," the priest pontificated as the ashes of the corpse of an unidentified man, or perhaps a dog, were sprinkled into the ground below. "A friend, physician, healer, and salt of the Earth who many communities will miss. The community of medicine, the community science, and the community he lived in..."

"Where the hell do I live now?" John thought as the eulogy went on in words sincerely written but mechanically delivered. "I'm supposed to be dead now, but I'm supposed to find Erica and then Vincent, then, somehow, save the world from getting destroyed by a Terrorist Organization that knows more about biological weapons than scientists do. And what's worse, they know how to dull the human spirit with drugs, wirelessly transmitted electrical frequencies, and, according to Erica's latest theory, top forty musical melodies and lyrics. It's bad enough that AM radio programmers are killing the collective human soul with sound waves in the form of top-forty hit melodies. Maybe they don't know how devastating the expansive soul 'happy' tunes are, or they are the victims of the poison they inflict on the public. And as for the Internet, who can say what subliminal messages are spreading out there? It's bad enough that kids these days are flatlined into geekdom by computer games or fascinated with inflicting cruelty on their fellow humans with guns, knives, chains, or cleverly designed words put on the computer screen."

"And then there's the ultimate conspiracy...mischief infused into people who should initiate a revolution. Keep people thinking that they're making big, major holes in the

System's Wall by kicking their heels up at the country bar dance floor, or getting drunk on illegal booze or zonked on 'smuggled' drugs, and you have them dead tired and submissive by Monday Morning after a hot weekend of partying...And then there's the--"

"Ego!" a familiar woman spoke softly and assertively from behind, causing John to turn away from his thoughts, agonies, and speculations to its source.

Erica never looked more determined and interesting. Of all the mourners, she wore orange, the color of courage. Underneath the tight jeans and spandex top lay a figure a 22-year-old model would die for. But between the bangs of the platinum blonde wig, eyes that would kill anyone who dared look at them with the wrong reason or motive.

"It's only an egotist that comes to his...or her..own funeral, me lad, Jack," Erica said out of the side of her mouth to John with more of an Irish Brogh than Highland roll to the tongue.

"Or someone who wants to see what I did leave behind," John countered. "I had to see what my old life was all about."

"And..." Erica added, letting John fill in the blanks.

John was struck by something he had never seen in the faces of the people who came to send his soul to a better place. He knew them all too well from his pathologically comfortable, overly sheltered, and highly accomplished life as a biomedical researcher and clinician. "My life experience so far has been...small, I think, Erica," John noted about his now officially ended life. "John Baldino may have been the biggest status symbol for Westchester General Hospital and Columbia Institute of Neurological Research, but his life was small. A plethora of research papers got over-rated, and many patients were cured as much by Mother Nature as by 'Doctor John. Curing people in a small part of the world where nothing really changes. But..." trying to find a cure within the disease, he speculated again. "Doing what you can within your safety zone is a start, right?"

"As long as you keep on moving," Erica countered with a strangely assertive yet clandestine subtext.

"What do you mean by that?" John dared to look into her despite the risks of being looked at himself.

"And what do you mean by that?" the woman of Fire and Warmth slurred out from the side of her mouth. Her gaze was held hostage by the flesh revealed by the wind blowing John's kilt upward. "Black on gray is such bad color coordination, and that Scottish plaid is so...Irish," she noted. "Though I have to admit, from the thighs down, you do look like a very hot lad....or lass." A hidden agenda grew behind her eyes.

"I'm impressed," John sighed, with a Scottish accent that felt convincing, to him at least.

"A man's legs always look more sexy than a woman's after we reach the big 35," Erica noted enviously.

"I thought our relationship was going to be...professional, Erica."

"First, John, I have to know if that surgeon removed some flesh between the legs after he finished rebuilding your schmuck'd up nose and cheeks."

Jack smiled.

"How does it feel not to be the one wearing the pants?" Erica asked with a whimsical smile.

"It's a bitch. No pun intended...But it does feel...different," John noted, then gave voice to, turning his back and gaze from Erica's stare.

"There's gonna be a lot from here on in that feels different, John."

"In what way do you mean....?"

John turned around. As quickly as Erica had appeared, she vanished. In her wake, she left a whiff of perfume that said 'yes' in John's reconstructed nostrils. In his hand, she left a note that said 'Absolutely!'. On the envelope, inserted under his belt, "Place of Change Number One" scribbled in Latin. The colorfully curved cursive handwriting was only understandable to a Pre-Microsoft physician-trained eye. A glance at its contents was even more cryptic, beginning with "Beaver goes to college with Tonto and shares a Tombstone pizza."

"The SouthWest," Baldino surmised.

"Flagstaff, Arizona," echoed from behind him. Was it Erica? Was it the wind? Or was it yet another case of crossing the life-death line, a warning from a ghost beckoning, as translated into 'still in human body form' talk, "All that enter here, lose all fear, or pay the consequences!"

II

"Apaches Dying of Newly Discovered Peyote," the National Inquirer headline read. "Southwest Epidemic: Contagious Killer Carcinogen on the White Mountain Indian Reservation," the Star reported. "Arab Terrorist Agents Behind Resurgence of Ancient Apache Suicide Cult," the Post boasted on its headlines.

The readers in New York, Chicago, and even the Flagstaff Shopping Mall believed the stories about what was decimating the most isolated and belligerent band of 'Injuns' North of the Rio Grande, mis-spellings and all. But the eagle overlooking the desert high country knew better. So did the Apaches in the 16,000-acre track of arid hills known now as "Rez Zero." The dead knew even more but could say nothing except to the eagle.

The losses in the last three months were staggering. One in ten Apache dead, another two dying on this 'fine day, the rest asking the most painful question of all--- "Why?"

The symbol of American freedom and Apache defiance watched from his perch in the knarled pines of the high country, passing up his chance to get easy prey in the early morning. He would eat a different kind of meal today---grief.

Today's burial was for a boy, barely nine years old. His muscles had been reduced to empty sacs that lay over brittle bones. His face looked ancient, wrinkled, and burned. His hair was gone, save for a few strands of three-feet mane spared from the chemotherapy. Jay's grandfather, Kurtis

Thundercloud, was determined not to let the boy die at the hands of the doctors in Flagstaff, even if the healers with the bottled medicines and white coats were well-meaning. The octogenarian never trusted the White men, particularly when they had good intentions. The cost for implementing any well-intended 'deal' by 20th or 21st-century cowboys would always be paid by the Indians.

Kurtis was only a boy when the Apache Nation was allowed to return West after their thirty-year imprisonment in Florida and Alabama. Geronimo knew that fighting the White man was futile. Eleven Apache against a quarter of the US Army was not good odds. But the battles of the 1880s were waged for the generations to come. "Someone will remember," the aging contemporary Geronimo assured the then-young Kurtis. "And someone will do something to make it better than it ever was. The Eagle Clan is watching over our Mountains for us," the old Chief had related to the young Kurtis, in secret, hoping that those the Apaches thought dead were still holding up in the Arizona hills. And that they were keeping the traditions alive and their identity hidden. So many had lost their lives when they came out in the open. As for the original Geronimo, he died drunk as a lower-rank Reservation Policeman under White jurisdiction in Oklahoma.

Old, well beyond his years, Kurtis didn't look into mirrors much these days, no matter how much Native buckskin and moccasins were made available by the resurgence of the American Indian Movement that made him look handsome to White and Indian standards. But, he saw too much Geronimo in his aging eyes whenever his stare was held hostage in a reflective surface these days. He knew well that if the First Nations' movement for basic survival wasn't going forward fast enough, it was going backward.

The eagle was honored that one of his feathers was tied into the remaining strands of hair still left on young Jay's head, Kurtis' last surviving grandson. The bird hoped that the deer whose hides provided the buckskin shirt and leggings for the still somehow living older man and the tragically dead young boy felt the same way from its new home in the afterlife. The Eagle clan had been in these hills for as long as the eagle's ancestors had. Lineage was lineage, and family was family.

Jay's family was the entire tribe, something expected of people with the same word for relative and friend. After losing a loved one, chopping off a lock of hair and sometimes a finger was custom. Not one of the mourners had a full complement of uncut topknot and ten unmutilated digits. Still, they paid their respects with an offering of flesh, hair, or something precious that was more practically spared--- turquoise rocks, beaded necklaces, and autographed Babe Ruth baseballs.

Jay was barely nine when he died. He had been the kind of kid who wouldn't turn to booze, cocaine, or cruelty when he reached teenhood. Suicide came as a thought to him three times a day but had never been an option to follow through with, somehow. So many of Jay's brethren at other reservations did succumb to dope, firewater, and cruelty, as did most of the Indians who tried to make a go of it in town.

Of course, there were 'successful experiments.' Several Apaches entered White society as lawyers, bankers, graphic artists, and businesspeople. However, few of Geronimo's ancestors became doctors, and fewer became writers. Kurtis Thundercloud wanted someone in the tribe to be a doctor and a writer. While he was alive, Jay seemed to be that special child who would become that combination of skills and perspectives. But, maybe there would be someone else to fill that critical role, a bridge between the Arts and Science that would connect Whites and people whose skin was not of that hue. If it were still alive, the Great Spirit would provide a physician-poet somehow. Maybe he wouldn't have an Indian skin, but he would have an Indian heart.

The eagle watched again and listened. The drumbeat and prayer chants echoed against the canyon walls protecting this ancient burial ground, where no white man had ever stepped. Not even legendary Indian Scout Tom Horn knew about this place where the rocks had faces easily seen by those with open eyes. The Shaman Kurtis leading the chant knew that this was where the birthplace of his people was. The stories about the Ten Messengers and their descendants were known and sung but never spoken. In Canyon Rock, it was here where some of Sitting Bull's Ghost Dancers flourished after the buffalo were gone. They also sought refuge after their brethren were wiped out in Montana, Wyoming and the Dakotas. Finally, here, the Apache could bury their dead in peace and privacy.

The eagle knew this, as did the other animals of the desert. No bird of prey or passion ate of the flesh consecrated here. But one kind of bird ignored this rule.

A crop duster swooped overhead. Kurtis ceased chanting and yelled up to the yellow-green vulture in the sky. "Get away, demon!!! Get away!!!" he screamed from the top of his lungs. They were now parched and fragile sacs due to what was happening at stage one of what was becoming to be known as MID, Mad Indian Disease. Stage two caused stereotypical hallucinations. Even in empty skies, the victims of MID saw planes looking like prehistoric vultures with four eyes and eight pairs of wings. The hallucinations would continue, forcing the fleeing victims of MID to see them land on the backs of white buffalo, which turned into locomotives that went off the track and kept chasing them. Such was in keeping with the stories passed around the campfires and the reported visions seen by every Apache in the psyche or chemo ward. No matter how fast you tried to run or drive away from them, the long-horned, yellow-green tanklike buffalos gored you in the chest, head, and eyes. Stage three of MID 'gifted' the afflicted with 'the shakes.' Grand mal seizures of a special nature. The kind that left you shaking AND conscious. Stage four was death, and an autopsy report that typically read "association cortex tumor of astroglial nature, with octagonal inclusions connecting microfilaments."

Kurtis' hand shook as he lifted his rifle and aimed it at the crop duster above him. "The vulture will not get me like the mechanical buffaloes got my grandson!" he vowed. "They will not get anyone else!!!"

A hand swiped across Kurtis' shriveled and shaking arm, the shot missing its mark by miles instead of meters. "They'll find us here if you shoot at them now," Jake Cuthand related to Kurtis 'Old Man' Thundercloud.

"If you fight a war halfway, you will always lose it!" Thundercloud admonished Cuthand as the shots ricocheted against the rocks, making an even louder sound than the original bullet. The Old Shamen felt weak, cold, out of breath, and fearful behind his fiery eyes.

Cuthand knew that Thundercloud was right. He put a blanket over the older man's now shriveled shoulders and gave him one of the ancient herbal agents that, sometimes, made stage 3 of the disease easier to deal with.

Cuthand's mental focus shifted to his youth. His 'voluntary' enlistment in the US Army decades ago, after the judge in town gave him a choice between 15 years in jail for being an 'ecological ethnic terrorist' or 2 years in uniform. A tour of reluctant duty overseas to maintain 'American economic interests and democratic Christian values' abroad should have taught Cuthand the price of fighting the enemy from a defensive-only position. But he had been forced into a defensive war against the Whites as an American Indian Movement activist upon returning home. It was a movement he was still trying to fight for as the most armed and weapon-smart member of the ancient Eagle Clan.

"We must take care of ourselves and preserve our culture," Cuthand reminded Thundercloud. "If even one of us survives and remembers, we all survive. Didn't Geronimo say that?"

Kurtis knew that the harder you fought the Mad Indian Disease, the faster and harder it hit you, most probably because of a release of norepinephrine from the locus trillions and the adrenals. Still, he had to do SOMETHING as the crop duster approached again for another look at the funeral procession below or to make another deposit of what some still believed was urine and feces from the pilot's piss bottle.

The older man snatched a bow with his trembling right hand, inserted an arrow guided by eagle feathers, then pulled it back with all his strength and sent the arrow upward. He said a prayer as it made its way towards the plane. A cloud came between the earth and the plane.

"It is a good day to die!" Thundercloud proclaimed to his people. "I will be joining you soon, my brother," he related to Jay's two-day-dead corpse and the soul still a few hours away from leaving it.

The arrow hit its mark, sending the humming left propeller into a loud buzz, then a febrile crackle. But the plane emerged from the other side of the cloud. The pilot seemed to have gained control of the other propeller, then headed North, the direction from which the cropdusters were coming that week. This time, the canisters that typically dropped yellow smoke on the ground below were ablaze, bursting into a blue and red cloud that blanketed the ground.

"No good deed goes unpunished," Jake Cuthand smiled proudly as the injured plane lost altitude, smashing into a landing beyond the mountains that owned the Apaches. "I look forward to our punishment--no, next challenge," Cuthand continued. That challenge lay ahead of Jake, literally. His life assignment now was saving the remaining White Mountain Apache and their way of life. As a member of the Eagle Clan, he had no choice. Getting to the bottom of what was causing the deaths of anyone who stayed on the Rez or left was hard enough. The 'why' would be an even more agonizing answer, probably involving a 'who.'

That 'who' materialized within what seemed like minutes. A military convoy armed with machine guns, decontamination suits, and orders from the Communicable Disease Agency had somehow found its way through the booby traps set by Cuthand. And somehow, it found its way to this, thus far anyway, unknown to any paleface burial ground.

Every Indian with a non-shaking, or intact, hand grabbed a gun, knife, or shovel for what would be a last stand. Thundercloud, having emerged victoriously from this bout of stage 3, cracked a warm, somber smile, returning to 'reality.' "Those pale-faced demons came here to honor the dead?" Thundercloud said whimsically to Cuthand.

"They ARE the dead," Cuthand related to Thundercloud as he saw the Masked Men emerge from the trucks. They bore masks that hid faces, eyes, and identity, particularly the soldiers in contamination suits carrying body bags and medical supplies.

"We are here to collect the bodies of the following individuals," Major Wentworth delivered in a very English accent from behind American Army I.D. He gave Jake the names of those he was assigned to bring to the hospital and the recently expanded medical research facility in town.

"I don't recognize any of the names on this list," Cuthand related.

"The English OR Apache names, Mister Cuthand?" Wentworth inquired.

"That's Captain Cuthand to you, Major."

"Dishonorably discharged for cowardness and inefficiency in the line of fire!" Wentworth blasted out loud enough for all to hear.

"Compassion turned into political convenience. I saved innocent non-American non-Christian kids from being massacred by American bullets in my tour of involuntary duty to bring YOUR brand of free-market American capitalism to people who didn't want or need it," Jake countered to whoever would believe him. "Or at least I tried to..."

"Your commanding officer was Black. And the kids were saved by Jesus and are working for us now," Wentworth shot into Cuthand's face.

Maybe it was true, perhaps it wasn't. For Cuthand, this stand-off with Wentworth and his legally sanctioned goons was a defeat. For every Apache with a rifle, there were three 'military medics' who whipped out machine guns. But, though this battle with him was lost, the war would continue. "How did you find us this time?" the overdecorated, then demoted to civilian Apache US Army veteran demanded of the Major.

Wentworth lifted his mask, then took in a deep, leisurely breath, taking his time to effortlessly shoot back the reply to where it would hurt most. "Indians are the hardest people to help, but we are obliged to do whatever we can, medically, to keep your people alive."

" Alive is about the spirit, not body!" Cuthand shot back.

"Tell that to the people here, who you buried, 'Captain Cuthand,'" Wentworth blasted back, who YOU took away from OUR facilities. Some of whom were still under our 21st century treatment protocols."

"Treatments and protocols that were killing them," Cuthand grunted through a mouth that had been relieved of several teeth after heated arguments with the Cops and doctors in town. "And for those who died before you were finished 'curing them,' their souls belong here. Didn't you do enough damage to us when you stole our children to 'educate' them in Residential Schools in treatments and protocols? But you always want to help us on your terms and agendas."

Thundercloud blasted out his horrific experience with said schools in his youth in Apache.

"What is he jabbering about?" Wentworth inquired of his Half-Breed interpreter, Corporal.

"He says you are a liar, Sir," the interpreter replied with as much assertion as his rank allowed through his mask. "Most particularly about wanting to help them."

"What can I do to convince him, Corporal Johnson, and you, former Captain Cuthand, that I'm not?" Wentworth asked with a sincerity he seldom showed even his own men.

"Take off that mask for a start," the very naked-faced Cuthand demanded. "And make your cropdusters go around our mountains and over the valleys, hills, and pastures that you THINK are legally yours. "

"The planes are the only way to monitor and control this epidemic!" Wentworth blasted through gritted teeth.

"By keeping our people here, keeping your people out, desecrating our sacred places with your hateful and dead eyes, and---" Jake's eye caught something even more frightening.

Thundercloud went into grand mal shakes and a terrifying scream. It was the scream of death, with a rattle loud enough to hear as far as Phenoix or Albuquerque.

"What the---" Jake muttered indecisively.

"He's dying," Wentworth said as his emergency team ran to the old man. The remainder of his detachment sprayed machine gun fire to ensure that there would be no resistance this time.

"This is sacred ground!" Cuthand asserted, never more resolute. He was terrified of what was being pulled out of Wentworth's holster---Syringes with mind-numbing biological bullets that no doctor or medicine man could take out.

"This is a cemetery, Jake," Wentworth reminded Cuthand, with the concern of a brother rather than the blasting from a pissed-off father. "And everyone here is going to be dead very soon, just like---"

"---Get that injection needle away from that old man, NOW!!!" Cuthand yelled out, seeing two men holding Thundercloud down, a third pushing the air out a syringe that was about to be inserted into the Old Shamen's shaking arm. Thundercloud's eyes fixed on yet another visit from the White Buffalo. Cuthand pulled a knife out of his leather casing and held it to Wentworth's throat.

"Do what the man asks," Wentworth calmly related to his troops, armed and ready to follow whatever order given.

The troops held their ground. There was not an unsteady or undiseased hand amongst them. Still, for the moment, 'Captain Cuthand' outranked Major Wentworth. "I want your people off my land. Or I swear to your God and ours that I'll cut those protective suits off you and scalp every one of you!"

"Even the ones with the crew cuts, Captain Cuthand?" Wentworth smirked.

"I can give you a trim two inches below the scalp you'll NEVER forget," Cuthand grunted. "Now, get those trucks off my land!!!"

"Perhaps you should ask his judgment first," Wentworth said calmly, his firm hand pointed at Thundercloud.

The older man took a last breath and then collapsed. His eyes said dead, his face saying one previous battle cry in silent desperation--- 'why'?

Jake felt the power go from his hand and his heart. Wentworth's half-breed Corporal pushed down his wrist, the knife Cuthand had on Wentworth's throat falling to the ground. Wentworth's men restrained Cuthand and every other Apache who posed a potential threat.

"Now then, our investigation requires that we take back with us the bodies of the following individuals for medical examination." He gave Jake the list.

"Some of these people are still alive," Cuthand noted.

"No matter. You see if you don't surrender these individuals, we'll take everybody, living AND dead."

Jake pondered the odds, chances, and scenarios.

"If one of your people survives and remembers, everyone does. I can and WILL make sure that the only thing left of the Apache nation is a page in a history book," the ambassador from the White Nation assured the present operating chief of the Indigenous one.

"In the interest of survival, I can help you, I think," Jake conceded.

"And there is something else. We need the members of this Eagle Cult, living and dead." The Major took out his remarkable book. He kept a black notepad private from his men and his unauthorized superiors. "All of the Eagle Cult members," he continued, handing Cuthand a pencil.

"It is the Eagle CLAN, which is part of our religion," Cuthand shot back, grabbing the pencil. He snapped it in two, then three, then four pieces, throwing it into the blood-stained dirt below him.

"A 'clan' which was outlawed in 1885, and still is, legally, Jake," Wentworth replied by way of 'friendly reminder.' That 'this is a warning, the next time it will be the slammer' tone, which Cuthand was all too familiar with.

Jake had pondered the matter for so many years. What would the benefits of sharing his people's secrets be vs.

keeping them secret? Some said that the 'go with the flow' method worked for all misfits from the Old West who needed to fit in with the new one, even the Mormons. When they became assimilated into American culture, they gave up polygamy but still kept their special relationship with Prophet Joseph Smith. But at what INNER price? "Some things have to stay with us," Cuthand stated in carefully chosen words, pre-rehearsed and re-evaluated.

"Please," Wentworth said with a sincere, even human voice. "Your religion is killing your people. So is your stubbornness."

"Tenacity and faith keep our people alive. What's keeping you alive, Major?"

"Very well, then. Tell ya what. You locate the people on that list, and I'll leave the rest of you to die in the sweat lodge." He signaled his men to spray another round of machine gun fire.

Jake held his ground, as did most of the men. But children huddled in their mother's arms.

"I'll take that as a 'yes" Wentworth said. "We'll start with that old man, Thundercloud, you said his name was. We'll take his brain; you can have the rest of the body. A fair White-Indian exchange."

"Do I have a choice?"

"Neither of us has any choice in this matter, Jake." That conclusion was firm, as it was clandestine.

Against the pleading and curses from surviving relatives, Jake Cuthand identified the remains of those on Wentworth's list. When it came to the living afflicted with MID, identification was easy enough. Four of every five Apache exhibiting stage 2 or worse were 'escorted' into the trucks. Why some were left behind was a mystery to Jake and the eagle. But it was something to hold on to. Cuthand, and even the most White Apache, knew that without something to hold on to, you become nothing, very, very painfully.

The eagle watched as the trucks carried off the dead and soon-to-be-dead. A bird amongst avians, he knew what the next step was. Indians were the hardest people to help, but some White men were better at this thankless task than others. A poet-physician from the land beyond where the sun rises would probably be that man, the eagle pondered. It was as good a plan as any other as the sun set over a dark, gloomy desert horizon.

III

The West Side pier at 79th Street wasn't as scenic as the jetties at Montauk. John Baldino recalled the events at the off-season resort where he first saw visions of beyond worlds during his last two-week 'vacation.' It was indeed a 'break from samo samo reality' generously flavored with hallucinations from the living and the dead, him not knowing at the time which was which. It was there that he was monitored powerful, clandestine, and international cartel BITE, and watched by his landlord, almost lover, and nearly executioner, Kathleen, during the two-week hospice 'vacation' where he was visited by the ghosts and real personas of so many people from his past. Indeed, Montauk Point was a special place for many reasons. But there were enough elements of 'The Point' on the West Side of Manhattan to keep him going on this next stage of his post-death 'life.'

Between and betwixt the garbage atop and bodies below the Hudson River, there was still sky, water, and winged creatures. Seagulls have always fascinated John since he could say and remember their Latin name. They looked so clean, so pristine, so regal. Yet they ate any garbage the ocean, 'trash disposal' boats, or junk-food-bearing people gave them.

"How could so much garbage turn into so much beauty?" John asked himself as he watched the sun setting over the Western sky featuring winged creatures dancing in the air, making the New Jersey skyline seem like bucolic mountains with a light show behind them. As the sun set, sending a constellation of colors in its wake, apartment roofs turned from steel gray to brilliant silver. Factory chimneys became pillars of tall pine. And then, at a magical moment, one of the gulls seemed to become an eagle.

"Here we go again," John mumbled loud enough to hear himself, like the homeless bum he was supposed to be for this leg of the assignment, a role that fit all too well. "The hallucinations BITE made me see in Montauk are back. I saw people who died come back to life. Some were alive, and I only thought them dead. But which one are you, my fine feathered friend?"

The eagle swooped down on the railing. A German tourist snapped a shot of the bird, but John took its real picture inside his mind.

"You are real," John said to the bird. He offered it a piece of his authentic Hebrew National hot dog, according to the overly tattoed crucifix-wearing Hispanic vendor. "Mustard and relish. Is that Kosher with you?"

Despite his love for birds, John was always afraid of them. They flew in a third dimension, which he could not navigate. Or maybe it was about the time at the lake as a kid when he was trapped on a porch with a raven who fancied a piece of his hair while brother Vincent and his buds enjoyed a laugh at young John's terror. Or maybe that bat flew into 10-year-old John's room alone during that otherwise enjoyable summer vacation in the Catskills. Or perhaps it was a bad dream after seeing Hitchcock's "The Birds" once too often. But now, it was a time of overcoming fear, embracing it, and letting it feed you something....beyond what you had.

The eagle remained still, perched no more than three feet before John. It flapped its wings just enough to warn his two-legged humanoid observer that it could fly if it wanted to. The avian visitor showed off its beak with enough tenacity to reveal to anyone, even with half an eye open, that he could rip open any throat he had to. This ghostly bird, or bird-ghost, was a visitor from the past or perhaps a future. The mind-altering effects of A137 during the initiation week in Montauk made John able to recognize 'ghosts' with messages. But he was not yet versed in deciphering whether said ghosts were from the land of the living or the dead, or both.

There was one way to find out. "A bite out of my hot dog?" he inquired of the generously winged visitor. "You want it? You can take a nip off my finger if you want, but not the third digit. I think I'm going to be needing it for the kind of people I have to deal with. Or maybe you have a third finger claw of your own that you---"

The eagle interrupted John in mid-ramble, cleanly taking the hotdog from his hand, leaving something very significant behind as he stepped onto his right wrist, leaving a brand that felt like a hot iron.

"A signature that looks like...something...familiar?" John intuited regarding the half circle with a stem sticking out of its base that was imprinted on and into his wrist. The burn felt like ice as he looked at it. "How did you do that, and how did I know what this was supposed to happen?" he asked the bird, feeling past, present, and future somehow merged.

The avian visitor squawked out something that felt like 'you'll know on a need-to-know basis.' It was with the same tone his superspy brother said when requested to know WHY he needed John's help in getting biological intel, toxins, and 'medications', only obtainable by the academically, economically, or politically elite.

John regained his composure. He fell back into the part of his brain that was more New York than Wild West or Ozian. "I suppose it's an eagle 'cult' or 'clan' thing, right?" he asked his winged uninvited dinner guest.

The eagle reached a congratulatory 'yes' to John's wild guess. It then flapped its wings and disappeared into the sky, leaving behind a trail of crumbs and manure that fell near John's head. And a feather that fell into his right hand.

"Thank you, I think," he said, remembering that the eagle feather was a sign of courage in traditional Aboriginal cultures. But his left hand found something else when he leaned on the railing to regain his physical balance on what had become his favorite observation spot in the world that week. Beneath the railing was a key, an address, and a single word of instruction from Vincent in inverted Baldino-ese script. "Go West, young 'man'"

The original plan, according to Vincent and the other messengers from the land of the living and/or the dead encountered in Montauk, was for the (by necessity so he could become an accomplished biomedical researcher) sheltered John to visit the places of change in the world on occasion, staying at the well-guarded hotels rather than the dives where the commoners laid their weary heads at the end of the day. John never expected the journey to start this new adventure at the Plaza Hotel in the Big Crab Apple. He never expected to enter, according to orders from Erica, as a homeless bum, offending the doorkeepers, guests, and other guests with his odor and multi-themed wardrobe. He was shocked when he emerged from the shower in his paid-for 'do not disturb' room, relieved of his clothes, wallet, and all of his 'Jack McFarlane' ID and wardrobe. They had been burnt to a crisp in the fireplace.

"Selena Horowitz, a reporter assigned to do a story on the scientist's mind, " John read on the paperwork sprawled on the bed. "In Flagstaff, Arizona?" He asked the man who had a Roman-style haircut and an ultra-sleek leisure suit waiting for him.

"My name is Leonard," the effeminate man with the assertive voice answered. "I was assigned to assist you, Selena. For your trip out West, Sir."

John didn't know what to think when he saw Leonard take the clothes out of the suitcases bearing her name, items that would hardly be appropriate for any Old West Cattle Drover unless said cow boss was a well-dressed bitch and/or babe.

"Erica said you had great legs," Leonard commented, pulling out a breast-length dark brunette wig. He put it on John's head.

Confused, wrapped only in a towel, John looked in the mirror.

"It fits your facial lines, eyes, and aura," Leonard commented with a masculine tone...

"And you think I have a great ass?" John answered, smart-assed and determined, noticing Selena's new 'wardrobe' in the closet, lady-like and sexy, hung up with orderly precision.

"Let's hope the scientists at the Klasen Institute think you have a hot ass and you know how to show it off with the right clothes," Leonard said, adjusting the loose curls on the wig, noting that the color and style did elegantly embrace John's jaw lines. "They know your face, which the plastic surgeon did not change much at your request. And your name and your work, Doctor Baldino. You were a science star. Now, you have to be a groupie. And a Matahari spy who's the only one who can find out what's REALLY going on in that institute."

"Who will be discovered the moment I open my mouth!" John protested.

"Not after I get through with you," Leonard said. He threw a pack of razors at John. "Clean and smooth, toe to neck, sideburns to chin, Sir. And after I spray this specially formulated mouthwash down your throat to adjust your vocal cords," the short-haired man who carried himself like an officer in the Gay Pride Army continued. He then sprayed five generous squirts from an unlabelled aerosol spray can into John's throat.

"Was this Erica's idea? Vincent's?" John asked in a high-pitched voice he didn't recognize as Leonard escorted him back to the shower. John's temporary handler placed the razors on the shelf and generously lathered his body with depilatory shaving cream after inactivating John's protests with a punch in the good doctor's belly.

"It would go easier if you let this happen to you and figure out what it is later Sir," Leonard said, followed by other requests to allow John's body to be handled. Leonard's "Sirs" tone, with which he appended each request, indicated that he didn't know or appreciate John's real identity while he was officially alive.

"Do you know who I am!" John finally blasted back at his half-male, half-female handler.

"Someone more central than Erica and Vincent are orchestrating this operation, Sir. Someone who…." Leonard held back the rest. He instructed John to shave his face and body closer, then apply hair remover just in case. "God knows that…"

"God?" John asked as he, at Leanard's request, scrapped the chest hair that had sprouted out when he was not even a lad of 12. He watched it fall into the bathtub. "Is God behind this?"

"Someone more powerful and more human, Sir."

"Living or dead, Leonard?"

"Living…Of course. You're asking bizarre questions."

"And you're asking me to do very unusual things." John didn't like what he saw in the mirror. It brought up fears and prejudices he thought were above his education, station, and intellectual development. "What if I say 'no' or change the name on this passport and press pass to something more in keeping with my real gender, which is very male and very heterosexual!" John asserted.

"Then you won't connect with Vincent," Leonard affirmed calmly.

"I'll risk it," John put out in Machismoesche with quivering lips. As soon as the words penetrated the air, they were stabilized with lipstick rammed onto them by Leonard's hairless, manicured yet bear-sized paws.

"And an entire tribe of Apaches will die if you don't do what you are told and what is needed to be done." Leonard was serious. He backed up his claim by pulling out the most recent newspapers from Phoenix, Chicago, and New York, pushing them into John's soon-to-be even more feminized face. They contained bold headlines that distracted the reader from the newsprint underneath them. The no-nonsense black and white print proclaimed with exclamation marks a contagious cancer named Mad Indian Disease.

"I'll improvise my way to save them." John grabbed the wig, threw it back on the bed, and shook the 'female' out of his pounding and worry-laden head. But he was unable to shake it from his voice.

"And Maria will not reach her sixtieth birthday." A tear came to Leonard's eyes, real ones, for any gender.

"Who's Maria?" John asked, Leonard's empathy connecting him to his own.

Leonard showed John the picture beneath the headlines. It featured a young Apache woman who had escaped Flagstaff and arrived in New York to embark on a career in acting. "Maria got invited into an ensemble company on her first audition. Her first performance was on a playground in the West Village, where she battled a hallucinated flying 8 winged reptile that turned into a white buffalo that turned into a laser-shooting locomotive that went off the tracks trying to run her over. Along with the kids, she was babysitting," Leonard said, relating the varied facts to what he seemed to believe was the truth. "In full few of a crowd of tourists, the cops and a specially-chosen team of paramedics who took her straight from the ER to a very underground room at Saint Vincent's."

John was moved by Maria's eyes in the photograph taken in the West Village 'Injun show.' It jumped out of the page and penetrated through his own ocular portholes. "She looks like she's suffering," he noted.

"That was stage 1 of the disease when she arrived," Leonard related. "By the time we got to her, the only photo was this." He produced more photos, revealing a young woman in a blood-stained hospital gown whose face was old, lifeless, and pale.

John's stare was absorbed by the picture of Maria taken at her autopsy. Her skull had been opened, the brain inside removed. From her 'resting place' in the morgue, Maria's eyes spoke to him yet again.

"She was still alive when they cut her brain out," John noted, recalling his own medical experience with too many comatose patients.

"We got some medical records out, too. The blood work is very bizarre. So is the histology of the tumor." Leonard pulled out the proof of his claim from a locked briefcase. He handed it over to the hopefully to be more than just 'good' Doctor.

"Astroglioma with octagonal inclusions. I've never seen this," John pointed out with his now hairless knuckles.

"Maybe you have," Leonard replied prophetically as he pulled another file under the mattress.

John studied and felt the essence of the photograph. It was an MRI. He let the tissue talk to him on its terms, a skill he begged so many of his medical students to develop but which few, if any, learned. It all came together now. "This looks like my X-ray when I was diagnosed with a temporal lobe tumor."

"Which you had until Erica cured it," Leonard reminded John.

"Why can't she cure these kids? And Maria?" John demanded to know.

"We find a cure; they find a new kind of poison. That's how it works now, Doctor J, or rather, Selena,"

"And that poison?" John inquired, trying to keep the conversation medical rather than experimentally transgender. "The toxin that's killing them?"

"Is probably coming out of the Klassen Institute. A second-rate research institute outside of Flagstaff that the Fed and the CDC have built up into an overly funded grade-A think tank. If we can find out the 'whos' about all of this, we can figure out the 'what.'"

"And Selena Horowitz will figure out the 'whys'?" John surmised.

Leonard held back. This time, he chose his words carefully, answering in a very affirmative, masculine tone. "We need a scientist, poet, and writer for this one."

"A poetESS?" John said, looking at his new ultra-female 'battle gear' in the closet. Skirts, blouses, and dresses that said 'ultra-fem and ultra professional.'

"Two spies in one. You heard the story about a French Duke who posed as a woman to spy on England?"

"Yes...Racheloue? Or maybe it was Journead. I forgot the name, but remember that the story was true," John related, trying to connect his past memory with his present life. Such was an increasingly difficult task ever since that all-too-revealing two-week vacation in Montauk that was anything but restful.

"He---she--got closer to the Queen of England than any man could, then went back to France and waged war against her at the head of his army," Leonard related.

"No offense or cowardess intended, but I'm not gay or a general," John shot back, his thoughts still held hostage by the feminized voice coming out of his mouth.

"We know, sir," replied the handler, who still refused to address John by his first name, Doctor, or even Doc. Leonard swiped a healthy hair remover on John's face with firm strokes and a gentle touch. While it settled in, he pulled out a pair of tweezers, turning John's thick Italian man's eyebrows into something less masculine and more culturally generic. "You'll have to be much more than a fag, general, or a rat, Sir," Leonard continued. "Maria's sisters, brothers, and people depend on it."

Leanard instructed 'Selena' to sit down. He quickly re-applied lipstick, followed by mascara and eyeliner, appended by a painful thinning of the eyebrows with catlike black warpaint painted around his eyes. Next was a layer of dark botox on John's face and a dark foundation to make his skin younger and ethnic enough to be 'interestingly Caucasian.' Leonard then handed John the blonde wig, a chain of pearls, snap-on earrings, and a white blouse and skirt that said 'ladylike' to the fingers, eyes, and nose.

Like it or not, John had to 'man' up and be as many women as possible to fill the accessories and hair pieces. When putting on Selena's wig, he felt like it was a helmet, preparing for a primal battle. The blouse and skirt seemed to be a uniform. The pearls and earrings are an insignia. Men, women, and children he never knew, and many who he did, would live or die according to how well Selena Horowitz accomplished their assigned task as an undercover scientist-turned-visionary.

John tried 'Selena' on, avoiding the mirror and allowing Leonard to make the final adjustments.

John closed his eyes. "YES," he surmised in a flash of brilliance. "It's A137 working again, and I'm part of this 'dream,'" he speculated silently. "And I DO recognize Leonard from someplace. And, interestingly, ALL of my senses are active in this criss-cross trip to someplace that seems very important." He felt dangerously lighter than his authentic self as the conversation in his head got more assertive and softer, both simultaneously. "It will pass as soon as the lights come on, and I come back to reality, such as it is."

True to John's speculations and well-founded assurances, a flash of light opened his eyes. "Smile, Selena!" Leonard said, a camera in hand. After this, he flashed several photos of John in different poses. But would the smiles John forced onto his strange-feeling face be convincing enough to hide the fear in his overly mascaraed eyes? That fear of being 'found out' about what he was had haunted John his entire life. And, as he considered, being recognized as John Baldino in drag to the scientists and administrators at the Klassen Institute who knew him as a celebrity award-winning MALE scientist who was supposed to be officially dead.

John recalled the difference between being a buffalo and a cow. Bison walked head-on into a storm to bash through overwhelming challenges quickly and assertively. Cows AND bovine bulls walked away from windblown pouring rain and got their asses wet, sore, and painful all day. But.... buffalo had more hair and thicker hides than cows.

IV

"The only real rest is in motion itself," John tried to recall to himself as he entered the airplane and was guided to his seat by a hot-looking female flight attendant, 'Lorena.' She was a head-turning babe in any culture. But John's attention was somewhere else. He noted that his leather mini-skirt, satin blouse, and 4-inch stiletto heels made him appear more sexually appealing to the men around him than the attendant did.

"Seat 1A, Ms. Horowitz," Lorena said warmly.

"Thank you," John replied with the hushed voice in which Leonard coached him, which had been severely under-tested since the eighteen-hour-long training and make-over session at the Plaza.

"If there's anything we can get for you, let us know," Lorena offered.

"Thank you, I will," John replied, thinking that the last thing he needed now was a flight crew that paid attention to its passengers. He gazed at the briefcase that described Selena Horowitz's background. And the notes she had collected on Mad Indian Disease. John did not know which portion of the intel fit into any of those categories for data verified, assumed, or projected. After looking up to see if dead air would provide such answers, his stare was held hostage by a mirror showing the body and life he had been dropped into. "I look like I would date myself and hopefully not get pregnant afterwards," he thought as his fingers felt the smooth nylons over his now hairless legs. "I do look ten, no twenty, years younger and feel a lifetime lighter; I think," the mental ramble continued as he caught a glimpse of the face in the mirror that said, "Barbie or bitch, your choice." From his luscious ruby-red and nearly quivering lips, he boldly ventured a full-voiced, high-octave reply to the attendant who seemed so desirous of pleasing him. "I have a lot of reading to do," he said to Lorena, hoping she would tend to and/or analyze the other passengers on the plane.

The Attendant seemed convinced that she was catering to a fellow woman rather than a man. Indeed, Leonard was a good coach. John was passing as a female. Such was more deeply confirmed by the fact and feeling that Lorena related to John as an 'insider' to a world in which he was very new.

'Selena' smiled back in the mirror to John, apparently impressed, perhaps even enticed. So were the business people in the first-class compartment. Particularly the ones with wedding rings on their fingers who gazed twice at John's legs. They were elegantly displayed by sheer hose and stiletto heels. Complimented by a firm C-cup pair of breasts beneath the twirls of blonde hair flowing over them.

"It's in the softness in the voice, not the octave range," John Baldino recalled from Leonard as he adjusted the leather miniskirt in a ladylike manner and crossed his legs in the prescribed manner that was becoming instinctual all too quickly. John hoped it was due to his ability to empathize with the female condition rather than embrace it permanently.

John Baldino began the dive into yet another read of the research data and profiles of the scientists at "The Klassen" with the ferocity of a lion---AND lioness. "Lying is lying. If the way to find the truth is to lie, so be it---I think," Baldino muttered to himself, in Italian, with a closed mouth. He was careful not to smudge Leonard's handiwork on his lips. "A real man doesn't lie, cheat, or apologize, but this is about real work and real life now," he pondered very expressively. "Under all the macho, most men are geeks or nerds and, with enough power, become Dorks. Witness Uncle Bill Gates, who could turn the whole thing around for us if he uttered seven magic words---' Do you want fries with that, Sir,' or 'Ma'am' or even 'Miss.' Women are bitches, whores, or sluts. A slut cheats, a whore steals, and a bitch lies, I think."

"Or lies with whatever nerd she can steal the most alimony from," a baritone voice said, in Italian, into John's left ear. It echoed throughout John's 'new' body, causing him to become frigid in terror. "May I?" the man with the 1B seat assignment said, in English, in the English accent.

Having assumed that his mouth had indeed accidentally said what he had been thinking, John smiled, Selena style. John noted that the pen in his hand had dropped to the floor. The expressiveness of feeling rather than voice was the agenda now. John noted the US Army insignia on the gentleman's uniform.

"I'm Major Wentworth," he said with chivalry that was very upper-crust, cultured and White. "And you?" he continued, picking up John's pen from the floor. Wentworth handed it back to 'Selena' in such a way that Baldino had to touch the Army Officer's flesh and pen. He had used that pen for his entire life to fight back against the world. "And you are?" Wentworth repeated, inviting and, in some way, demanding an answer to that inquiry.

"Selena," John self-observed, coming out of his mouth. He felt himself being coached by the honest Selena, who, according to the intel related to him by Leonard, had died while investigating and/or reporting Mad Indian Disease. He gently retrieved the pen from Wentworth's hand, a task which required some kind of 'handshake' afterwards. John said that the fake ultralong nails would make his fingers look and feel thin enough to pass as a member of the gentler and perhaps more manipulative gender.

"Harry," Wentworth replied. He sat down in seat 1A. He adjusted his tie, cleared his throat, and then took out a fresh copy of the Wall Street Journal. Before reading it, he smiled at Selena. No soap opera middle-aged hunk could have been hotter and more accessible.

Listening to the body was the best way to keep the mind working safely and effectively. John felt powerful signals from his gut, belly, AND tummy. Something was very wrong about Wentworth. He was too sure of himself, too contented with the world around him. Yet, he seemed to be a man who knew the global score all too well. Anxiety was topped by terror when John noted the leisure reading Wentworth pulled out of his briefcase. The International Journal of Communicative Diseases. Followed by...

"I don't mean to be presumptuous, but you look familiar," Wentworth abruptly inquired of John as a no-nonsense question.

John dived deep into himself and Selena. "We all look familiar," the reply, punctuated with a tastefully flirtatious smile.

"Quite," Wentworth replied with a whimsical smile. "I thought I recognized you. In my line of work, you meet a lot of people."

John cued into something. Ever since his 'gone fishing' vacation in Montauk, nothing was coincidental. Why was this British Major attached to the American Army sitting next to him? Why were his eye movements so... sinister? They displayed shifts downward, upward, to the right or the left, but seldom were on center. Why was he so interested in him? Was it as a woman, maybe a man, or perhaps as a soon-to-be corpse? Was school called into session this early?

Wentworth's 'coincidental' handshake had been cold, but it was real. This was no visitor from the dead, but he was perhaps connected to a lot of dying. Something that probably all military men experience, including John's brother Vincent.

"What kind of work are you in?" John asked in a Selena voice that said flattery and admiration. "It looks essential."

"Quite," Wentworth continued. His eyes turned upward and to the right. Visualizing plans with the occipital cortex, John surmised.

"You're a doctor, I see," Selena offered, noting the medical insignia on his uniform, turning his body Wentworth's way. John 'accidentally' showed a bit more leg in a gesture that somehow he felt was appropriate AND necessary.

"And, contradictory to what all women and most think, not all of us Doctors are rich or even solvent," Wentworth replied.

"Yes, I know," John volleyed back as Selena. He recalled his own experiences with gold diggers who thankfully took their shovels to other doctors who were better at over-charging patients than curing them.

According to the psych books, the English gentleman's eyes shifted down and to the left, a sign of self-reflection and agonizing re-assessment.

"Keeping medical truth alive is dirty, but someone's gotta do it," Selena commented, gazing at the medical journal in Wentworth's hand.

"Quite," Wentworth's reply, with eyes turned downward. Shame this time, then straight ahead---frustration, anger, and then---closing of the emotional gates. The male animal had gone into its cave, ready to come out when it was ready. It was something that God knows John had done so many times to women.

"I'm sorry," the apology offered by Selena, accompanied by a body, turns away from the cave door.

"Medicine and politics used to be so much easier. Now it's...painful," Wentworth delivered to dead air before his sorrowful eyes.

"How so, Harry?" Selena's reply, daring to define the necessary relationship to continue. John saw a cracker crumb on Harry's shoulder. Selena moved John's hand gently to it, whisking it off with the lightest of touches. John and Selena explained the reason for the incursion over the Angst line with a simple, civil, and Platonic smile.

From then on, Wentworth talked, John listened, and Selena gave the signal to deliver the occasional 'ahhuhh' or, when required, 'that's fascinating' or 'really'?' into John's inner ears. The tales of Wentworth's medical career and life achievements had no shortage of jokes or ironies. They required the listener to chuckle or laugh. John remembered it all too well. There are three things that a man really wants from a woman---loving respect, passionate sex, and someone to laugh at his jokes. But laughing at his sexual skills under the sheets is not one of the jokes to be allowed.

Harry Wentworth's jokes about his days in the British Medical Corp, the UN Communicable Disease Agency, and the off time between gigs in every continent of the globe seemed not only irrelevant but...crude, at least to Selena. Paula Poundstone's Three Stooges theory was correct. Men laugh at pain. Women pity those who have it or perpetuate it.

But under all the trans-body and trans-dimensional transformations were the memories of others John held onto. Maria, and the people who had died, and who would die on "Rez Zero." Harry related little more than what John already knew about MID, the euphemism for 'Mad Injun Disease,' which terrified whites more than it did redskins. The official story that the Press got stuck in the back pages of the newspapers was that it was due to the ingestion of something only found on the Rez. Something that somehow got into the food chain of the Apaches as part of the resurgence of an ancient, and still outlawed, Eagle Cult, rumored to be a new species of peyote.

It produced bizarre brain tumors, which were of the astrocytic variety. Along with induced stereotypic green and yellow hallucinations of strange creatures and, ultimately, death, with the primary emotion of helplessness as the final chord for the life opera. The causative agent had not been identified. However, the current theory was that it was a latent and most probably contagious virus living in a herb known only to the Eagle Cult. This could spread to white kids in town who were bored with shopping malls, street drugs, and their parental culture and who would try anything to experience the kind of lives their burnt-out Yuppoid parents WEREN'T living.

However, there was something new to the tale that Wentworth felt compelled to relate to his fellow passengers. A top secret revealed to an outsider was always the cheapest way to impress a man or pick up a woman. And under the pressed collar and 150 dollars a drop after shave cologne, Wentworth was still a working-class stiff from Liverpool, no matter how many semesters he had spent at Oxford. He couldn't resist Selena's charms or, perhaps, John's humanity.

While listening to 'Major Harry's' small talk and big boasts, John recalled and visualized some of the stories that got buried in the back of the newspaper articles. These were explained in further detail by Erica's written accounts of such, which never got published anywhere. As always, stories about important people were heard, while even more important stories about 'commoners' were seldom printed or shared.

Senator Jacobs had lost a son to MID when said prodigal son was doing his summer "Indian" trek out West before starting law school in the East. Mike Jacobs Jr spent a painful and embarrassing two months in the psych ward till he committed suicide. His mind was too bright not to figure out a way to do the deed, and the hallucinations became too real to endure. Federal funding was supposed to be released to start a special investigation. Still, instead of funds allocated to specialized researchers nationwide, it all went to the Klassen Institute or whoever would relocate there. Mike Jacobs Sr. died of a heart attack two days after his bill for more funding was turned down.

"Heartache is sometimes confused with heart attack, but the result is always the same, Selena," Harry related to John as his eyes were shaken back into seeing that which IS in the 'real' world rather than what was going on behind the scenes in the envisioned one. "You look too pretty to be a journalist, and your eyes are too kind," he continued with a more respectful than flirtatious tone. "Still, I'd rather this stay between us."

As any self-respecting traveler with residencies in the land of the living and the dead could see, it was now time for John to let Selena do the talking. There were several options. Some of the choices were turning the head, shifting the pupil line, rotating around in a clockwise circle, and batting the long eyelashes in Southern 'little ole me tell anyone?' mode. But a direct attack might work best here, John thought. A blank stare, eyes fixed, nothing moving in the optic portholes except the thoughts behind them. "It must be hard for Senator Jacobs' losing a son as he did in Arizona, a story I read about just last night," Selena said, and John felt, changing the subject abruptly. "All children are precious" came next.

The plane jolted before John or Selena could assess what Wentworth was thinking behind his started face. "We're hitting a bit of turbulence," flight attendant Lorena said over the loudspeaker. "Please fasten your safety belts."

John tightened the belt around his waist, noting a sagging in one of his blown-up 'man boobs,' which were now full-sized regulation female breasts. He adjusted the cleavage as discretely as he could.

The attendant looked at John's hands, then into his best poker face. "She knows who and what I am," John told himself and Selena. "She has to. I've always been a terrible liar."

John contemplated the entire situation once again. He glanced at the mirrored reflection in the window and said goodbye to Selena. Then he picked up the complimentary Pheonix Gazette left behind for all First Class passengers. It featured two stories. Ignoring Wentworth, who seemed also to want to ignore him, John read the stories in the popular rag that, according to its academic critics, invested more resources in colored ink and photos to attract readers than into the pockets of reporters who wanted to share facts rather than opinions.

On page two of the Phoenix Gazette, one story was about a murderer-rapist on the run from the law, with all too familiar pictures. They were of John Baldino---himself, in every 'look' since high school, with variations in facial hair and a top knot, describing him as a fugitive, to be killed or apprehended, with a new name. Either John really did have an evil twin somewhere West of the Mississippi. Or, most likely, someone on the legal side of the badge wanted him to be arrested upon arrival in Arizona. Or shot dead if found anywhere else in the country. Such required John to stay being Selena.

The second story, buried on the pageback of the local rag that was believed to be gospel by most of its readers, was about two deaths at the hands of MID, Maria's mother and sister this time.

John pondered the matters, being sure that his ruby red did not move or quiver when he was conferring with the ghosts inside his head. And knowing that the claim that MID was caused by Pagan Savages eating a rediscovered species of carcinogenic peyote spread around by a Cult of bloodthirsty 'Injuns' had to be investigated or disproven. This was only possible by discovering the REAL story behind MID and everything else happening around before the localized epidemic spread into a pandemic that would kill men, women, and children of all races.   Slowly and painfully.

V

Willy the Weatherboy on the hotel room lobby TV boasted a day of snow for the skiers on the mountain and sun for the citizens below. His more maturely dressed and presumably more educated supermodel anchor, A. Cathrine Williamson, recapped the top stories of the day for those whose interests and investments lay outside the resorts and shopping malls of Flagstaff. The menu today included a new war in Africa, an impending shift in the Pentagon Research and Development staff in DC, and another bank robbery in Phoenix, perpetuated by an escaped mental patient claiming to be a deceased miracle Doctor, John Baldino.

"That's a twist," John said to himself while the staff checked the reservation. "In 'The Fugitive', the Doctor, accused of murder, gets a chance to escape from a train, and at least gets to keep his underwear. But I have at least some cash. At last count, whoever my friends are, they left me a whole five dollars and..--"

"Did you say something, Ma'am?" Tom Robinson, head clerk and night manager, offered with a smile featuring a peachfuzz moustache which he sported like a well-waxed cowboy handlebar.

"Were there any messages for me? Maybe from a tall gentleman named Vincent, or a more friendly, dark-haired guy who called himself Vinny?" John asked in a business-like Selena voice and subtext. He wondered what his brother would think about his feminine voice, look, and evolving new perspective.   He showed Tom pictures of his brothers Vincent, Vinny, and Vince taken in better and less 'classified top secret' times.

"There was a Vince who checked in here, Ma'am," the 'down home country' replied. "An interestin' man with a lot of history behind his tired eyes," Tom said. "Sort a looked like him."

"When?" John asked eagerly, motioning for the all-too-eager clerk not to take Selena's bags to the room.

"He's your husband, Ms Horowitz?" Tom inquired. "Or fiancée? Boyfriend? Manfriend?" he advanced, colorfully and politely, while gazing at Selena's interestingly-framed cleavage.

"We were...are...a lot closer than that," John/Selena answered, averting his generously eyelashed eyes, and the experiences he recalled behind them.

Tom looked down at John's hands, which he instantly withdrew. But he did catch a white ring of white skin under the finger on the 'Ms. Horowitz's left the fourth digit.

"Some marriages you don't forget, or put aside," John related, silently remembering his first and only wife, who died when he was twenty-five. "Sometimes wearing a ring can help you remember someone, or even bring her back if you call out hard enough." John stopped himself, noting Tom's smile turning into a disapproving frown. "I mean...well...sometimes a woman can give another woman the kind of love a man can't, or won't," John said by way of explanation.   "In any case, you have to know when to let go of who you used to be, and used to be with," John continued regarding the wife he still held onto for 25 years after the bus accident, the young physician couldn't save her from.

"Of course, Ms Horowitz." Tom kept his distance, withholding or perhaps losing his interest in John's complex backstory. Taking hold of the bags himself, in a gentlemanly manner, he led John down a dark red carpeted hallway with white stucco walls decorated with photos of old cowboys, young soldiers, and Walmart variety security cameras toward Selena's room.   It was an offer she could not refuse, particularly as the next guests entered the hotel lobby, uniformed Army Officers from the US and two other countries they didn't recognize. "Your room is ready, accordin' ta specs. And at this hotel we're very discreet," Tom continued as he opened the door to the royal red-carpeted corridor lined by half-busted vending machines containing soda, chips, and candy.

"No one is going to peek into my keyhole to watch a lesbian two-for-dumb sale", John thought snidely. "You're sure you haven't seen Vincent anywhere around here, or know anyone who does?" he advanced, stopping to lay down his bags. He retrieved a Benjamen from his fringed leather purse. He noted the rough shape of Tom's boots and rips in his jeans, NOT made by a fashion designer.

"And if I do, see him, anywhere, by accident, anything I can should tell him, I'll tell him you were askin' 'bout him," Tom's final pledge, taking the C note into his hand as discreetly as possible. "Thank you," he said, picking up Selena's bags and proceeding down the dimly but elegantly lit hallway featuring autographed photos of cowboys, pics of celebs, and military heroes, all short-haired and White. "This way, Ma'am," he pushed out of the side of his mouth.

Tom's 'Ma'am' sounded just as insulting as his disapproving smirk, which John noted through a reflection in the mirror. As for the possible source of Tom's new tone, John could feel the beginning of a five o'clock shadow coming under the foundation of his face. The hair remover was top-A quality, but sweat and worry always made his facial hair grow faster. Or maybe it was the flashing of the C-note as if it was a Washington that put more distance between the tastefully groomed Selena.

John smiled a polite 'thank you' and bent down to pick up the two small suitcases that, at this moment, were all that John--or Selena--owned.

"Do you want me to carry those in for you, Miss?" Tom asked with a polite tone that was more insistent than inviting.

It wasn't a 'babe', 'hon', or 'chicky', but it still reeked of macho mean, something that neither John nor Vincent Baldino ever indulged in. "I'm fine, thanks," came through Selena's lips in a helpless Southern Belle tone. Tom bowed slightly, satisfied with the extra gratuity of a smile, and went on his rounds of getting through another day as best as he could towards goals that were maybe obtainable, or maybe reserved for luckier or craftier 'commoners'. "Interesting," John and Selena shared with each other. "Ouch", the next sensation from John's wide, hot, and aching feet.

It had been a challenge for John to walk in heels after an entire day of thinking on his feet. But his feet seemed to adjust to it very well, the usual backaches after a long day of walking flatfooted, not experienced at all. It was frightening to know that his only possessions were now in the bags marked 'Selena', every piece of wardrobe in it being a skirt, dress, or something to accompany such.

Upon arrival in the room, John closed the curtains. He put on the lamps and looked as carefully as he could in every corner. The beach house in Montauk had been bugged with three video cameras, seven mics, and motion detectors that could pick up a cockroach having an erection. BITE had gotten him on tape, mumbling his memoirs, and memories and talking to the hallucinations, or real people, that revealed so much about his deceased super-spy parents and his super-guy brother Vincent. A brother still thought to be dead by most of the world. But BITE didn't seem to be on the tail of Selena Horowitz, even though Major Wentworth leaked state secrets in an attempt to get a piece of her ass.

The room had mirrors, lots of them. Wherever John looked, he saw Selena winking, wincing, or wiggling back at him. "Who is this person I am supposed to be?" John asked himself. "Why am I so...enamored by her?" he asked himself silently. Giving life to Selena with the will of his mind would undoubtedly make her come out of the mirror and touch him, but the relationship was deeper than that. He WAS Selena, and perhaps she was him, too. "I'm the brains, and you're the body," he proposed to her by way of an offer. A firm 'I don't think so' came from her eyes.

"Okay, then. You do the heart stuff, I do the head stuff," John proposed.

"Unless things change," Selena replied.

"And things always do change, don't they?" John's counter.

"You only find rest in motion itself, John," she offered. "And you do look tired and exhausted."

"We have work to do," John said back.

"Quite," Selena answered with a smile, averting her usually captivating stare.

Maybe he was experiencing the residual effects of A137, the mind-altering, and brain-changing 'special spice' he was fed by still beloved landlady BITE agent known as 'Kathleen' in Montauk during his week there, still with John. Or maybe he was just using his own self-manufactured endorphins that enabled him to get into people's heads, be they in the land of the living or the mysterious realm called 'dead'. But…as Erica reminded him…who else was more qualified to dissect the inner workings of anyone else's mind, brain, or Soul? And who else could crawl into that mixture of qualities that makes homo sapiens 'human', with such sheer force of will and compassion? John had always had some ability to read minds. Still, Selena would help him read feelings, which, theoretically anyway, would enable him to do that now, an even more critical task than ever. Mix a little data from the real world and push the conversation with the 'mark' and/or 'victim' in the right direction, and you'd be able to uncover the innermost secrets from even the most honest liars on BOTH sides of the Rainbow.

"You know," John said as the final word to Selena. "I know people who are so used to lying that they don't know when they are telling the truth."

"Am I looking at one now?" she challenged.

"Not yet," was his silent comment and conclusion. "But we have to find out which men--or women science is lying at the Klasen Institute, and why!"

Dinner was delivered, on the house, or perhaps out of Day Manager Tom Robinson's meager paycheck. It was, after testing it on the cockroaches who chose to be John's roommates when the lights were off, free of hemlock, cyanide, arsenic, and taste. As well as any trace of A137. But there was little choice in the matter, as John's body needed to be fed for Selena to do her best or worst. The four hundred bucks could only go so far in a Western town plagued by inflation and Eastern vacationers, which was becoming more Aspenized by the minute. And the credit cards, all in Selena's name, with picture ID, had technical problems that Tom promised to clear up by morning.

It didn't matter much, anyway. Selena had 1-800 and an FAX number to send all important information to, and all of her needs seemed to be taken care of so ominously well. She also had a tight agenda for the next four days at the Klasen, allowing precious little time for her, or John, to do unscheduled snooping. Listening and watching would have to be done fast, in style, and with maximal intensity.

Leonard, or whoever Leonard talked to, had sewn microtages into John's new clothes and accessories, indicating what was to be worn on what day, and where. At first, still 'Doctor' Baldino thought that Leonard didn't trust his 'fashion sense', and that he would give away his real gender with a mismatching of colors, shapes, or textures. But there was a deeper madness to Leonard's tastefully fashionable agenda. John could feel the beads inside the sleeves, bracelets, chokers, and even the bras. They were all state-of-the-art non-metallic metals. High--tech things undoubtedly were connected to highly-placed people. These were some places connected to 'the places of change and influence. Maybe mini voice recorders, or maybe not.

"Do whatever Leonard tells, or told, you," the note under the char-burned steak delivered to the room said in Baldinoese from Vincent, a language of inverted and contorted letters/phrases that John and Vinny invented as kids when trying to keep messages between them unreadable to their Catholic School Nun teachers, girlfriends and, they hoped, parents. "I'll contact you when I can. But this ain't no casual bank robbery day," the rest of the hypergraph read.

"Indeed, it isn't, Brother Vincent," John said as he went through the assigned garb. No trousers, no shorts, not even a tie or a sports jacket adopted for power-bitch fashionwear. Everything was elegantly and unmistakably female.

With no other options left for his field of vision in the mirror-filled room, John gave in to the most understated pastime of American egotists. "Guess you win this first round, Selena," he said to the woman in the mirror, addressing the brain behind her big, baby-blue eyes this time. "You get my body, and everything that goes on it."

"You need a shave, John," she said back.

"Do I get to keep my balls?" he asked.

"We'll BOTH need them. We have a busy day tomorrow. Time to get some sleep."

"Which side of the brain do you want?" John inquired.

"The one you're not going to use."

John smiled. "Goodnight, Selena,"

"Goodnight, Johnboy," was Selena's heartfelt reply.

VI

"Life isn't a battle, it's a dance," was John's first conscious thought of the day after a night of bizarre, vivid dreaming. He woke up in the more lush than functional hotel room, sneaking a look out the window from a small slit in the curtains. Such a panoramic view provided a panoramic view of the mobile homes occupied by the working caste, the condos owned by the rich, and the loudly speaking mountains behind them, which hid secrets from the citizens of the valley. Those secrets included the whereabouts of untold numbers of still-alive and defiant Apaches. He couldn't remember the details of the nightmares that woke him up prematurely, but only the texture. The dreams were in color this time, not just black and white, but they were about something very, very important.

Fighting demon death was at the center of it, as was always the case with physician Baldino as he sought the advice of the wizards on the Ozian side of the Rainbow. But the issue at hand now seemed to be how to trick the demon death out of more victims. Maybe it was a Western thing, perhaps an Apache thing, or maybe something Selena was trying to suggest. Her eyes were sad, and seductive and could use another touch of mascara and liner for John to see what solutions were incubating inside them.

Or maybe it was something even more basic. John recalled the arguments his father would have with his mother when dealing with the newsworthy and non-news-worthy civil injustices that afflicted the residents of Yonkers, New York, every day. Iron Mike Baldino, a decorated veteran of WWII and silently-valued soldier of at least five undeclared wars thereafter, would ask his sons upon returning home from unnamed places of change with a camaraderie, 'How goes the battle?'

Five-foot-two, 98-pound Helena, an ex-Nun who still maintained her missionary status privately. Upon returning from overseas (or over on the darker side of town), she would greet John and Vincent by name, with a broad smile and some kind of hug, a touch of the hand, or a peck on the cheek. In matters of husband-wife disputes, Mike would win every battle, but it seemed that Helena won every war. It was that way in mother-son arguments, too. She never had to raise her voice. If Helena wanted her boys to do the lawn, paint the gutters, or get a haircut by the weekend, Vinny and John would use every stall, trick, and manly boast of defiance at their disposal. But by Friday, 6 pm, the manicured front yard, bright red roofs, and tastefully trimmed topknots were the pride of the neighborhood and the Baldino bros.

Born to the "just the facts, Ma'am" sign of Aires, John Baldino was never comfortable with getting what you wanted by manipulation. Yet he knew that the nurse who suggested therapeutic approaches and treatments to upcoming residents usually was far more effective as a doctor than an attending physician who TOLD said residents what to do. "Do you think that we're dealing with a bladder infection instead of a brain tumor, Doctor?" was far more effective in getting scalpels out of the skull bone and eyes onto the organs that presented the real problems.

John recalled that teaching and ruling from below was more gentle and effective than the "Herr Professor" dictator approach, which was, interestingly, being distorted by so many senior male physicians. Tragically, it was adopted by many women doctors, particularly the ones who had been nurses. Healthcare problems in the US of A were going to pot for more reasons than bad communication between hospital administrators and HMOs. And more people than ever were suffering and dying. Even Iron Mike Baldino knew that veteran Sergeants suggested orders to wet-behind-the-ears Captains in the field before the chain of command was officially passed on. And even in war, politics is politics.

The situation in, and apparently around, Mad Indian Disease at Rez Zero was even worse, and getting more Apocalyptic by the day. It was reported with the most extreme indifference by the White newscaster who blasted it into John's ears, replacing the sustaining sound of Silence that was John's constant mantra, even amidst the most crowded airports or subway cars. Two Apache youths were shot today as they broke into a pharmacy. The youths were armed and reported to be dangerous. They are reported to be in serious condition. Further report at 6."

"'Reported,'" John said to himself and Selena in the mirror next to the T.V. "Whenever you want to tell the world that something is said to be true but really isn't, you say 'it is reported that'…That's the way it works in the scientific literature also."

"And, apparently, the real world outside the lab," Selena replied with a face appearing in the mirror that looked more Barbie than bitch, more purr than a pariah. "Stop staring at me and look out that window, you pervert!" she shot back at John straight to cerebral cortex areas 10, 2, and several others that had lain, by necessity, dormant for most of his adult life.

Outside, in a public place in full view of the dark and dingy alley behind the University Hospital, provided by a smaller window on the opposite side of the room, a very private affair was going on. An Apache elder in torn jeans, mismatched cowboy boots, and a tattered Army surplus jacket were doing what seemed to be a death dance in the middle of a circle delineated by assorted junk, including used cans, empty cleaner bottles, and boxes of bloody tampons. His jerky hand motions and eye movements indicated that he was in Stage Two of 'MID'. The chants were in a language that John could not understand, but which he could somehow feel. The carved tattoo on his chest bore a striking resemblance to the semi-circle mark left on John's right wrist by the Eagle back in New York. It was the only part of John's body not taken by Selena. A distinctive brand that Leonard insisted on covering up with a foundation that would even out skin and body tone, making Selena seem dark enough to be 'exotic' but not 'wetback' to the Anglo Caucasion scientists John Baldino had to interview

"Don't you think we'd better cover that up?" Selena said to John in a soft voice from inside, John's aching but still hungry for expansion head.

"I told you that area 14 was off-limits, Selena," John shot back. "We have to ask that old man some questions. And we have to do it NOW! I'LL go if you won't." John reached to pull off the Selena wig from his head, but her long dark brown locks were stuck to his own hair, apparently with clip-on extensions Leonard had put in while John was asleep back in New York.

"Leonard does great hair," Selena said. "It looks so…natural."

"There is NOTHING natural about this!" John protested, trying to untangle the knots and pins Leonard had installed so well. "I'm going to demand that the Indian out there talk to me!"

"Fine. We'll ask him."

John threw a bathrobe over the hairless body below his neck, noting that it was getting a bit more tanned than the previous day, perhaps more Mexican, or perhaps more

"He's out here!", Selena screamed from the cerebral frontal lobe area 6.

John carefully edged his way down the fire escape to a balcony one story over the Elder. It provided a full view of the morning rush hour in downtown Flagstaff and the desert beyond, saying to any frustrated driver stuck in a traffic jam and gridlock life---"just leave it, if you dare". Selena saw trouble from her observation post in occipital lobe 19 of John's head. She and John then noted a convergence of at least eight green sedan cars at a single entrance and exit point of the garbage-infested alley where the Old Indian was dancing.

"We'd better be careful out there," Selena warned as John, holding him back from sliding down the balcony to the garbage-covered alley below, where the Elder continued to dance, not taking notice of John, or the rats who were avoiding getting stomped on by his hole-ridden boots.

"I'll show him my hand, which has the same insignia as the brand on his chest," John said, wiping off the foundation from it as best as he could. "No coincidence that..."

"The claws of an Eagle feasting on garbage dumps in New York are the same as those swooping around the mountains here?"

"It's not a coincidence," John pointed out to Selena, voluntarily surrendering his consciousness to a voice from the 'decal from the Infinite' on his wrist.

"Maybe so, but those visitors from the REAL world may have something to say about your 'coincidences. Selena blasted out, diverting John's stare into the infinite' to the guns, hospital masks, and generic military attire on the men who got out of the largest green vehicle that stopped in an alley behind the Elder. "I know that guy. He looks familiar," Selena said regarding their leader to John, using John's lips to SAY it this time.

"We all do," John added, regarding the man who bore a striking resemblance to Major Harry Wentworth. "But, first, I have to show this Indian, who seems to be a Shaman, this impression the eagle made on my hand when I was in New York."

"We'll blow the entire Mission if you do, John," the ghost of the most recent investigator of Mad Indian Disease warned her successor.

"Why, Selena?" John inquired.

"I don't know. But...eh..."

Serena's reply, or John's assessment of it, was interrupted by a stream of Japanese tourists in China Cowboy hats migrating into the alley, not aware, or not caring, about the procession of green sedans. Three of them filmed and photographed the Apache death dancer, with awe and fascination on their faces. According to what John could translate from their comments and decipher from their heavily accented English, they thought it was a rain dance.

Upon hearing and seeing the tourists, the old man froze in his position. All of the tourists took out their cameras to record the 'authentic Indian'. After this, the old and soon-to-be-deceased Apache elder noted something in the sky that was visible only to him. This resulted in him picking up a broomstick that had been sharpened at the end, appending to it a feather from his back pocket, and going into what, to the tourists, was a colorfully choreographed defensive battle against a mythical beast, using the broomstick sharpened at one end. The G-men hid their weapons, their leader instructing his men and the drivers into green sedans with government licenses to back away from the dancer and the tourists.

"What's the Apache word for 'friend', again?" John asked himself as he searched the cubbyhole of his cranial vault regarding the crash course in Apache he read on the plane. "You have to know it!" he asked Selena.

"No, I don't," she replied. "And don't do what I know you are thinking, John," Selena replied, reading John's mind, heart, and emerging agenda.

"I didn't ask what you say to your friends, or prospects, Selena. I asked you what the Apache word for friend is, which I am sure you DO know," John muttered as silently as he could.

"Ya know, or should know, I didn't ask to be assigned to help you, John!" Selena blasted out from inside John's head.

A momentary glimpse of 'total picture' hit John like a clenched fist in the belly at an Irish drinking match gone bad. "'YOU were assigned to help ME, Selena?'"

"We're both assigned to help each other, John," Selena replied.

"I assign myself what I do," John balked. "And," he said, looking at the claw mark the eagle left in his right hand in New York. "I think that old before his time man has something in common," he continued to Selena, pointing her attention to the same impression on the Elder's chest through the opening in his coat.

"Friend", John said to the 'dancer' in English, as the frightened of heights ex-Doc jumped down from the balcony. Upon landing, he stumbled on a discarded hospital mattress, which he hoped would have a paucity of bugs, needles, or body secretions. With his eagle-stamped right hand, extended out to the Old Indian, John edged his way towards the MID patient, who could perhaps give him the first honest answer as to what that affliction was about. The old man, whose tremors were getting worse with each affirmative step in this 'war dance', was getting worse.

'Friend,' John repeated, from a collection of native languages he somehow recalled from his youth when watching Cowboy and Indian Westerns. He of course ignored 'kimosavi', which he found out later was Mohawk for 'poop face'. But the Elder kept on fighting the demon that only he could see from inside the circle of mixed 'rocks'... He shooed John away from him with his non-armed hand, protecting John from whatever or whoever he was fighting. Or, perhaps, John thought, it was to keep John from entering the circle of assorted objects, fashioned into what John recalled could be a medicine wheel. A sacred place of power and protection.

"Okay, I'll fight this demon with you," John offered from outside of the improvised medicine wheel. "I'm just going to get a spear of my own," he said as he picked up a discarded mop handle and walked towards the circle of assorted rocks. "And fight that demon with you."

John quickly noted that the older man's wrinkles were more profound than they appeared from a distance. The whites of his eyes were yellow. John placed himself between the old man and the demon he was fighting, then dared to look at and into his ocular portholes. The Elder's pupils finally stopped rotating when John gently touched his shaking right hand, causing his tremors to stop.

"You and I, talk?" John asked in a voice that was partially Selena's and partially his. "Man to, sort of anyway, man?"

The Japanese tourists laughed at the joke from the brunette babe to the distorted Old Indian. Then broke into applause. John turned to them, asking them with hand motions to curtail their clapping. The youngest of them, a teenage girl who seemed to be brighter than any of the adults around her, googled something on her phone, smiled, then said to John in her best English. "Word for a friend in Apache is…"

As the wonder child struggled to wrap her Asian mouth around the First Nations word, the older man disappeared as fast as he emerged, leaving a cloud of black dust in his wake. The head tourist, who seemed to be more of a film than tour director, said something in Japanese that meant 'find him, or this movie will never be filmed and none of you will be paid now or when we get home'. His underlings spread out in all directions to find the older man.

"I needed to talk to the Old Man," John muttered to himself.

"We will," Selena affirmed. "Man to man," the follow-up, said prophetically.

"But as what man?" John asked.

"The one who better get my and your ass upstairs and out of range of those feds, cops, and/or military goons behind you before we BOTH get arrested," Selena answered, as loudly as ever, into the ears inside John's head. He scurried towards the black and now white cloud that lingered in the Old Indian's absence. A set of sirens was then audible to John's outer ears, coming from 2 police cars and as many military ambulances. "And that smell of dust the old man left behind, it's meant to confuse as well as blind any enemy trying to put you into the ground, jail, or a hospital bed in a permanently locked psych ward," John heard from Selena, or perhaps himself, or…as he considered…another woman trying to keep him alive, so he could die after he saved more people. The right people anyway.

John's inner nose could somehow smell the kind of death that inner voice was speaking of, along with an aroma that he could not define that made him feel lighter than air, somehow able to fly into the sky and merge with it.

As for Selena….There was something about the Eagle Cult that was not part of her world, or perhaps her gender. Then, there was the all-present practical side of things she never lost sight of. "We have to be ready to interview the scientists at the Klasen Institute at nine, John. Everything's arranged. Vincent's orders," she informed John.

"Maybe...But, fuck, it's only seven, Selena."

"That gives us two hours to get ready," she informed his still body-occupying partner. "And there's no need to curse at me, John," Selena continued, conveying a world of hurt under her subliminal hush.

"I forgot. The damn girl make-up and wardrobe thing, according to YOU anyway, doesn't go with expressive expletives," John replied.

"Fucking right, John," Selena affirmed from behind prefrontal area 3.

"And…I get to think, and you get to do the wiggling!" John shot back.

"Yes, John," her meek reply from behind every motor neuron in John's brain.

John knew that women were better at listening than men, or at least they pretended to be. "I'm going to need some of your 'sensing' apparatus, okay? But only when I ask for it."

"Yes, John," the submissive reply that ruled from below.

John took long strides on the way up the thankfully not observed stairs on the fire escape to the penthouse but remembered to keep them narrow. He recalled that women were about feeling, not thinking, at least according to the books written by most men, and some women. At least that was the way it was with traditional women. And bitchy as she could be, Selena was traditional. She held on to the estrogen receptors in John's brain with the desperation of a protective mother and the love of a young girl enamored by her first real boyfriend.

"Who is she?" John asked himself regarding another female presence attempting to get into his head, mind, and heart, remembering that his crossing over the life-death line during that fateful fortnight at Montauk was about more than just visualizing other souls. But it was also about bringing them to life, and perhaps, becoming them. Listening to the visions kept him alive during that two-week 'vacation' when he was writing his memoirs. Trusting the wrong ones nearly cost him his sanity and identity.

"This is bullshit!" he said after assessing the absurdity and familiar strangeness to it all. He reached the last staircase to the Penthouse and found his way to the thankfully still-open escape window he had crawled out of. "This is shit, crap...I'm going to swallow a big bottle of beer, glass and all, and wake up from this dream and---" He stopped, stumbled, and looked down at his hand. "Darn it, I...I...shoot...I chipped a goshdarn nail," came out of the lips.

"And we both have a lot of learning to do," Selena said hauntingly from the window reflection. "Tempus fugit."

"Time flies," John replied, silently. His affirmation came from an Eagle, who perched up on top of the gutter just above the window. The bird flapped its wings, showing off a six-foot wing span. It seemed to know that John still harbored his fear of birds, almost as much as the Indians feared the iron horse or, in the case of MID, the white steel buffalo. "I'm okay with this," John said with every brain cell in his head, heart, and gut. "I'm really okay with this!" was the repetitive mantra.

"Coming, John?" Selena's voice said from inside the hotel room.

"Yeah," John said. The eagle displayed a final show of its wingspan. The black hole between his beaks emitted what seemed like one of those 'There ya go, guy' nods Iron Mike would give Vincent after a well-earned touchdown. Or an 'ada boy' he would give John after his 'too much of a genius to risk putting him into combat' son pulled another trapped patient out of the woods. Then, without letting John figure out who he was or where he came from, the Eagle flew away.

"We're running late," Selena related in a dominant tone infiltrated by the kind of fear John had not heard from her.

"We may run a little later," John replied, gazing at a feather the Eagle left in his hand. And felt a recently-wetted urine-soaked crotch under his lace panties.

VII

Selena knew more about the Apaches than she was telling. At least that's what John intuited from his right association cortex in the private time behind closed doors in the hotel room, which he hoped was not bugged. Every time John Baldino thought about getting the Apache perspective on MID, 'Ms.' Selena Horowitz would divert his thoughts to the left parietal lobe, to matters of scientific data written up in the Journals, or snuck out of the morgue.

John perused the research records of investigators from the Klassen Institute no less than five times, who had published far more than their officially declared grants could support. With happy faces of the researchers on the Klasen Quarterly featured the happy faces of researchers that reeked of professional confidence, academic bliss, and effortless success. But it had a rancid odor between the lines that was worse than the Secaucus exit on the New Jersey turnpike, still the smelliest stretch of over-industrialized road on the Eastern seaboard.

John and Selena agreed on one thing so strongly, and painfully, that they never had to talk about it. The real deadly and contagious disease at the Klassen and the town around it wasn't cancer, MID, or anything biological. It was the deadness of spirit. A contiguous humorless lifelessness leading to the insensitivity of mind, and inevitably to a machine operating on indifference, myopic logic, and no real agendas except short-term self-interest.

John recognized some of the faces in the Klassen Quarterly Magazine that had been dropped off at his hotel room by the official liaison. Some he didn't. It had been years since Doctor Baldino had attended conferences with these guys by day, sipped brandy and martinis with them by night, and, on rare occasions, peeked at nude dancers with them in the wee hours of the night. However, answering some off-handed baiting questions by inquisitive graduate students who wanted to work for his research competitors, John always found himself being discreet concerning getting the dirt on his fellow senior research colleagues while they were colleagues.

"I know that nerds and geeks can become dorks with enough power, but we still need nerds, geeks, and even dorks. Without science, spirituality is blind, " John asserted in carefully spoken words to himself now, and his new 'colleague' and on-skin companion, Ms. Selena Horowitz.

"And without spirituality, science is lame," Selena's echoed comeback between John's ears, which were still hurting after having been pierced for the first time. "You know better than to use half an Einstein quote against ME."

"And Einstein was a woman, Selena?"

"The part of him that was interesting," was her reply. "And, eventually, right. Some men and women say that the real scientific brains and inspiration behind Albert was his first wife, Mileva. And when the always-alone Albert became a politician for peace, it was his second wife who did all the.."

"We don't have time for this," John pressed. "I...as you...have to find out what my colleagues have been doing with their time, money, and reputations. I can't believe that a scientist dedicated to investigations in the Life sciences is behind all of this dying at the Rez."

"Yes, you can," was Selena's reply. "You left research because serving humanity as a scientist wasn't human enough."

"And I...I mean…eh… Selena Horowitz...is supposed to do a story on 'The Soul of the Scientist'." He read from the assignment sheet and accompanying forgeries of Selena's glossy-printed resume, that Erica had left with Leonard. "The

Klassen Institute has more Nobel Prize caliber scientists per square inch than anywhere else in North America. Science is the new religion. What is this New Clergy in White Lab Coats and, interestingly, Whiter skin, really all about?"

Selena smiled. John looked inside his brain for a bigger question underneath all the fragmented ones.

"I can write this any way I want, Selena?"

"As long as I, Selena, get the byline, John," she replied to him through a clear and alluring reflection in the mirror.

John pondered the issue and the strategy. "With the way I write, 'my dear Selena'. Sentence fragments. Hard, mostly visual descriptors with no flowery descriptions of what is smelled, tasted, or touched. Terse and confrontational dialogue. They'll call you a lesbian."

"I've been called worse," Selena answered, from the mirror in the room, and those within John's ever-growing multi-dimensional mind.

"When, and by whom? It sounds like you have a history, Selena, a very fascinating one I'd love to hear."

"No, John," she said, withdrawing into an even more silent whisper.

"What did I say?"

"The 'L' word, 'love', and you didn't mean it. Then, I'll tell you about---" she stopped.

"Tell me about what, Selena?! You can trust me, I'm a doctor. Or at least I used to be a---"

Selena disappeared again.

"Women have caves, too, I suppose," John thought to himself as he looked into the mirror to try to find the mystery woman and/or spirit. But all he saw was gender-neutral flesh, a human face looking like what most humans called 'female', but not being anything at all. His attention was diverted to a wrinkle of crow's feet under the eyes and a side view of the upper thigh that made him want to sprout a third leg. "What the hell do I do now? Fuck me?" he asked Selena as he searched for her in the mirror and inside his head. He asked the question but really didn't want to know the answer. John's experience with the first generation batch of A137 taught him that some questions you don't want answers to.

Drug A137 had been designed to break prisoners by making them insane first. Then to reveal truths or memories hidden in the recesses of the mind. It displayed moderate binding to five serotonin and sigma opioid receptors. It was a competitive agonist to dopamine type 2B sites and had some residual alpha one activity, elevating arousal levels in a brain that let everything in. Only the most highly disciplined minds could handle it. Or, as BITE found out, only the most empathetic spirits, empathy being a discipline BITE severely underestimated. The dose of A137 given to John by BITE just before his 'gone fishing' trip barely a month earlier was supposed to make him spill the family super-spy beans on day one, reveal past childhood memories about places and facilities he had been by day two, recall conversations between Iron Mike and Helena that took place across bedroom walls by day three, then the truth about Vincent's whereabouts and activities by day four, followed by suicide that night.

However, John's complement of 'Empathy Neurotransmitters' was higher than anticipated. Baldino sensed that 'ENT's' did exist in the brain, and were more powerful than the thalamus as modality mixers, more potent than the reticular activating system as arouses, and more effective enhancers of the senses than even the top-of-the-line sensory deprivation tanks. What's more, the half-second delay between the operation of the conscious and unconscious mind could be seen, and manipulated, somehow enabling the user of said brain to redefine time itself. Add some active visualization to prime up motor-sensory coordination, add a few cc's of iron will, and crossing the life-death line would be child's play. No one understood John's new ability to hear SOS messages from animals, people at a distance, or recently killed corpses, even himself. But Erica trusted them, as apparently did John's brother, Vincent, wherever he was.

Somehow, exposure to the serotonin disinhibitor A137 allowed John to jump into different areas of his brain, consciously. He could see, feel, and project different things about the world. No one born or man, woman, or anyone in between had survived its use. He owed ex-colleague Erica, who provided him with an antidote just in time, a suicide undercover mission into the most heavily guarded and most probably surveilled institute West of Nutley, New Jersey. He owed Vincent, wherever he was, a lot more. Most importantly, he owed Maria, the 'case study' Apache victim who died of MID in the ugliest and most painful of deaths, with the mutilation of her beautiful body and most probably a more beautiful mind.

Though working with Selena was a dangerous and bizarre alliance, John knew he had to stay the course. A debt he owed to a thousand other Apache and Valley girls like Maria, who would die painful and premature deaths at the hands of MID, or whatever was the reason for that debt. Whether initiated by BITE, the CIA, KKK, the Eagle Clan, PBS, or PMS, MID had to be stopped. Retroviruses were the deadliest of microbes, and this one, apparently, tentatively called MID virus, ate up the human brain AND spirit, on its own time, very quietly.

The uniform of day one required to gather intel for Selena Horowitz's "Soul of the Scientist" article on the "Einsteins of the Klassen" was appropriately picked out by Vincent and Leonard. The instructions were in Leonard's handwriting, the approval signatures in Vincent's distinctive penmanship. It was simple. Black pumps with sheer hose, a tight blue suede skirt with a hemline four inches above the knees, a wide turquoise belt, an off-white blouse with a pronounced V-line with color-co-ordinated vest, and a silk scarf around a Rhinstone-studded choker. Earings were to be large but elegant, somewhere between party-girl and three-hundred dollar-a-night hooker. Hair was to be worn with big bangs and an even bigger body.

"I can't do this," John said to himself when seeing the final result as the clock ticked down to the arrival of the pre-arranged ride to the Klassen. "Someone is going to find out," he said to his reflection AND Selena as he looked in the mirror again.

But, the time for Halloween rehearsals was over. It was November 1st, and winter was about to arrive in a minute and a half. John's legs shook with fear as well as cold. "Selena!" John called out to the only agent who could help him maintain his cover, and, he hoped, composure. "I've got all the facts down, what do I do about the feelings when our escort from the Klassen Institute gets here?"

"You'll let these science-sleazoids pick you up," her voice rang back.

From John, a grumble.

"That was supposed to be a joke, Johnboy," she gently said.

"I'm not a boy! I'm not a fag, either!"

"I didn't say you were, Doctor John."

"And I'm not retreating from my responsibility as a man."

"Of course not. It takes a real man to do a woman's job."

"I'm serious, 'Ms. Horowitz!" Dr J screamed back at the woman he had become or had to pass himself off as.

"And you are arrogant, Doctor Baldino," she countered.

"This may be a good day to die, 'Selena', but if I'm caught dead like this..."

"You'll go to the pink circle of hell?" Selena mused.

John ran his fingers through Selena's blonde locks, adjusting the 'doo' so it would have the desired effect. He stroked the skin of his forehead, eyebrows, and arms, noting, even more intensely, the softness of the hairless skin, and the presence of something else---

"Pacinian corpuscles, John," Selena explained in John's language. "A theory is that we women feel more than you men do because we have more vibration, pressure, and maybe even electrical field receptors on our hairless, thinner skin than you do."

"I never thought a mission to save the world would feel so...disgraceful."

"And fun?" Selena interjected as she noted John's lips moving up in BOTH corners. "You like being me. It's easier to get inside a woman's eyes, heart, or cocktail dress than into her reproductive box with an ugly-looking penile organ you only use for---"

"---Okay...Okay, Selena," John conceded.

"And, in a gentlemanly manner, you may need to adjust those boobs, so I look like a tease, not a cunt, " Coach Selena replied. "And your lipstick is smearing."

"I'll give you a fat lip if you don't," came out of John's mind, but not his mouth. Then---" What's happening!?" he screamed from a head in the mirror that was not his own. A barely recognized woman's face, matching no other that he recalled from his experience or recent investigations.

Selena now had control of John's mouth. "Shut up, and listen!" she said as the knock from the Klassen driver echoed from the hotel door, for REAL. "I'll get us in," she assured John.

"Coming", John, as Selena, said in an alluring manner. True to her promise, she let John see very clearly where she was driving both of them. As his, now her, feet did the model-walk towards the door, in a manner that would make even Leonard proud, and perhaps even horny. John felt that he was in good hands walking in Selena's heels. But there was something else in the arrangement he didn't trust, or couldn't link to any Λ137 'ghost connecting' effect imaginable with his still-scientific brain.

"What do you want?" John's mind screamed out to Selena from Broca's area 4, the only region of speech from which he could still hear his own voice. "What's YOUR agenda in all of this? It has to be something involving someone other than Leonard, Vincent, or even Erica."

From Selena, a chuckle, knowing far more than telling.

In the hallway outside the hotel room stood a pleasant-looking gentleman sporting a "Chemistry Club" tie, blue blazer, and a firmly fixed Roy Rogers Western smile. Brillcream fixed the greying hair covering his head and temples in place.

"Miss Horowitz? I'm Doctor Tompson. Administrative Director of Public Relations at the Klassen," he said in a tone so simplistic and uncomplicated that it was scary.

"A nearly geriatric nerd," John noted from a part of his brain somewhere below the temporal lobe, very close to the amygdaloid rage center.

"Please call me Selena," came from Ms. Horowitz's 'mind', out of John's mouth, with a perky smile that said 'available'. Selena extended Dr J's hand out for the pleasant businesswoman's handshake/palm touch, a gesture taken to be far more than that by its recipient. "I'm so glad to meet you, Doctor Tompson," she continued with a subtle Southern lilt to the voice never shared with her cerebral roommate John.

"Aren't we acting a little too cordial here, 'Miss Selena'?" John steamed up from his brain stem.

"I can help you," Selena silently spoke back to John. "I really want to help you," she repeated sincerity behind her silent voice.

"I don't want your help. I can do this myself, thank you," John rebuked.

From Selena, John felt something very human---pain and hurt. Who or whatever she was, Selena Horowitz had as much to risk in this as he did, whoever she was, and whatever she had to do. According to what Leonard and Erica wanted John to believe, Selena was a real person once, her body buried in the ground someplace, her 'ghost' seeking to make a final statement in the world. It was a very real A137 possibility, as was possible something else…Perhaps 'Selena', when or IF she was once alive, didn't have the same agendas as Leonard, Erica, or Vincent. But 'she', or 'it', seemed to have John's best interest at heart. Such appeared to be the case as Selena carried on 'pleasantry' conversations with the Liaison from the Klassen about the gorgeous Western weather and terrain that meant so much to the Geek with the nameless name of Tompson. An "I just follow orders' administrator who was hired by still-to-be-identified Dorks who had the real scoop on MID disease, and more.

"I'm sorry," Dr J said regarding his daring to think that Selena was never a real person, or if so, she may be working for John's enemies. Or worse, strictly for herself. "Yes, my dear, I am truly sorry for even thinking that…"

"No, you're not," Selena's unspoken rebuke.

"Yes, I'm sorry. I'm sorry, Selena."

"You're sorry for what?" Tompson asked, having heard John's inner voice push something audible from his mouth.

John felt the bioelectric fields and auras around him, as well as inside his head. Selena had gone, leaving him alone. But with the script and stage directions, he needed to pull off this investigative drama. Still, he breathed in a sigh of relief. Acting like Selena was easier than being her, or having her inside him. Leonard had coached him well in manners of voice, walking, and mannerisms of speech, and as a clinician, Dr John had previously made himself well-versed in the "Men are From Mars, Women are from Venus' books. All was under control, as he found himself walking quite naturally in the stiletto heels toward Tompson's car, sauntering from point A to B as a graceful dance rather than a machismo march, with, yes, he had to admit it, an element of 'fun'. The biggest problem ahead for John playing Selena would be longer lines to get into the toilet at the airport, opera, or stadium. Or so he thought until he took notice of the two men behind Tompson.

"This is my brother Daryl, and my cousin Daryl, really," Tompson said by way of introduction of the six-foot-ten redneck cop and the three-hundred-pound National Guardsman packing enough rounds to wipe out the White Mountain Apache, John Baldino, and even Selena Horowitz, ten times over. "They do some security work for us, and I offered them a ride to work."

"No problem," John said in a strained Selena voice which he hoped would be in keeping with his newly acquired gender.

The vehicle John was so graciously led to seemed like a standard civilian sedan from the outside, but was a limo on the inside. The most comfortable seat and the seat of honor was the middle passenger seat, between the closed and locked doors, and the doorkeepers.

To "Selena's" left sat Daryl number one, apparently a doubt-first and trust-later kind of cop. Daryl number two, home after a long Army tour in the Middle East, glanced at the Baldino's boobs. Thomson looked straight into John's baby-blue eyes from the rear-view mirror. "Have we met before, Selena?" he asked.

"I don't think so," John replied with blinking eyes, finally cueing in on Thomson's MO. By the way, Thomson held his chin, carried his clothes, and lived 'behind the line' of an otherwise erect spine, he reminded John of an underachiever resident he went to medical school with who seemed not important enough to listen to or remember. One of those scientists who was a technician, any notability he had being the result of the genius or marketing prowess of the Senior Investigator. A 'yes' man who soon would be replaced by a robot with even less life in him than that mobile machine who was just like other carbon-based robots John recalled from...

"The Neuroscience Meeting in New Orleans! That's where I've seen you, Selena." Tompson flashed on. "New Orleans, somewhere, maybe---."

"---Maybe New Orleans, but not at the Neuroscience meeting," John countered, cortical fear center 5, begging Selena for help, but the bulk of his motor cortex determined to be a better woman than she could be.

"Where, then, Selena?" Thomson pressed, determined to figure out why the middle-aged woman in his back seat really did look so...familiar from his youth.

"We all looked familiar to each other than," John said in his best maternal-all-grow'd up 'Selena-ese'."

Thomson chuckled. The Daryls scratched their heads. The car moved down the sun-baked road through patches of desert. It was converted into shopping malls and identical 'individualistic' housing for the newest invasion of California software designers, New Jersey construction workers, and retired Canadian snowbirds. But there was still something in

Thomson's mind that seemed to bother him about Selena. The puzzle-solver that Thomson seemed to be, the comfortably aging 'Tonto' Technocrat, would not let go of a memory he had a long time ago. That memory was connected to the eyes of the 'guest' in the back seat of the car.

The reality hit. John Baldino was more of a superstar than he realized in his youth. A, so everyone else said anyway, 'golden time' when he was chronically complimented by his Elders, secretly admired and envied by his peers. And maybe Thomson was one of those 'nobody's in progress' who had Baldino dismissed as a brash, arrogant young scientist. Then again, there was another hypothesis to be advanced here. Technocrats remained so because they were afflicted with a dull-out virus, and enjoyed living and thinking 'inside' the box assigned to them, be it in the lab or on vacations spent away from the workplace where the simplest of pleasures were the only ones sought, or experienced. Reading into Thomson's possible history assigned to spawn simple-minded offspring rather than a discovery-seeking humanoid. A 'skill' that would have never made it into his resume. No wonder 'Selena' became someone who this man who studied but seldom experienced life recalled from the brief time he experimented with Living, big L.

"New Orleans was a long time ago for all of us," John sighed in Blanche Dubois mode to quench Thomson's curiosity, and futile hopes of reviving something in his past that would never materialize in his future. "We were all young, adventurous, and…foolish."

As predicted, Thomspon's eyes turned downward and inward. He cringed into his seat like a boy caught with his hands and genitals caught in the cookie jar.

John sat back, crossed his legs, and gazed out the window, warmly letting his not-so-baby-blue-anymore eyes linger on a young couple displaying their romantic affections for each other on a bus stop bench. "We both have families and professional lives now," John breathed out firmly, being sure to restrain its fire with a soft, distancing, dignified 'whisper' around the consonants and complex vowels. It was that 'hushed female lead' voice so many actresses used to ensure they would be hired in those B-level Cop, Lawyer, and Medical shows that remained on the air longer than the A-level quality dramas that got one season before getting axed off the tube. "Some things are intended to remain discreet. Is that not so, Doctor Thomson?" the Selena/John duet continued to the guilt-ridden and apparently very-married Dr T.

"Yes, indeed," Thomson concurred, clearly, courteously and concisely.

Upon arrival at the Klassen parking lot, everything was back to the 'normal' schedule, both inside and outside. Thomson offered to carry Miss Selena's bags, catching a glimpse of the reflection of what was under her skin in the patten-leather pumps, unaware of what kind of balls Journalist Horowitz really had.

As John sauntered down the hall, he felt proud. Lesson one about lying was learned and implemented. Assume that the other party is guilty, call them on it, see them fall, stick your boot, or in this case, high-heel, into their groin and declare victory.

"You're supposed to say 'great job,'" John muttered to Selena in their private room between Dr J's ears. "Now, if you can tell me who I should visit first, and where they are on this map, that doesn't tell me which way is North or South," he continued, gazing at the map Thomson left with him.

Selena didn't answer. Too much was going on outside John's ears to deal with inner business on the home front with his…wife, lover, girlfriend, mistress, or whoever Selena really was, or was becoming.

"Fine, then!" Selena nagged, finally emerging. "You didn't want a road map, so when we get lost, it will be all YOUR fault."

Selena was right. Nothing inside the overfunded think tank matched the maps Thomson or Leanard had given John. The entrance to the Klassen was filled with art. Costly art, commissioned by sculptors who put the healer-scientist-patient dynamic into stone and metal in wonderous and sensitive ways Baldino had never seen before. The kind of entrance plaza that only well-stocked Institutions could afford, or less-than-ethical ones needed. Or maybe both. But whatever compassion and commitment the sculptors put into the statues, those expressions were lacking in the white-coated Priests, and Priestesses, of the Scientific Research Station in the middle of nowhere that was, according to Insider Reports in Science, on its way to becoming the 'hottest hodown homestead for Medical Minds West of Nutley, New Jersey'.

John still felt in control and brave enough to ask the question he was not supposed to ask, but which had to be answered, for better or worse. "I was supposed to meet a guy here," John said, recalling the man who promised to reveal what the Master plan was, finally. "Six-feet-two," he said to his Host, Thomson, brushing him lightly on the shoulder to ensure his attention and delay the entry into the metallic complex that said 'Technology' louder than 'Science'. "An ex boyfriend. Body of a fullback, the mind of a tank commander, the courage of a lion, the mind like a computer, the smell of a sausage grinder..."

Thompson clamped his lips closed. His pupils looked upward to the right, then downward to the left. He pulled his hand to his chin, saying nothing. Feeling…threatened, or so it seemed by the tapping of his feet.

Leaning back, John let Selena handle the rest of the description. "He's sort of a pig, but he's more ham than hog," she let loose from John's lips regarding John's brother. "He goes by the name of Vinc----"

John quickly took control of the reins with alacrity when he caught a glimpse of a newspaper lying on one of the foul-smelling 'trash disposal units'. Its headline read "Mass Murderer Seen After Drunken Brawl outside Rez Zero---MID suspected." The suspect had a very white and familiar face. It was his own, under the alias of Jack MacFarland. Wanted for murder and multiple rapes in Brooklyn and ten other cities else that valued the lives of helpless 7 year old girls. How and why was John being framed for murder, and in so many places now? WHO could have been behind this 'event' that burnt all of John's bridges to his comfortable and contented past?

"Where the hell is Vinn----" John self-observed, slipped out of his chattering teeth, and Selena's magenta red lips.

"Did you say something, Selena?" Thompson inquired.

John shook his head no, holding on to anything that would anchor reason to reality and optimistic possibilities. Maybe it was a hoax. The pictures of John Baldino as a killer rapist looked real. However, trick photography often looked more authentic than the real thing, and some people still believed what they read and saw in the newspapers. Who wanted John arrested, or shot? .

But one thing was certain, as he was stuck here alone. Sure, Erica or Vincent would contact him. But the knot in his stomach said it would be from the grave rather than in the flesh. And though John was far more comfortable and trusting of ghosts than real people, he still found himself fearing death! I wonder how long it would take for him to become a voice in someone else's head. However, such came with advantages such as not having to pay taxes, not worrying about paying rent, and not having to endure catching a dull-out disease by being around carriers of that all too common ailment like Thomson.

The real-life vector of that under-diagnosed disorder that makes people and what they produce lifeless, dull, expressionless, and humorless, brought John back into the 'real' world. He gave John a 'to-do' list, indicating who he would interview for the 'Soul of the Scientist' article 'Selena' was writing for the times, with room numbers and times to be there, instructing John to go to the Security Office first to check in... "Standard Operating Procedure, for all of us," he said by way of explanation.

Said SOP included a swab to check for viral infections, an X-ray machine to check for firearms in any bags or backpacks, and a full body scan which, so John was told, 'assessed any irregularities in the bioelectric field of the major organs'. After being cleared, it was 'smile to the camera', after which a tag with your smiling mug was given to you as a visitor's pass.

The names of the scientists on Thomson's 'suggested agenda' were very different from the names Leonard had scribbled down for him in New York, in Erica's handwriting. Dr J contemplated the omens, options, and opportunities as he did a complete body and mind check in the, thankfully unoccupied, women's bathroom to ensure that the world would see Selena, not John Baldino.

Passing by the morgue en route to the first 'human interest' interview didn't help allay John's fears. A137 made him highly sensitive to bioelectric fields, which, according to those less scientifically inclined, could be called ghosts. The spirits of those in the morgue were recently detached from their body, and they died agonizing deaths. John could feel, even from a distance, their agony at the time of dying, a collective scream which was mostly Indian, and, perhaps, a little White. The 'holograms' lingering over the corpses, seeable by only John's eyes, were all yellow-green, In the brief time John had to pretend that he was 'lost', he knocked on the skulls of the numerous darker skinned corpses and the few with paler complexions, focusing on the ones whose eye revealed the most fear and agony, hearing an ominous echo from inside the empty skulls "Anyone still in there?" he said to their faces, after which he heard variations of "I'm still floating around here and are as lost as you are in finding my way back home or wherever I'm supposed to be now, you idiot."

After having partial conversations with the dead, John was interrupted by one of the soul-dead 'living'. "Looks like you got lost, Ms Horowitz," Thomson said, the two Daryls, in lab coats that matched his, behind him. "It happens to lots of visitors here. They come in, and can never find their way out again," he mused. "I can escort you to your first interview."

"That would be appreciated," John said, as Selena. Not hearing or feeling her around or in him.

With that, John allowed himself to be escorted to the interviews with Klassen's scientists and technicians assigned to him by Thomson, or more accurately, his still unnamed boss.

John didn't find out anything new about the Soul of the Scientists at the Klassen except that they seemed soul-dead. However, the data John collected in Selena's absence revealed some new facts about MID. It was spreading fast. Every one of the scientists assured John that they were doing everything in their power to stop it, as well as the myriad of diseases that usually plague humans and animals.

"I got some shrugs of indifference from the techs on the way in here," John said to Selena, and perhaps a third visitor intruding into their midst thought as he looked through the bullet-proof glass between the security office and the common hallway from the lunch room where Selena was guided to a specific area of the establishment. A portion of the multi-roomed eatery where all the diners were professionals and, because of such, mostly white. "Maybe these overfunded, sheltered, and boring as odorless shit researchers don't care what they saw or who I really am," John reported to the now two inhabitants in his head."They probably don't know very much, anyway. Any brilliant scientist keeps his techs underpaid, hungry, and in the dark, particularly when the experiments are secret, and the data forged." John then flashed on something, the rightness of "you only find the real reason in mental motion itself, fueled with a little anger to break out of orbit."

"Falsification of data! THAT'S the look I saw in the eyes of the head techs, the ones who really ran the labs, and the ones who gave me that 'we've seen you before' look, I think," John screamed to himself, in Silence. He finally put the face to the name of one of the White Coated victims of a dull-out disease. She was standing next to him at the salad bar with a chart in her hand, a pager in her belt, and that mentally anesthetized look on her face which was deader than any of the corpses inside the morgue. She was a woman who was very much in the world of the living, from his past. Another 'nobody' back in NY who was apparently a powerful 'somebody' here.

Janet Olston, mother to all and friend to only a few, had been a whiz with machinery and even better with people ever since she apprenticed as a test-tube washer at the Rockefeller in New York. She owned cats, preferring their company to most men and, despite the rumors, to any woman. She knew when to keep her mouth shut, and how to keep her job. No hyphenated name would be appended to hers except 'Chromatography', 'Crystallography', or 'Columnseparatorextradinarie'.

The authoritative look in her eye and the fact that she moved in and out of so many labs at the Klassen with such ease and familiarity revealed that she was the leading dealer of technical favors in this place. If she couldn't fix a piece of machinery, she'd trade it or replace it with something else that would work. Somehow, Janet always knew how to rule over molecules and tissues without letting them rule her. Maybe it was because, back in the Big Crab Apple anyway, she let booze become her beloved master on so many Friday and Saturday nights spent watching network television and movies far below her level of intelligence, and class.

"I'll ask her about what's going on here next time I see her, out of range of the cameras, the cop soldiers, and the surveillance mics," John pondered. "We'll have a girl-to-girl talk, or, if she's drunk or trustworthy enough, something more honest. Janet always respected honesty. Although in this place, it's a luxury I can't afford to---"

"---Miss Horowitz," one of the Daryls abruptly whispered into John's ear. "Your boss is on the line."

"My boss?" John let slip out as more of an unexpected question than an acknowledgment of his place as a person of power and influence.

"The guy you're working for," the reply. The meeker yet still strong and dumb enough to toss you into the clink if you piss him off Daryl leads John to a courtesy phone on the wall.

"Hello," John said into the receiver, anticipating that he'd hear a voice to connect him to something he could trust and use. Maybe it was Leonard, with makeup and fashion tips. Maybe Erica, with a coded message about the biological work, or workers, at the Klasen. Or perhaps it was Selena, having taken on human form through occupying some other still-living host. Or maybe Vincent, the real owner and operator of the Freedom Post, the most respected alternative newspaper in the West of Philadelphia. Perhaps Vincent was alive and well, talking from a phone atop a mountain overlooking the Klasen with a free lift ticket to get John out of the valley and Selena Horowitz's life---but---

"Selena Horowitz, is that you?" the voice at the other end said, a male voice, very non-recognizable.

"That's what my ID card says," John flippantly, whispery, whimpers replied. He contemplated yet another enemy in his midst, or worse, a destructive and dangerous friend. The possibility was that it was one of Selena's family members who was told her whereabouts, not knowing she was dead.

John swallowed his breath, feeling Adam's apple pushing away the scarf on his neck like a lemon, ready to bleed yellow blood. At the other end of the line, there was nothing except for the clearing of the throat from what was probably a male caller.

"---I think this conversation is over," John finally said to the man on the other end of the phone. After hanging up the courtesy phone, John heard the phone ringing in his purse. The call display on the phone didn't match the 1-800 number given to him as a contact by Leonard et al, nor even the published number of the Freedom Post, which was part of Selena's cover. "I don't know who you are, but if you're one of my paper's competitors trying to find me---" she said to the voiceless caller.

"Lesson two," John contemplated the lying game. "Assume incompetence and punish them for it." "My journalistic competitors," Baldino whispered with batting eyes to yet another who took Daryl's place. A smaller framed Daryl 3 this time. "Competitors make life interesting, don't you think?"

"Beats boring, Ma'am," the guard volleyed back with a genuine smile and a 'Ma'am' which was culturally genuine. A Western Ma'am rather than an Army one.

The route down the hallways, clearly outlined by 'darling' Daryl #3, sent John down the prescribed routes to the next prescribed destination. Of course, John pretended to get lost colorfully at the first turn. It forced an unscheduled detour to a quieter corridor. One with less of those colorfully tasteful, probably camera-containing, portraits and sculptures on the walls. From the recesses of Selena's overstuffed fake cleavage, John pulled out a list of scientists assigned to him by, he hoped, were the REAL editors of the Arizonan Freedom Post, perhaps Erica or Vincent. Who, according to Leanard anyway, wrote articles for that fact rather than fib-infused newspaper that, presumably, was Selena's employer before she died in the car 'accident' not five miles from the Klassen, which burnt her vehicle and her body to a crisp.

Rightly or wrongly, John Baldino spent little time reading newspapers back in New York. The excuse he gave was that he was too busy reading medical journals or writing his own. In reality, he was, even then, too sensitive to handle what the people outside the labs and operating rooms were reading. News about the pathology of the world, rather than the body. News that continued to be news about famine, poverty, misery, cruelty, and its precursor, War. A phenomenon, and perhaps an inevitable pastime for humanity, which had one common denominator no matter who was wearing the white hats, black hats, or who had their hat-bearing heads beheaded. Made very real by a set of sepia-toned old photos of locals who had served in 'Great Wars' from 1917 onward.

"War---long periods of terror punctuated by brief periods of terror," John recalled, but this time with a female voice and inner ear that made him pity its victims more painfully than he ever remembered.

"I heard it's that way in science, too," Selena said, with the kind of understanding and respect she had never shown John.

"Or so we'll both find out?" John asked as he wandered the halls, on his own terms, not caring who was listening. Selena certainly was. Finally, she understood that John's innermost agony was survivor's guilt. Living so comfortably in Westchester County and 'safe' neighborhoods in the City. Sweating blood and tears over a research lab bench to discover wonder drugs for diseases in, admittedly, an air-conditioned facility in summer and a heated set of rooms in winter. The details for distribution were left to 'lesser minds' in more dangerous places. Those 'Places of Change' that Dr John avoided, or was not assigned to because he was too valuable a genius to risk becoming a dead hero. Death or the pretense of having died, of course, being an occupation hazard encountered daily by his parents, his brother Vincent, or his almost-everything-else Erica.

John offered a warm Selena smile to the reflection of a glass in the display case featuring 19th-century medical journals and tools to implement the cures described within them. This time, the reflection was her face, and not his. The 'moment' was courteously and coincidentally acknowledged by a Daryl 4, a beer-belly Bubby with a wide Buddha smile. "Miss Horowitz?" he asked. "Ya look lost."

"Not any more than any of us are," John and Selena said to each other, and Daryl 4. "But I'm sure you can tell me where I'm supposed to be next. Sir?" 'Doctor Selena' inquired.

"My pleasure, Ma'am," Daryl 4 offered, pointing away from where Dr John and Selena knew they needed to go after Selena told him the room number, but not the name, of the first scientist John had to bond with as a human interest journalist and perhaps suspect who was responsible for letting MID run rampant.

"That would be nice," Doctor J said to Daryl 4. "Thank you, Edward," Selena added, bringing up the rear, noting his real name on his ID.

"Well," John said to Selena. "It's back to the old methodology."

"Mouth open, ears shot, 'John'?" she challenged.

"No…it's not where your eyes are open, but how open your eyes are when you are there," John related in the silent-speak with his new ever-changing 'hostess' which was becoming progressively louder, and more complicated inside his head.

VIII

The inner sanctum of the Klassen had no shortage of "Warning, Radioactivity", "Infectious Agents In Use," and "Chemical Hazard" signs around. But they were all on very official-looking doors, not irreverent foreheads or hot-looking asses, as was the fashion in every graduate school worth its salt and/or sodium chloride.

'Tourguide' Tompson popped out of nowhere to assist Ms. Horowitz. Complete with more stiff body language, use of passive tense grammar, and non-expressive words when it came to interacting with Selena, keeping his emotional distance this time. It was as if he feared opening up a can of worms with a romantic flame that had returned from obscurity and seemed to know more about him than he knew himself. Or so John and Selena let him believe.

On the way to the first prescribed visit for the 'Soul of the Scientist' article officially intended to bring even more research dollars into the Institute, Tompson explained the reasons for the extra security in this wing of the building, having noted Selena's disapproval of the semi-automatic, guns, uniforms, and security clearance checkpoints along the way to the first interview.

"Animal rights activists," Tompson explained. "Misinformed, naïve, and dangerous activists are stealing research animals and destroying labs that are our only hope to find new cures for numerous deadly diseases. Including those that affect their own sacred dogs, cats, horses, and llamas."

John, as a former prolific researcher himself who hoped and prayed that God wasn't a white albino lab rat, agreed with the moral mathematics in Thompson's head and proposition. The dog, cat, and even cockroach-loving Dr J, even at an early age, saw no problem in sacrificing a hundred rats to save a thousand dogs or a million people.

To John Selena never tried to change, healing on a one-to-one level was about feeling. Healing on a global level was mathematics. And even on a one-to-one, every new patient was a new experiment. A medical hypothesis did not kill more than 5% of patients when applied. Actually, it helped 45% of them or at least some figure about the 35% mark that represented the placebo effect for anything. Medical theory had a higher benefit-cost ratio, and by the time you got to medical fact, it was written in stone. And the most prestigious research institutions were affiliated with teaching hospitals, which were more accurately learning hospitals.

Thompson's pager rang. He answered it with a few 'yes's, 'no's, and 'I don't know's', hiding his eyes, then face from his lovely, and apparently bright, guest. Then, a final question came over the line, to which the basically honest nerd-turned-geek hummed, hawed, and answered in a very businesslike tone, "I'll be there as soon as I can."

With a courtly and brief "Ms. Horowitz" bow, he went on his way, leaving his guest in a well-guarded hallway with one way out, a desolate smoking area balcony six stories above harsh pavement. It was vacant and windblown, collecting and amplifying wind rather than protecting its inhabitants from it. Undoubtedly another one of the 'punishment' pens for those who still indulged in the 'dirty' habit of tobacco use, at an institution that John knew was well funded by a major Cigarette Company. John wasn't sure if Selena smoked, but apparently, she did, as Leonard put several packs of Virginia Slims into each of her handbags.

While pretending to puff away, John looked at Selena's watch, which was digging into his recently shaved and moisturized wrist. He still had ten minutes left until the first appointment. A bird cawed at the ledge, a crow to the biologically-oriented reductionists in the 'real world'. An eagle, if you looked beyond the black silhouette with the third eye, rather than the two on its side that you could close at will. The eagle yet again cawed something at John, which he felt, but didn't quite understand. Followed by what seemed like mad laughter, and a departure back up onto the stratosphere.

Before going back into the inner sanctum of the Klasen, another secret had to be figured out in a room John never imagined he would ever visit. Nature was calling John from a more basic and biological level. Looking for the restroom with 'kilts' on kilts ' on the signs rather than pants, John resigned himself to what had to be taken care of first before any other business.

"It looks the same as the men's room," John commented to himself as he looked around this ladies' washroom, designated on the door by the medical symbol for women. "Except for the lack of urinals, presence of a couch, and a more subtle brand of graffiti scratched into the walls, not much difference." But maybe there was a difference that couldn't be ignored.

He ignored the mirrors, appreciating that they were, in essence, unnatural devices that repelled the viewer with low self-esteem or hypnotized the viewer with high, superior self-regard into narcissism. After relieving himself of a large volume of urine and lose feces, he retrieved the mini-non-metallic detector Leonard had inserted into a small canister of powder in his 'James Bond' purse and scanned the room. Nothing there. No one is listening. Most probably, but....

He went into the stall still smelling of fear, removed a transistor radio from his handbag, put the Country Station on loudly, and dialed the most recent number Leonard had given him to call ONLY if there was something big that had to be related, or it was the most dire emergency. It hit him that if the numbers were converted into letters, it read "1-800-FUCKUPS. Whoever it was at the other end had to answer one critical question.

"Yeah, talk to me," the voice said abruptly after letting John hang on for at least nine rings.

"I have one question, Erica," John asserted to the woman, and friend, who had started him on this Westward Pilgrimage and Crusade.

"And I might have one, or many answers," the reply.

"You sound so....close," John said, putting past Passion before immediate contemporary business.

"And you sound so...different," Erica noted. "And adventurously rather than merely academically inquisitive," she appended as a compliment. "But you have a question."

John cleared his throat and then asked the question that had to be answered. "Who is, or was, Selena? The real Selena?"

"Someone who died doing the right thing by trying to stop people from doing the wrong thing," Erica advanced. "Who really IS dead? Confirmed as deceased because, well…You hear and see only dead people, John, right?

"Which is….the working hypothesis in this experiment right now," John replied, his open scientific still speculating about hows and whys regarding his ability to talk with and be trusted by the dead as a 'mystic; and his ability to connect with the dying as a still in body human doctor.

"It's public record," Erica explained. "Lots of men, ones you know very well, read her work but don't remember her name. And even fewer have seen her face. Or remember it anyway."

John gazed at the articles from five years ago in his Selena kit. "I'm getting way too many 'you look familiar' stares since my arrival here, Erica," John pointed out.

"Lots knew Selena of people, good ones and bad ones," the answer.

"But was she one of the good ones, or bad ones?" John pressed. "And…there seems to be another Selena who wants to talk to me from the other side of the veil. Wanting and needing me to take chances that 'Selena 1' is holding me back from." John pondered the matter, deciding to push his further speculation into humor-infused 'discourse' so it could go where no man, woman, or anyone in between has gone before. "Does, or rather, did Selena have a twin sister? Or maybe she had a split personality? The other personality luring me, and you, into a trap where I would, me, Leonard, and Vincent would wind up being ghosts talking to schleps who have been 'gifted' with the ability to talk with the dead?"

Erica answered with silence. And the kind that yogis and metaphysical thinkers hear in the deep woods in winter, which connects them to the Earth, Mother Nature or Spirit, big S.

"Erica, are you there?" John asked, demanding an answer. After a long silence, he heard a click.

"The colors up there in Canada must be marvelous this time of year, don't ya know," Erica replied with a Newfoundland accent, tinged with a generous portion of overly accented Irish delivered with a baritone voice. "And if ya got the misfortune of bein' strongarmed into becomin' the fifty-first state, know that ya still got a home in Newfoundland. Where ya wake up to the smell of squid in the mornin', kiss the cod for lunch, and down a pint of Screach after supper. A magical place where every bridegroom comes to the altar experienced and every bride comes as a virgin, don't ya know. And when ya go to the Walruss Casino in Toronto, don't ya know, put all yer chips on number forty-two and you can break the bank, don't ya know. "

"Yes, I know," John said, looking at the first name of the scientists to be interviewed by Selena for his 'Soul of the Scientist' book, which was written by John Baldino, author of the often read but not understood 'Heart of the Healer' book, which he wrote about the people who made him what he had become before his official death. The sequel would be far darker and had to be read by the right people before the wrong people got hold of it.

IX

John walked down the corridor leading, according to the directory anyway, towards the first scientist assigned to him by Erica et al to flatter, interview, inform, or perhaps take down. He felt assured in his quest to find out what and who was behind MID on his own terms, while still listening to Selena 1 and 2 for their suggestions, being sure to be careful about which ones he took, and which ones he didn't. Above all, staying on the best of terms with them. After all, behind every great male fugitive-crusader-physician-psychic was a persistent woman looking to take over his body. It had been that way for centuries.

John tried to initiate a conversation with Selena, starting out with some jokes that he thought would be in keeping with the articles she had written when alive. But she didn't answer. Perhaps because he had become too nosy. Or probably because his humor was tasteless to her, or so she feared, lame. Or maybe she was jealous of Erica.

But, to be truthful, John was relieved to be rid of the woman who called herself Selena, as he redefined his own manhood and womanhood. His manner of lying was truthfully getting better by the minute. The little things all of a sudden described the bigger things. Like eyelines, again. When a man sizes up a man, he starts with the eyes, then pans downward at the shirt, belly, and shoes, the final affirmation of what the mark is really all about. When said man scans a woman, he starts with the feet, goes up to the hips, then the waist, the bust, the neck, the mouth, then the eyes, not forgetting to linger on the hair along the way. A woman astute enough to know this can see what's in a man's eyes before the male opponent has even moved up above the waist.

No wonder Erica took special note of John's legs at the cemetery, and Leonard insisted that nothing in John's wardrobe cover anything below the knees. Under the hairless, artificially softened skin on his face and body, the big-banged blonde hair, and the elegant $400 lingerie, John was still Dr. Baldino.

Dr. John had always been a loner. Even as a young man, isolation sustained him and his love of humanity. To be a loner was to be segregated in neutral times, ignored in bad times, and admired in good ones. But 'alone' still felt lonely. Such was the feeling in John's aching heart after 'Selena 1' left. Maybe he loved her, maybe he admired her, or maybe it was just another after-effect of A137 as he felt another woman trying to talk to him from the other side of the grave. A gentler and younger soul who spoke to him in brief phrases in a soft voice, with words in a language John could not understand, but certainly felt.

It had been a while since John paid homage to posters scientists displayed in large auditoriums displaying their work to their colleagues, potential funders, mistresses, and competitors at overpopulated scientific meetings. Said posters lined the hallways of the Klassen Institute, perhaps to impress the researchers, their families, their mistresses, or their funders, whose identity was still a mystery to John, Erica, and Selena. Each lab displayed the latest papers presented at meetings, with multicolored, glossy graphics as impressive as the data. There was no room for Rembrants, Picassos, or even an imitation Van Gogh in these hallways. It all looked academically fascinating, biologically intricate, and financially expensive.

As for what was required for mortals in the material plane to discover how their human bodies and brains worked, John remembered the credos. The ones that never made it to print in the intentionally humorless and expressionless Medical

Textbooks that John, truth be told, had written in his pre-A137 days.   But he did put them into print in his 'Heart of the Healer' book with a plethora of jokes, witticisms, and satirical prose which offended most of his former scientific colleagues, but inspired enough students to keep them Alive, Big A.

Credo 1   A mind that lets data find its natural slots perceives the real relationship of things to each other and the whole.

Credo 2 Everything is subject to question, and change.

Credo 3. A mind moved by urgency and passion will always lead you to the center of the problem.

Credo 4 Nature never gives you a problem without a solution."

Again and again, John let the data on the posters nailed to the wall percolate through his mind. Which of them was relevant? Which of them mattered? And how did techno-play with molecules relate to the real-life human condition? Then, something flashed inside his oversized head. Klasen's research dealt not only with drugs but also with drug delivery systems. Liposomal technology allows you to put a molecular pill into a microscopic ball of lipids. The liposomes were coated with proteins that would direct them not only to the cell but also to the organelle in that cell. And they could pass through the brain barrier more easily than the son of a Russian Oligarch gaining entry into a sold-out rock concert, waving around American C notes to the doorkeepers.

The material carried by liposomes was tracers, antibiotics, and a few hormones too large to pass through biological membranes. But what about genetic material? Could the gene missing in a child destined to be diabetic be inserted by injecting a liposome into the mother's vein? Probably. Could the ability of an adult neuron in the spinal cord of a 40-year-old with spinal cord trauma be instructed to become a whipper-snapper stem cell again, growing neurites up and down the spinal cord, linking together what a break, crash, or stab had separated? Hopefully. Could a bacteria or virus be inserted into a liposome, dropped by an airplane over a population of unsuspecting people who would become patients, then find its way to the brain and---

"---Now we're thinking," the unidentified and uninvited female guest in John's brain whispered, this time in English.

"Who are you?" John asked as he turned the corridor toward the first appointed interviewee, eyes fixed on the agenda.

"Look at me when I talk to you, John," she said.

"I'm tired of looking into mirrors," he volleyed back in an inaudible yet loud murmur to the inner ear. "I need to do some work in the world outside of me, you, and whatever partnership we had."

"Had?"

"Yes, it's over between us, Selena 2, or whatever your name is."

"Not until I say so!" she screamed into every part of John's sensory and motor cortex.

John stopped dead in his tracks, frozen, unable to move.

"What do you want?" he demanded to know.

"The same thing you do, John."

"I want to go home," he self-observed, admitting from the most tired part of his Soul. "To give patients drugs that do what they are supposed to do, making their lives more bearable and longer, and providing me with a sustainable purpose. I want to talk to the world through a phone, dictating machine, or even a lectern instead of the silent screams in my head. I just want to be a normal citizen who has access to magic wands on occasion. A MALE normal citizen again, even if I can't get a woman."

"No, you don't, John," echoed in from the younger, yet somehow wiser woman inside his cranial vault relative to the middle-aged, super bright and now, for better or worse, absent Selena. "And there's a deeper reason why you volunteered for this Mission."

"My brother Vincent, who did something about the cruelty in the world instead of theorizing about it," John muttered to her. "Who neutralized the worst asshole in places of change.   Rather than try to find, stumble upon, or unintentionally steal scientific discoveries in a comfortable lab in places of comfortable stagnation, which elevated me to being called a 'genius saint'. That's why I'm doing this!" John asserted. "I think," his somber conclusion on the matter.

"And for the common people? Or maybe, I pray, a common person," the nameless female 'entity' spoke back in a language only a 137A-exposed brain could understand, and a subtext only John Baldino could feel.

John pondered what she said and how she said it. "Probably. Maybe. No. Yes! A patient you choose to heal is an obligation, for life."

"So is a group of patients who call themselves a people. Or call themselves The People."

John considered the comment, in Silence, big S.

"I'll take that as a reconciliation, John?"

"Only if you tell me your name!" Dr J insisted, not backing down this time.

"At the time of… resurrection," she said sorrowfully.

"Yours of mine?" he asked.

An answer formed behind John's empathy center 3, in the caudal temporal lobe. It moved slowly through the visual, auditory, somatosensory, and vibration cortex towards Broca's speech center 8, when---

The clearing of the throat came from a real-life person next to the poster John had migrated to. "Are you looking for me?" a very real, baritone voice asked.

John's body unfroze. With a feminine circle, he turned his torso around, then tightened again. He looked at the name tag on the pressed white coat, then gazed up at a plain, nonoffensive smile, above which were blue eyes and a full head of perfectly combed blond hair. The owner of such proudly pushed his chest out, proudly allowing John to read his nametag. "This work of yours, Dr. Renkin, is...is..." John moved out of a mouth that was gone dry with exhaustion and salty with terror.

"Humbly submitted for the approval of your readers, Miss Horowitz. Please, do come in," the six-foot-tall man with a pale white complexion and aristocratic Nordic bearing said, inviting John to follow him.

Why mild-mannered William Renkin, Ph.D., M.D., LLD, was named 'Wild Bill' on John's 'must investigate' list of scientists was as much of a mystery as why Commercial disco replaced intelligently written Woodstock folk-rock just as the Revolution for Peace, Love and Harmony was about to take hold. His office was well lit by natural sunlight, the kind that made any visitor squint for the first ten minutes of his casual fireside talks, by the bunsen-burner talks. The walls were lined with ultra-G-rated family photos that would make Norman Rockwell seek refuge in the arms of an S and M hooker. Jesus was his publicly overstated Savior. By-the-numbers science, his Salvation. His ticket for entry into the Klassen elite seemed to lie not so much in his work in an Institute that boasted 'bold, dynamic breakthrough' science as in his Mission Statement. It was scientifically sound but certainly not biologically innovative, the nature of which fit his personality like a sterile surgical glove. 'Wild Bill' was clearly a classic case history of dull disease, the unrecognized and most widespread pathology in North America and Europe. It mainly manifested in scientists and clinicians, with symptoms that made its unknowing victims lifeless, dull, procedural, expressionless, and humorless. An affliction which John did his best to avoid when he was amongst their number, with a variable degree of success.

As for the particulars of Renkin's work, it was standard enzymatic analysis on glucose and lipid metabolism in the neuromuscular system, measuring the activation energy for each of the multiple pre-established reactions in those chemical cascades. But someone had to be able to withstand long periods of boredom. Ironically, Renkin wore a Western shirt with a plainly fonted "Be Compulsive" button over his heart. His imitation cowboy boots had no scuff marks on them from being around ANY horse, cow, or even canine. They were worn under pressed dockers, complemented by a crucifix around his neck. Indeed, he was a classic upper-crust victim of academia-induced dull-out-virus who didn't really know how dead he was.

"Would you like something to drink, Miss Horowitz?" he asked John in an offensively non-offensive tone.

"Selena," came through John's mouth from the mystery woman who seemed to be battling for his attention with all the physiological and metaphysical tools at her disposal. John watched his body move and his mind think, as he let this strange new woman do the talking. "Coffee if you have it, with creme and sugar?" she requested through his mouth, somehow knowing that John preferred unsweetened tea.

"Your body is a temple, Miss Horowitz," Renkin gently admonished in a monotone that reeked of boundless contentment, which catapulted him into complacency. "I have apple juice, grape juice, or spring water."

"From what Spring?" John thought in New York. "All this 'happy' can't be good for his health, or mine. Maybe I should go straight into the questions and ask him about---"

---" Apple would be great, thanks," John interjected in his voice.

"I also have some pastry. I don't know what kind of nuts are in them, but what's life without going a little nutty?" Renkin smiled at the remark, thinking it to be a joke.

John replied with a forced chuckle. It seemed to satisfy the Nordic gentleman's wants and needs. He delivered the goods with maximal grace at a pace so slow that it was painful to watch. "This isn't a food fest, Selena 2, or whoever you are," John silently related to the uninvited guest lingering in his brain. WE have a schedule to meet. Which I HOPE will involve finally meeting my officially dead brother, Vincent, in the flesh."

John felt a jolt in his neck, forcing his eyeline to be fixed upon a photograph of Renkin with a wife and four 'youngins'. They all looked alike, clad in their white Sunday best attire with matching, big, broad, happy smiles. With, as John could ascertain, no lobotomy scars on their foreheads.

"You have a nice-looking family," John said. "Lovely children," he continued, feeling some disapproval coming from his new bodiless 'advisor'.

"They are good boys, solid citizens, and dedicated Christians," Renkin said proudly, and very slowly. He handed John a glass of orange juice, then an all-American pastry. Apple pie converted into German strudel.

"Make him tell us something I don't know," the ghost inside of John demanded as he smelled the treats offered to him. Avoiding the temptation to fill his empty and vocal growling stomach with a generous bite of the strudel, he forced himself to take small, ladylike nibbles. While doing so, he noted that Renkin was indulging himself in larger man-like gulps and bites. After finishing a small portion of the pastry which just made him more hungry, His left hand was pushed into reaching for the list of questions he had written in his notepad the night before, his neck gently rammed into looking at the issues dealing with MID rather than into Renkin's face to come up with more witticisms. The fifth question seemed to be the one worth asking first.

"If you were to list three things that you valued most, what would they be?" John inquired, not having any pushback from the ghost.

"As what, Miss Horowitz?" the even more offensively non-offensive reply.

"As a scientist, a Christian, and a man…Bill? Wild Bill, according to many of your colleagues," John asked, the ghost discreetly instructing him to expose a few more inches of his leg, then sit back to await a reply.

"You're fishing with dangerous bait," John warned the ghost woman who was Selena's alter ego, or perhaps not. "Scientists like him have no sense of humor and even less respect for emotional directness. It's something in the air ducts, or maybe from wearing all that white. This guy definitely looks like he stopped being a virgin only after having his third kid. And as for dulling out fever...Selena, Selena...are you listening to me?"

"I read in your background that you're from Salt Lake City," John noted, getting back to the business of the real world. He recalled the year that the Neuroscience Society held its meeting in that Mormon-ruled city, perhaps because of the lack of distracting entertainment that non-Mormons usually enjoy.

"Yes, Miss Horowitz," was the reply, with a strange mixture of humility and pride.

"It's a lovely city. The kind of place that's pure and clean. No graffiti. No smog," John commented. "And nothing of interest to the thinking and artistic soul," he thought but did not say.

"Ah, yes, Miss Horowitz," Renkin remembered fondly.

"And no riff-raff," the duo or perhaps trio of women said through John's lips with a big, wide Sunday school country smile. "No gangs. No drunks. No Indians who disguise dangerous cults or Pagan customs as New Religions."

"Yes, Selena," Renkin replied, with a nod of appreciation, averting his eyes so that he could revisit his homeland with images behind his pathologically contented ocular portholes. After this, he quickly turned his head toward John and gently blasted out, "But I'm surprised to hear you talking about Salt Lake like that?"

"Why?" John replied, placing as many lead walls as he could to protect himself from being seen by Renkin's strange brand of X-ray vision.

"Your attire aside, my dear Selena," Renkin replied with restrained disdain. "You talk like a Follower of the Church of Latter-day Saints."

"The Mormons," John noted silently from the sidelines.

"But your name...Miss Horowitz," Renkin noted, scratching his clean-shaven chin in a professorial manner as if there was a manicured, grey beard in that location.

"It's from my husband," John improvised. After rubbing his ringless, left fourth digit, noting that it was mildly discolored after having removed, at his own rather than Erica's or Leanard's instructions, Selena's wedding ring. "A good and honest man who is….deceased."

"Yes, you do look like you have lost a loved one. I see the pain in your eyes," Renkin noted after a pensive delay just long enough to make John squirm for a moment or two.

"I guess this guy IS more than a Geek for Jesus," John conceded, silently. "He sees that I've lost...hopefully temporarily...a brother. And he knows that I still am a more found than a lost brother." John turned his head toward a mirror, hoping that the reflection on the other side would tell him what he needed but didn't want to know regarding the real whereabouts of his 'officially dead then alive then officially dead again' brother Vincent. But no answer came. Only the realization that it was time to tend to the job that Spirit Big S was assigning him at the moment.

Yes, better to focus on what Renkin was doing scientifically before he came to the Klassen. When he was perhaps someone else, and when John certainly was something different from what he was now, or in the process of becoming. He turned to Renkin, as the very established and comfortable investigator helped himself to another piece of apple strudel. "Doctor Renkin, my research team told me that you were at one time the most published scientist working with rodent models of learned helplessness," John noted.

"Yes. It is an intriguing biological tool," Renkin said, the corners of his thin lips breaking into a fond memory of the past, the details of which he was visualizing behind his brightening eyes.

"How exactly does it work? Learned helplessness, that is," John asked, leaning in towards the life-tired middle-aged man who suddenly felt like he was an eager, idealistic graduate student again. "Your funders and our readers, who pay taxes to your funders, would like to know."

"It's actually quite simple. The biological will to survive is instinctual," Renkin replied with renewed vigor, perhaps due to flattery, social duty, or financial greed. He led John into another area of the lab. It was a large room full of people with contented faces doing what looked like state-of-the-art work with state-of-the-art equipment. Such included the newest TLC, crystallographic, and column separators, many of them from companies that John's mental Rolodex didn't even recognize... The Never-Get-Dirty Dozen under Renkin's command knew their orders before Renkin gave them, and perhaps before he even thought them. "Maybe the instructions of the day come from demonic Orwellian programmers who write the Christian Rock tunes they bop their heads to," John mused. "Shut up, Groucho, and get with the program!" his new bodyless partner screamed back at him.

"Every creature is born with the instinct to survive," Renkin related with a cordial smile as he approached a shelf filled with rodents munching on pellets that smelled more edible than his apple strudel. "But if you take this rat with, of course, the permission of the animal care Committee, and the Blessing of the Lord, and place it in a tank of water where there is a submerged platform that it knows about, it will swim to safety, shake the water off his bum, and---" He proceeded to place the rat in a water tank, in which there was a submerged platform the rodent swam to with alacrity, boldly splashing the excess water on its back, the lion's portion of it landing in Renkin's face, drenching his glasses and cheeks.

"The caged rat praises Jesus for sticking it back to the cage master?" the ghost woman, or women, inside John, forced out of his mouth, with his permission.

Renkin's smile sank into a consternating frown. He retreated into himself, disappointed and offended. John saved the thread of communication with an apologetic smile, blaming the rest of the transgression on too much exposure to MTV at the airport while waiting for Selena's luggage. And, of course, too much coffee, tea, and chocolate on the plane, which, as all clear-thinking Mormons know and all people everywhere should know, are toxic to the mind, body, and soul.

The very Christian scientist continued in a non-offensively clinical manner, which smelled offensive because of that quality. "But if you take a rat and put him in a maze and teach him that every time he finds the way to the cheese he gets it taken away..." Renkin put a fresh rodent into the maze, shutting the door to the cheese each time the rodent figured out a new way to get it. "This poor creature has experienced this situation many times.   As we humans so often are prevented from getting what we want or need, as part of God's plan in so many cases."

John saw frustration and an even more painful emotion in the rat, a creature that, to most scientists, is an expressionless animal.

"You take this animal and put it into the water in which he knows where the submerged platform is..."   Renkin dropped the rat into the tank. It sank to the bottom like a dead stone. John reached into the water and grabbed the rodent, pulling it to safety, but not before the water had filled its lungs, sending it to what Jenkins no doubt would say was 'rat heaven'. As long as, of course, the rodent had surrendered to Jesus with his last breath.

"We can induce learned helplessness with a variety of drugs, now. We're working on a model that mimics human depression and learned helplessness." Renkin related with pride.

"What about the cures!!!" the ghost woman protested in a silent scream as John tried to revive the rat back to something resembling health. "I'd be very interested in seeing your papers, and the data, if you have it, regarding the cures for this," John said on her behalf through his lips, and what seemed to be a permanent feminine voice, thanks to spraying Leonard's 'specially formulated' mouth freshener, or something he implanted deeply into John's throat when he was sleeping back in the Plaza in New York.

John looked around the lab, letting whatever found its way through the eyes find its natural slot into his now hyperactive brain, which struggled at warp speed to connect many fragments of data into one working hypothesis. He recalled Erica's last words as a Newfy fisherman determined not to have the American flag flying over the Provincial Government office in Saint John's. "To break the bank at the Walruss Casino, put everything on red 42."

Renkin got a call on his cell. "Yes?" he said to the caller. After a few 'Hmm's and yeses and maybes, which lacked any sense of concern or urgency, he hung up. "I have to tend to some business, but if you wish, have a look around at the lab that the Good Lord provided for me and feel free to talk with God-fearing, and loving staff I've been blessed with," he said, after which he went into his office, intentionally leaving the door open. Meanwhile, John took note of the faces of the lab assistants, noticing their complexion was all male, mostly white. Two of them Negroid. And three Asians. All were clean-shaven, without any indication of recently removed hair on their upper lips. But as for 42 red, nothing bearing that number or color was present. On the drawers, ID tags on the cages of rodents, or numerically labeled elixirs on the shelves, nothing bore that number.

"So, why did Erica put this 'nowhere man' on the list of people I had to see?" John pondered, coming up with no answer. Except that perhaps Erica's intel was wrong. Perhaps John was wrong to think she was so right about this and everything else. Including MID. The clicking of the clock above John echoed increasingly loud drumbeats into his now aching head. Reminding him that there were other names on the suspect list.

X

John and 'the Selenas' were incensed at Renkin's insensitivity to the rats in his lab. Particularly the one whom he had convinced to give in to learned helplessness and drown, one stroke away from saving itself on the submerged platform. But the indignation was for different reasons than the men around and outside of them. "That animal was defenseless. How dare scientists like him drive animals into committing suicide like that!" Selena and the new mystery woman asserted to John. "It's not fair."

"Life isn't fair, or kind, once you become dead inside like Renkin is," John related with intense sadness to the woman, or women, sharing his brain box as he proceeded to the next name on Erica's list, chosen because of the largest of the font relative to the others. And, by 'coincidence', the operator of that lab is around the corner from Renkin's. And the corridor leading to it being uninhabited by Thomson's 'Darryl's', who would 'guide' John to investigators who would say and write good things about the Klassen. But en route, John couldn't resist informing his ghost women advisors about the realities of science in a technically advancing rather than humanistically growing age.

"The party line---passionless is part of science today. It's part of the discipline. The last person you hire to work in a cancer lab is someone who's been diagnosed with the disease. It sounds cruel, but too much passion can make you lose objectivity and send out a treatment that doesn't work or has side effects that bite you in the ass after the patient is cured. Side effects that can be worse than the disease. A solid investigator has to be, above all things, objective."

"And that's why you've been pushing us so hard, Doctor John, Hmmmm?" came from the young 'Selena' and the older one.

"I know you can move those feet of mine like a fox," John conceded as he looked at his watch, then down at the heels and skirt made for fashion rather than speed. "But can we motor like a... a...."

"Tigress? No problem," the new ghost's reply.

"You only find real rest in motion itself---as well as the solution nature gives you to the problem at hand," John noted as he became a verb, moving to the next challenge at an extended power march, faster than any run AND twice as stylish. The brain in his belly felt connected to the center of John's and the Selenas' energy chakra. Directing a body that was becoming miraculously transformed from heavy to light, passive to active, mass to energy. "I can't wait to find out where these feet take us next," he inquired of 'the ladies'.

"You have the list, John," the younger ghost snarled, revealing her pain at his rejection.

"And you have an unwritten agenda," John shot back. "One or maybe more than one agenda... That you're not sharing with my, my lily-white ---"

"I'm not Lilly OR white!" the new ghost protested.

"Then what?" John turned his head to the mirror. Perhaps he could see in his inner eye this new, rapidly becoming domineering ghost's real body. "I'll cross the line again if you show me what your body really looks like," John offered.

"Fuck you, John," her reply as she clouded John's vision with, to his perception anyway, a fog smelling like desert sagebrush.

"So then what DID your body look like?"

From the young ghost, ----silence and withdrawal.

"How long have you been...in transit," he pressed. "When did you die and when will you....ya know..."

"I don't know. I also don't know what's on the other side of, ya know..."

"...Death?" John gently offered the young ghost in search of a home, somewhere, preferably outside of his head.

"You have a gift, John. I do, too," she shot back, causing a headache this time on both sides of John's cranial vault. And we don't have much time left."

"Neither do they," John noted, glancing at the mostly dark-skinned corpses through the glass with a door securely locked, and noticeably unlabelled. The spirits of the departed lay uneasily over them; the astral fields, electrical to the scientist in Baldino, seemed scattered and still possessed by spirit. "Killed, according to the medical data available, green and yellow buffaloes," John noted. He felt the presence of people recently dead or dying behind another door, this one with no windows. "These beasts haunting our friends aren't normal representations of phobias. The nearest I can think, intuit, and feel it, the tumors find a place in the caudal temporal lobe and supratentorial parietal cortex, thalamic intermodality mixing occurring between the lateral and medial geniculate, so the people, now patients, hear colors and see sounds in a very stereotypical way.." In an attempt to pull more 'enlightened guesswork' from his head, John scratched his chin, his elegantly long-nailed fingertips, still thinking his scholarly beard was attached.

"You think those hallucinations are visions, John?" older Selena asked.

"Maybe the Eagle Clan does promote powerful medicine too potent for the normal human," he speculated. Maybe if I can get a little closer, I can..."

"No way, John!" older Selena blasted out.

"I can handle it!" John shot back

"No, you can't, John," said the younger woman, who still refused to provide John with her name and origin. "Not yet anyway."

"The visions of the Eagle Clan might merely be---" John speculated.

"--- the only thing the Apache has left that is theirs!" the young ghost ranted, possessed by fear, driven by the highest sense of urgency. "I think I love you, John, but you'll never understand what the Eagle Clan is all about until---"

"---I stop being me?" he bolted back. "Maybe I'll invade your head and find out for myself what your story is."

"I don't know what you need to know, John," she said. "I really don't---"

"---Know how childish you are acting, young lady?"

"I am not!" the young ghost woman inside of John's mind, and now soul, rebuked. "I am not a child! You, like, can't, ya know, tell me what to do. And, ya know, all I'm, ya know, asking and needing you to do it…" she protested, in a voice that gave away her actual age at her passing.

"I heard that pout," John said as the millennial invaded the right frontal hemisphere, crossing over the genderless no-mind zone. "Who are you?" he asked her, inviting rather than demanding an answer.

"Someone who…" The answer from the second mystery woman, now ID'd as an old and dead before her time millennial, was interrupted by Thomson startling John.

"So, that's where you are, Ms. Horowitz," the head administrator of the Klassen said. "Looks like you got lost on your way to your next interview." He looked at his clipboard. "We and, apparently, because you are in this corridor, you want to meet an interesting brand of new scientist who…well…is a master at new technology!" he boasted. After this, he led, with John in front of him, John et al., to the next scheduled destination. "A brilliant lad who is bringing us old farts into the new century, kicking and screaming sometimes, but for our own good. And the good of your readers. A wet behind the ears but smart between them, 25 years who, well…makes what he does look so easy."

"And worthless?" John thought. "Since 'effortless success is the best kind', 'overworking yourself is self-abuse," valuing who you are is more important than what you do', and of course, the most repugnant Code of the new generation, 'honoring your word and meeting deadlines is useless because everything changes and ya gotta, like, ya know, be total, like flexible," he recalled from the latest batch of under thirty students who he taught from a university lecture, the number of them who really wanted to make a difference in the world had dwindled to zero. "But," he thought to himself. "Getting a Ph.D. and a position of responsibility and influence in the Klassen had to involve some struggle and applied effort.

From the next assigned lab, the door opened by a crack, John did not hear the deadly silence but loud, rebellious noise. But it was not accompanied by an appreciation for Truth or Struggle accompanying real Revolution. It was a recording of a heavy metal garage-band rant that was more growl than words, and all of two repeating chords to accompany a 'melody' of as many notes. "You may need these," Thomson said as he handed John a pair of earplugs, then plugged a second set into his own ears.

"Yeah. I know I will," the middle-aged Selena said to John.

"I won't," the younger mystery woman who had hitched a ride on John's multipersonality-hosting soul added.

"I don't need these earplugs either," John said to the interesting woman inside of him and the actively non-interesting man next to him.

"Doctor Stone. You have a visitor who…has epilepsy, the frequency of that music stimulates that in there!" Thomson yelled through the half-open door. "Right. Ms. Horowitz?" he blasted out.

"Selena Horowitz?" a voice from inside asked. "The reporter from the New York Times and Boston Globe?"

"And Rolling Stone," Thomson added, winking to John and Selena.

The music was abruptly turned down, and the nearly closed door was pushed halfway open. Greeting John at the door was a creature devoid of a human heart or a human soul.

"Welcome, Selena," the robot said to Selena with a bow. It turned to Thomson, saying, "And don't you have ADMINISTRATIVE things to do somewhere else, Professor Doctor Thompson, Ph.D., M.B.A., B.S., while my bosses and I do innovative things here?"

"Yeah....I do, after I..." Thompson replied, with a clenched fist that he subsequently shook in the robot's face in a threatening manner. The robot responded with a raised third finger and a laugh.

"This isn't over, Doctor Stone!" Thompson yelled into the lab to the robot's 'master'.

Stone's answer to Thompson was music. A rendition of 'The Times They are Changing', a modern version by a punk band. "Dylan does that song better than any of you kids did, or could!" the former scientist who had been 'promoted' to an administrator as a means of keeping him out of the 'innovative in crowd' blasted back. "And Ms. Horowitz has other scheduled appointments in half an hour with....!"

Thomson's phone rang, making him answer it with alacrity and intention. "Yes?"

"The Committee has met and wants to nominate you for a Nobel Prize," John heard from the other end of the phone with his sensitive ears. "Are you available for a phone conference now, from your office to discuss the details," the caller continued with a Swedish accent.

"Certainly, I'm on my way," Thomson said as his legs carried him as fast as a walk could take him down the hallway. "And what part of my work do you want to talk with me about?"

"The door to the lab opened all the way by the robot, who moved aside, revealing to John the real identity of the speaker at the other end of the phone as he entered. "All of it, Professor Doctor Thomson. We have been studying your work for a long time and, after careful analysis, consider it," said Dakota Stone into his cell phone. The Millennial who was finally kicked out of his mother's comfortable womb no more than 25 years old with purple streaks in his jet black hair was clad in skinny jeans and a 'Fuck the System' black tee shirt and continued the prank call to Thompson in Swedish diction. "Solid, cautious, logical and…" he handed the cell phone to the robot, who, in a half-demonic voice, said, "So old and yesterday. And so behind everything new." Dakota's robot shut the door, locking the door behind it.

"Whoever you are, your generation has no respect for authority," yelled into his phone, loud enough for John and the ghosts living anywhere West of the Hudson to hear him. "And you, 'Doctor Stone', have no respect for your elders, and betters!" As the administrator whose wounds of regret and lingering bouts of failure ranted on, John noted pro-environment, pro-LGBT, Black Lives Matter, anti-Capitalism, pro-feminist and anti-gun, anti-fracking, defund the police, and, most notably, anti-bullying posters behind the mischief enjoying kid who seemed to get his jollies from torturing hard-working and underappreciated old folks. Indeed, John Baldino, the ever-thinking apolitical physician-scientist who of late was more critical of his leftist Comrades than the right-wingers like he's still "America love it or leave it/keep America beautiful get a haircut' brother Vincent, wondered if Dakota really understood what effective revolution was. And that Real Revolution involved doing what was right, rather than what was popular. Doing what is complicated to do rather than what is easy.

Behind the wonder child of modern technology was a plethora of computers, biochemical analysis machines, and distilling apparatuses that were being manned by robots. Those mechanical, metal penis-lacking men were assisted by a variety of hunchbacked humans of many ages and skin colors who were of a lower rank than Stone. John looked around the lab and into the many reflective surfaces, looking for Selena, or her new millennial ghost girlfriend. "Over here," he heard from Selena, from an oscillating cloud in the hallway, trying to get into the room. "We're both locked out," came from the new mystery woman.

Dakota closed the door, leaving the ghosts on the other side of it. With pride pole vaulting into arrogance, Dakota invited John to sit at a table. John was served a latte from the head robot. Then, a stack of research papers was dumped in front of him, bearing third-class assistants. They included a fifty-something glass cleaner who was either Mexican or Indian, or perhaps both.

"So, like, these are the most, like totally awesome, research papers I just got published," Doc Dakota boasted in a manner that John did when he came home with all A's to his father when he was six. "I've analyzed the DNA, cell structure, and mitochondrial enzyme composition of normal and some abnormal brain cells, including those from MID subjects, in ways they've never been looked at before. Using, like, totally awesome state BEYOND the art machines, Selena," he continued, pulling his unpaid new publicist into a tour of the machinery which looked like it belonged to the 22nd century, or the set of 'Star Trek: The Ultimate Cool Generation'. "Like this model 23A chromatography, version 3.9 NOT 3.8 aminoAcid analyzer, four D electron microscope and" Dakota proudly proclaimed. He then took in a deep breath, letting out more hot but ultra-cool techno air. "A new diagnostic machine that has more data in its circuits than any doctor's brain.

Just punch in the data here….and you have the diagnosis here. Effortlessly obtained…and since effortless success is the best kind…And…old ways of doing things like overwork and over-worry are abuse we get," he said, clearly identifying himself as a willing victim of Millennialism Disease. A new variant of the dull-out virus, or perhaps a different disease entirely. "Look at these, Selena!" Dakota went on, dumping more research papers in front of John's face.

While speed-reading them and absorbing their essence and details at the same time, something John was a natural at, another robot offered Selena coffee and snacks. She refused then, despite the sad faces emerging on the mechanical servant's face.

"And...Do these or anything else you're doing have answers for what's causing the cancers on the reserve, and cancers everywhere else?" John pressed. "With cures that....?"

"....Are still being investigated," Dakota replied, pulling back his lips, thoughts and 'like, cooler than you could, like, ever be' bravado. "But," he came back with after sampling what it was like to be a responsible, respectful, and humble servant of anyone but himself. "I and a few of my buds are making awesome breakthroughs, unlike 20th-century dinosaurs like Pastor Professor 'Mild Bill' Renkin and," he broke into a condescending chuckle. "And that old fart 'state behind every art', John Baldino, published about brain cancer, and put in print."

"Neither of whom you quoted in your research papers, I see," 'Selena' pointed out, in defense of John's work.

"Don't have to," Dakota replied. "Rules of the most read journals, finally, are changed. No need to quote any article written more than 5 years ago."

Doctor Stone snapped his fingers, summoning more robots to bring more drink and food to the lab bench in front of him. He sampled then, nodded with approval to the mechanical servants, and then dismissed them.

"And when someone repeats your work in five years and gets credit for 'discovering' it?" John inquired, putting aside his disdain for creating creatures made of metal, which were valued more than those made of flesh and blood. "They don't have to quote you? And....correct me if I'm wrong, but hasn't the human body and...test rodent biology been the same for the last 100 years?" he and Selena both advanced.

The 'hey, I'm so cool that nothing that anyone says offends me' demoted to a 'mortal' Millennial pouted. He then took in a deep breath, emitting from it primal rage, fueled by terror, his eyes lost in a blank stare.

"But," John offered as an approving Gold Star conferring still 'hip and cool' over a year-old reporter, Selena. As Selena, John gently laid his hand on Dakota's shaking shoulder, which was attached to a clenched fist, "I and I'm sure old ghosts like even John Baldino and Paster Professor Jenkins would agree that young people like to and should discover new things."

Stone's rock-hard fist loosened, as did the tightness of his lips.   "And discoverer and user of new methodologies," 'Doctor Stone said. Directing his eyes towards the stacks of his research papers which were written to show off the young investigators' technical prowess rather than providing inside into how the normal human body worked and how diseases sadistically fucked up its operations.   "After all…It's about the journey, not the destination," concluded regarding the reason why he was who he was, and did what he did. Or didn't finish doing what he should have.

"Medicine and science are about the process, not the product?" John put forth, quoting the credos of the most ineffective yet most funded teachers in medical and graduate school, that had made his experience in those training programs so frustrating.

"Exactly!" Dakota exclaimed with glee and pride. "The process of discovering something instead of what the discovery is."

"And discovering what killed these Indians?" John proposed as he pulled out a newspaper article showing pictures of the newest MID victims.

"Yeah," Dakota answered, taking a quick look at the photos. "But," he added as he stared at what he still thought was 'Selena' down like she was an old 'so yesterday' woman, from another part of his brain and, if he had one, soul. "That term in MID. The I stands for Indian. 'Indian' is racist."

John replied by pulling out photos of other patients and putting them into Dr. Stone's smug face, which was sent to him by Erica's still unrevealed contacts to his hotel room inside boxes of delivery pizza. "And how are we going to prevent these patients who are in the hospital right next door to here from dying?

"Where the fuck did you get these photos?!" Dakota shot back, angered at and scared of the parties who had given them to John.

"And how do you, and we, treat the heartbreak their families are experiencing after and during a painful death? And prevent them from dying of the same thing?" John proposed.

"Ah!" Dakota exclaimed with pride, beaming out of his eyes, his right index finger up in the air. "THAT we have covered!" With a snap of a finger and the surety of an overly literate Russian noble who has both control and an understanding of his illiterate serf, he called out, "Harrold!"

The most impressive robot in the lab wove his way to Dakota, giving his master a courtly bow. Stone pointed to one of the many computers lining the lab bench, the one with the largest screen attached to it. "Turn on computer 3, stat," he commanded to the robot in a foreign tongue. "That's Klingon, Selena," he explained proudly to the 'scribe' who would get him even more great PR to feed his ego, which would fill his biomedical treasure chest with more funding and buy more technical toys for him to play Doctor Wizard. As a result, I have been promoted from Associate to Full Professor and more.

"Yes, I know, it was Klingon," John replied, having recognized some of the words from his brief geeky past. His gaze was alerted by a flash of light coming through a window leading to an adjacent room. Selena's ghost, with more details of her face discernible than usual, pointed John's attention to her watch. Then, to a stack of open files on an adjacent table. "Yes, I know! Tempus fugit." John observed himself answering Selena with an audible voice. Thankfully, Dr. Stone didn't hear him. Or did the young hotshot technowizard care enough about John, or Selena, to take notice?

Dakota leaped to his feet and motioned to his staff in the adjacent room to bring his laptop in. It was delivered by a lowly human assistant three times his age with skin a quarter as white as his own. Dakota browbeat the hunchback halfbreed 'sanitation engineer' for shuffling with shaking feet and leaving his office in such a mess that morning.   This allowed John to take photographs of the multiple research papers on Dakota's desk with the hidden camera in his purse.

Dakota ordered the assistant to clean off the dust from his desk, around the stacks of carefully piled up research papers with a multitude of 'pleases' of course, delivered with a slow voice with no shortage of paternal condescension.   John 'accidentally' tripped the Old Man, causing his arms to display tremors, the pupils in his eyes to begin to rotate in circles, and his torso to knock over every stack of papers on his 'benefactor's desk.   John leaned down to help retrieve them from the floor, taking pictures of them with the cameras hidden within Selena's purse and getting shots of loose papers that lay in the waste basket.   Meanwhile, Dakota stomped his feet impatiently.

"Selena.   Ms. Horowitz. Let him do it," he requested. "You're enabling him.   And his people have to learn that…"

"Each gives according to his or her abilities, and takes according to his or her needs," John proclaimed. "We're here to help each other."

"And technology is here to help us all," Dakota asserted, after which he snapped his finger, calling out the door. "Harriette!   Astum!" he yelled out. "That's Cree for come," Stone boasted.

John was relieved of his janitorial duties by the business end of a long, metallic, and sharp rod.   Attached to it was the hand of a female robot, whose breasts were almost as large as the artificial ones glued to John's chest.

"Cleaning up messes is cyberwomen's work," Dakota declared, begging and expecting John to laugh.

John did his best to emit a ladylike chuckle at Stone's joke, as such was, of course, expected of most women from most men. While Harriette did her assigned task, aided by the flesh-bearing lab tech, Dakota moved the laptop to another area of the room, opened up the screen, and invited John to join him.

"Letter of condolence to Leon Red Cloud's widow, Harriette 2. Please," he requested of the computer bearing that name. "Presumed member of the outlawed Eagle Clan who's flying with the angels now...In English...and then in Apache."

Two letters were spat out of the printer in less than three seconds, startling John.

"And there you have it, Selena," the presumably neo-feminist man boasted as a member of the penile-bearing 'superior' human species, placing the letters into John's shaking hands.

"Ms. Horowitz!" John insisted, as even female ghosts deserved SOME respect, something he had been depriving more than conferring upon Selena since they had met. His eyes opened wide with shock and anger upon reading it.

"An AI condolence letter with more impact than even Hallmark can match, Harriette two!" Dakota said to the computer, reading the words, but not the emotions, in John's mind.

"And subconsciously relating to the font exactly what you want the reader to feel, Doctor Stone?" John replied.

"Exactly!" was the following boast from the young scientist who could correctly spell every chemical in an organic chemistry text but got baffled when trying to write 'humility'. "And for grief counseling, as well as providing a medical advisor so Leon's wife doesn't wind up like her husband and son did..." he continued, after which he rapidly typed out something on the keyboard.

Dakota stood back, revealing to John an image of himself as an older and darker-skinned counselor on the screen. Speaking in English and Apachie what seemed to be permutations of party line bullshit that smelled, to a blinded nose, like Shinola.

"Instant male therapist, more fluent in Apache than any Indian faculty member still left in the Native Studies Department at Flagstaff U. is," the explanation, and boast. "Who can also be..." More typing produced more councilors, with Dakota's face as the basis of their facial structure, of course. The first is 100 percent First Nations. The second is a gay black man. The third is a lesbian. The fourth is a transwoman, then a transmale, followed by a hermaphrodite, an Eastern European, then a Korean Asian therapist speaking in Germono's first and favorite language.

While Dakota overexplained how the machinery worked with impressive terms that he no doubt knew Selena would not understand, he was looking at Harriette. John snapped photos of as much printed material as his scanning eyes could see, or smell, nearly overloading the hard drive on the camera.

"Selena? Ms. Horowitz?" John could hear from the corner of his eyes, which were looking with disgust at the AI images of faces on the laptop that faded in and out of view. He felt a demonic presence come out of them, most particularly when they were projecting artificial 'kindness'. John then shifted his gaze to the rest of the lab, hoping his eyes and ears would bring in something that would have some relevance to finding out what was being done to stop, or perhaps perpetuate Mad Indian Disease.

Meanwhile, Selena's ghost in the hallway cleared her throat, motioning for John to get out of the lab fast! He did, just as a seemingly concerned Thomson appeared behind her, with two towering and well-armed Darryls by his side, working their way to the lab.

"You will excuse me, Doctor Stone," John said to Dakota, reaching for his purse. "An urgent appointment I have to get to, eh…" he blurted out of his mouth, proceeding to it with a fast walk that could not break into a run.

"Yeah, I know, Harriette," John heard Dakota say with disgust at 'the useless old generation' personified by the real possibly MID-infected lab assistant. And as well, probably by Baldino and Selena. "Some people can't appreciate new things, my friend," Dakota related to Harriette 2, stroking her shoulders, and perhaps sprouting a third leg between his two hindlimbs.

XI

En route to the next lab designated on Erica's list while Selena was officially 'lost' and not benefiting from Thomson's VIP treatment, John stumbled into an air-conditioned vending-machine-loaded unpopulated lounge with an interesting backdrop of the desert hills behind the Mega-Metallic complex. The cloud over John's bloodshot eyes started to clear. While checking his Selena makeup, he saw a face emerge on the vending machine, starting with the eyes. Those portholes belonged to a child of a most ancient people---or maybe the ancient eyes of a childlike people.

This vision, hallucination, or supplementary visitation became academic when John's two REAL oculars and single third eye beheld the appearance of an Apache Ghost Dance below the window from his protected perch amidst the endless series of hallways. Entering into John's ears was the deafening hush of silence, that universal sound that enabled Beethoven to hear the music of the Heavens, Einstein to listen to the rumblings of Nature, and, rumor had it, Steinbeck to hear the authentic voices of the American people even in the noisiest migrant worker camp.

Superimposed on the silence, and the openness of mind some would call "zen", the vision behind the reality happened. The dancer was the Elder who had vanished from the alley behind the hotel. This time, his chants seemed encouraging, his prayers elegantly spoken. He mumbled some words in the form of a question in a tongue John didn't understand, then turned to look at him.

"I know what he's feeling, but not what he's saying, yet again," John confided to the child's reflection. "What the hell is he saying?!!!"

"Loosely translated---help," she related. "Help!"

"Help" echoed in John's brain, ricocheting on every wall of it, until the silence left him and--

"Help, Miss? Can I help you?" came into John's outer ears from a dark shadow cast by even a darker man.

"Yes, please," John said, but this time with a woman's voice-guided, but not controlled by, Selena. "I'm looking for corridor 4F," John continued to his unexpected visitor after regarding the location of the next man or minion on Erica's must-see list to a handsome, dark-haired man of no less than thirty-five and no more than 50 years.   His clean physique tastefully framed by his real-life lab coat, made any movie version of James Bond look like Barnic Fife or Woody Allen.

"Corridor 4F," he said with a cordial chuckle. "That probably is the underachiever or the draft dodger wing," he continued, stumbling upon a pun that he tried to turn into a joke based on the classification of those deemed unfit to do mandatory military service.

"Sometimes, humor comes to you after you dive into the abyss, or fall flat on your face trying to leap up to the stars," John replied as Selena was assured and terrified that said pun was yet another 'coincidence' delivered by deities whose motives were benevolent, malevolent, or perhaps both.

"Excuse me?" the white-coated Priest of the New Age said in a deep voice that sounded like God, or someone even more frightening. "I'm Dr. Harvey Smith, and you must be---"

"Late, by five minutes," John apologetically said, remembering the Ivy League colleague he posed for pictures with for so many fund-raisers. And the competitor who challenged every one of his contentions at Neurology conferences, from professional to professional. He threw the man he used to go 'woman watching and catching' with between talks at Neuroscience meetings, a 'girls are obliged to be late' smile.

"I have a busy schedule today, Ms. Horowitz," he noted, looking at his watch. "But science is about serving people. And remember that their wages from slinging hash or pumping gas DO pay for our test tubes, chemicals, and visions of an expansive biological future."

"Smooth delivery, and a hot-looking ass, with a thick wallet in the back pocket...Hmmm", the new Selena noted.

"The dance before the sting," John warned.

"He has interesting eyes, " said, pointing out.

"And I see right through both of them!" John admonished from a silent place inside Selena's head, which was noted but not listened to. "I bet you think he's going to give us a compliment now, Ms know-it-all."

"I've been boning up on your stories and articles. It's an amazing thing when beauty and brains come in the same package, Ms. Horowitz," Agent Double O ONE delivered to John with a Bondish charm that would make any man want to be him and any woman want to be with him.

"Selena," John replied, opening the door to both possibilities.

"You certainly got the beauty part right," L. Harvey Smith shot back with a friendly grin. "The rest will come in time, I suppose. And we do only have an hour for me to show you some fascinating data."

L. Harvey led John and the Selenas down the hall, past more white-coated scientists who were far less Bondish. Their attire seemed more formal and more military. Never had John seen so many black Oxfords, white shirts, and cropped heads in one place. "I WILL ask about things related to MID," he assured his cerebral roommates. "Smith has his eye on the Nobel Prize for the prestige, not the cash," he went on. "He's in it for the glory, not the gold. I think it's a blue-blood family thing, having a rich and influential millionaire politico father who never says that what his son does is good or rather grand enough. But he's the best liposome neurochemist and neuro histologist I know---or knew. He's published more in ten years than anyone else has in a hundred. And scooped me a third of the time to press with any discovery I stumbled or pushed my way onto. How I don't know," he murmured behind a shut lip, ruby red locked in a womanly smile. "But I, no, we WILL find out," John continued, observing that his tongue pushed the words out of his mouth.

"We will find out what, Selena?" Harvey asked, apparently due to John's not controlling his mind, perhaps with a 'thought reading' detection device attached to the side of his head, or a keener sense of hearing that John had in his ear-tingled ears. "What will we find out?" Smith pressed, looking straight into John's eyes.

"I want to find out…everything about your work…that you feel is ready to share with and transform the world," John said with reverence. "And you, Doctor L. Harvey Smith," the appended, lightly stroking Smith's name tag. "The L must stand for Lion, by the stream of research papers you've published."

"The 'L' is a family secret," Smith related, stopping in mid-stride and gazing at the floor with a blank stare.

"And the work done in your lab? It's earth-shattering stuff. State beyond the art, so I've heard, and read," John's reply. "From your fans, Serena, and, so they claim to be anyway, your colleagues, such as ---"

Smith resumed walking, name-dropping famous scientists whom he envied as well as hated. He praised their accomplishments, then devalued their validity or practicality, finally ending with… "and there was John Baldino, the fool who thought he could pull merging 'above all do not harm' with 'make as big a difference in the world as you can' who…" Smith's feet and mouth came to a frigid halt. He lingered in thought for no less than ten seconds, which to John felt like ten hours. His face revealed a constellation of emotions ranging from love to hate, adoration to envy, respect to fear. Finally, Smith provided a concluding remark to it all. "Yes, John Baldino. Who…I heard he died after he went 'enlightened', then mad, and killed so many others. May he rest in peace, or…" Smith broke into mad laughter. "No, let's hope that Baldino, who won't sell any more copies of his most recent books in THIS town, can, as he wrote, 'REALLY only find real rest in motion itself.' Somewhere else, far away from those of us who live in the real world above ground.".   With that, Smith went into motion again, leading John and 'the girls' down the hallway.

En route, Smith allowed his eyes to gaze yet again at the reporter who would make him more famous than he already was. He checked over every part of John's body, from the shapely gams to the tight thighs, the ample bust, the elegantly hip choker, and the lips that would say 'yes' to anything. "I think I like you, Selena," he offered. "And of course, respect you," he added.

"Does that mean you'll tell me about what the L stands for?" John pressed.

"If you find out, I'll have to kill you, Selena," Smith mused. "But it would be nothing personal." Having arrived at the final destination, he opened the door to his lab. This high-tech training facility had written invisibly over the top "Abandon all dignity, those who enter here---". In contrast to Renkin's lab, the staff was working with the utmost sense of urgency. Posters of data and piles of files related to Mad Indian Disease covered every lab bench and every inch of the wall. However, what was most noticeable was not how white their lab coats were, but the skin color of 80 percent of those wearing them.

"It's good to see Indians working in a State-of-the-art research lab, most particularly working on a cure for MID, " John, as Selena 1, said to Smith in the most complimentary manner regarding the First Nations lab workers who occupied positions of glass cleaners to grad students, and the occasional post-doc. "MID. A disease that, curiously and interestingly, gives patients stereo hallucinations. Prehistoric reptilian birds with eight wings landing on the ground and turning into White bison that then become railroad locomotives which chase them, and gobble up their loved ones which---"

"---activate genetic memories of trains that took them to Florida after Geronimo's defeat in the case of Indian patients, and in Jewish White ones, Nazi railroad cars that took their loved ones, and them, in past lifetimes, to Auschwitz, " Smith interjected. "The locomotive goes off the tracks and chases them and their loved ones till they faint out of exhaustion, or lose the 'grit' to fight back."

"Like them?" John pointed out, noting from the corner of his ever-watchful peripheral vision, exhausted beyond dead tired, lab workers bearing mostly brown skin. Most of them had hospital ID bracelets on their thin arms containing multiple needle marks.

"Smart of Smith to have Indians promoted from High School dropouts to graduate students and post-docs," the new mystery woman inside John's head said of the lab workers who were focused 160 percent ONLY on their work and not on John, or each other. "Because he knows that---"

"---Research is an endurance test, for the sick and the healthy, Selena, and well-motivated people, and patients, usually have a way of getting better, in some way anyway," Smith related to John, overshadowing the voices inside his head and soul. "But one thing we do know is that Mother Nature doesn't and shouldn't release her secrets to people who haven't paid their dues. It's a matter of necessity."

John took another look around the lab, particularly at the darkest-skinned workers, and what they were doing.

"Descendants of Geronimo," Selena noted sorrowfully, focusing on the thinnest and most tired of the workers. "Sweeping the floor, washing the glassware, cleaning shit out of the rat cages," Selena added. "For...for---"

"---L. Harvey Smith," John said, out loud, to the Selinas as well as his former rival, and friend. Realizing that he said Harvey's name, he turned to his old rival, and perhaps most effective ally in the fight against MID. "Doctor Harvey Smith.

A scientist who is giving people a chance to save their own people."

"To save OUR people too," Smith offered. "With some innovative work that...well...I think your readers should know about Selena now. And some liberating discoveries they and the world will benefit from...very soon." Without further ado, he bowed his head slightly, in the manner of an aristocrat at a ball, rather than as a peasant to a master, inviting John to enter his office.

L. Harvey Smith's office was as ornate as any in Yale or Harvard. It boldly featured oak desks, wood floors, and only the best smoking tobacco you could buy West of Chicago coming out of a pipe, which was inserted into his mouth for the show, not smoke. He flunked off his lab coat, replacing it with a tweed jacket containing patches that were intended to make the eight-hundred-fifty-dollar coat look like it was a 'Struggling Scholar' special. Behind Smith was a poster of Einstein with no quotes underneath, Uncle Albert's eyes hidden by lush green plants. Apparently, Harvey still hadn't looked into the eyes of the physicist and humanitarian who was the conscience of all scientists and humanitarians.

"Sit, please," Harvey said as he showed Selena a chair. He was twirling his mustache, a facial ornament that suited his face, affirmed his social rank, and shielded the real meaning behind any of his words.

John adjusted his skirt, tried to remember how to cross his legs, then sank hard as his derriere fell toward the floor until it was stopped by hardwood on the tender ass.

"A lower chair than yours, L. Harvey," John noted, between his ears. "This superior eyeline problem is a bush league trick, and it is very crass, despite the fact that what you have on those stereo speakers is very---"

"Bach," John gave voice to regarding the music coming out of a thousand-dollar stereo system. "The Brandenburg Concerto. A lovely rendition. The flute is such a lovely instrument when it's played with so much---love."

"Enough 'I' words, John," Selena silently said to John through labored breaths. "We feel the 'I' thing, but we don't always say it."

"Bach is so civilized," Harvey related as he helped himself to a cushioned seat behind his desk. "I can, and have, bought the best electron microscopes, column separators, MRI recording units, and the top post-doctoral fellows in the world. Back home in Manhattan, even the glass cleaners know Bach's work by BWV numbers and Mozart's by Kirchleitner listings." He took a sip of brandy, lit his pipe, and then took a puff from it. "Out here, Fritz Kreisler is a new kind of car."

"And Mozart is pronounced with an 's' instead of a z?" John offered through Selena's charming lips with the snobbery of a New Yorker who considered everything West of the Hudson River inferior to anything produced or envisioned in Manhattan. "Wagner's Ring Cycle is passing around the wedding bands at the swap meet? And Beethoven's Ninth is a new brand of homebrewed imitation Bavarian beer?"

Beacon Hill bred and Upper East Side raised, Smith smiled at the home references. But underneath it---fear. His own quips could never top this witch of wordsmithing, this languisher of language, this woman who could out-cool him in his own culture. So, L Harvey, true to character, changed the game to one where he could change the rules and how one registered points on the scoreboard.

"I have a theory," he pronounced, leaning back on his chair and blowing a ring of smoke into the air, as if he were the Creator himself, making the world in his Enlightened image. "Pop music has a formula to it--we know this. The proportion of home chords and keys to minor and diminished ones is directly related to the stupidity of the people who are hooked on it, as is the consistency of the beat. The easiest job in the world is to be a drummer for a country band or a bass player for a rock group. Country, disco, techno-beat--"

"Disco for people too cool to sweat?" John interjected.

"Old rock and new rock, which merges to become mud, Selena," Smith, who in the past, stole rather than invented philosophical quips that came so naturally to John, asserted. With unbridled authority on the matter, of course not giving any credit to John's having come up with the 'mud' analogy five years ago. "And especially music from people of color. It dulls the brain, and noting what my graduate students play in their off time, this dulling-out virus is contagious. The next time you see a happy listener bobbing his head to the top tune of the minute, think about all those brain cells dropping out of his ass."

John faked a convincing Selena laugh.

Smith leaned back in his chair and mused on. "We tried it on the rats, and it worked. Let rodents listen to rockabilly, and they become an even lower life form---administrators."

John laughed again, with Selena's most girlish giggle, as Smith showed off his comedic follies. John used his third eye to look around the room for anything suspicious. The data on the walls looked prestigious enough, and in last night's reading, John revealed that Smith's work was solid. The most respected asshole in experimental neurochemistry had also made himself a brilliant pathologist. The electron micrographs posted on the wall showed the bizarre inclusions in the astrocytomas present in MID--with something even more ominous. Clusters of nine filaments revolving around one microtubule on top of them, with a dissociated molecular weight of 42. Erica's references about revolution number nine plus one, the answer to the universe is forty-two, and the ever-presence "it is the Walrus, kookoochachuu" were right. Maybe Smith, the walrus-mustached wielder of woes, was at the bottom of MID, which, when subjected to double-check of logic, led to---

"That's not an omen," John flashed on between his ears. "That's....a cross between a reactive non-cancerous astrocyte and a cancerous astrocytoma," he self-observed, muttering.

"Selena?" Smith inquired.

"I was looking at your photographs...They look very...artistic. I guess you're shooting to win the Nobel Prize for art as well as medicine."

"Yes," Smith replied, stone-faced and deadly serious.

John took a tape recorder out of his pocketbook. "I have no brain for science, and I want to get the details right. Do you mind if I record this?" Selena asked.

"Yes," was the answer, delivered with a smile and penetrating eyes.

John picked up a pencil and a pad, asking for permission to use them.

"Yes," Smith's reply, warmly and condescendingly delivered.

"You cure cancer here, is that correct, Doctor Smith?"

"We develop models of neoplastic diseases, Selena. With special pesticides and exotic toxins that I have access to."

"Which are?"

"Pesticides that your readers will find out about as soon as the patents run out. Which kills insects at high doses. And at higher doses turn normal rat brain astrocytes into… fascinating ones, enabling us to develop drugs that----"

"---Make the rats feel better?" 'Selena advanced through John's mouth, faining biological ignorance. "That can cure people?" John pressed.

"First comes understanding the disease, then the cure. That's how science works. It's a slow and tedious process," Smith advanced,

"Not with that army of hot shots, you have out there which…" Selena smelled the odor of something in the mini-cafeteria Smith had set up for his staff, mainly frequented by the Native and Mexican workers. "What smells so 'indefinably delicious'?" she inquired.

"Scientists and our support staff gotta eat," Smith boasted. "And with that renewed energy, we made, and continue to make, significant progress in many areas."

"Such as?"

"Your readers would understand the details, and with respect, I don't think even you could, either."

"You've been misquoted by reporters before."

"It's a disease that's more widespread than the common cold, Selena."

"Or MID, Doctor Smith?" the bold insertion from Selena 2.

"Now you did it!" John bolted out at the youngest and most enraged Selenas. "When you want an honest answer from a liar, you never ask him for the truth! You're a woman, you should know that!"

"Shut up and listen!" the Millennial ghost growled back at John. "If you men would shut up and listen, everyone would get what they want."

Smith stewed, contemplated, and then put on a very official smile. "I'm sure you have some other, more relevant questions. And answerable."

"Of course," John said. He shifted his left hip, showing a more revealing angle of his shapely thigh. Harvey raised his eye with renewed interest. Selena felt flattered. John fired off the next round. "Funding, Doctor Smith. Where does yours come from?"

"Huh?" from Smith's mouth, words hardly uttered in public.

John looked at the scribbling in his notepad, the figures all too well known in his head. "Ten years ago, the NIH spent barely 2 billion dollars and funded over 4% of new applications. Today, the money spent on research in the biomedical sciences is barely 2% of the defense budget, and everyone who wants to be anyone is dependent on the mob or the private corporate sector. Yet, your lab looks like a film set from Intergalacia General Hospital. And officially--"

"We get only a portion of what we need." The gates into Smithland were closing fast. The monarch folded his arms and turned slightly to the left.

"So the ETs are behind high-tech science," John delivered with a lightened tone.

"We have a few silent partners, Selena."

"The military, Professor Doctor Harvey?" the still Pacifist 'above all do no harm' Baldino pressed, as a direct question which his female compadres wanted him to propose more indirectly and deceitfully.

Smith pondered for a second, puffed on his pipe, and agonized over the right way to relate it. Finally, he edged his way forward, delivering "The US defense department---in THIS country, has trillions to spend. The National Institutes of Health has less than 4 billion in its annual budget. The cost of treating the average cancer patient is two hundred thousand dollars a year. Every year, two million people contract cancer of one sort or another. Less tanks for the Generals means more test tubes for us, and, if we're lucky and good, more cures for the patients."

The words sounded logical and even compassionate. But the subtext was suspicious. The sentences started out strong and ended weak, eyes turning away at each period. Smith had committed what, to him, was a mortal sin, and seemed to be spending all his waking time and money justifying this new brand of science he was conducting. But what had converted him into what he had become, or was forced to be, now? What could have been the turning point where a career headed for the Nobel Prize was headed to something more...dangerous?

"Fraud," blurted out from the Selenas from the frontal lobe of John's brain into his lips and out his tongue, without consultation of prefrontal gatekeepers.

"I beg your pardon," Smith asserted.

"In the generic sense," John continued with Selena's charm and Baldinoese restraint. "How bad is scientific fraud these days?"

"You're accusing me of fraud, Ms Horowitz?" Smith inquired, lifting his chin, and, no doubt, clenching his fist under the desk.

"No...But I've heard that your competitors are less than honest. Being first in science is everything, and being second makes you broke."

"The issue of fraud is severe, Selena," Smith asserted, leaning in towards John as if he were an ignorant and, for that reason alone, ungrateful graduate student. "And has been trivialized. Let me tell you the story about David Baltimore. "

"Wasn't he the cell biologist who made up data about a cancer cure back before Microsoft?" John enquired.

"Yes," the firm reply, delivered to hands folded in front of Smith's back-to-business face.

"I heard he was nominated for a Nobel Prize for the work," John said in his best non-confrontational Selena-esque. "His female graduate student blew the whistle on him. Her reward was getting kicked out of science for life. He was suspended from submitting research grants for five years, while he worked off of other people's money and taught---for a yearly salary that's more than most senior researchers here get."

"Yes, and his Cell Biology book is still read by medical AND graduate students," Smith noted.

"What's he doing now?" John asked.

"Getting funded again," Smith replied with an odd sense of pride for the thieving overly lettered bastard. "I was asked to review his proposal for a grant and the studies he did for publication in Brain Science. The background work is solid, the proposal sound, and the clinical application very doable."

"And your action will be?" John enquired.

"To sink it, of course," was Smith's frighteningly non-confrontational reply. "I'll have one of my graduate students tear it apart. It's good training for them," he continued, even more calmly.

"And, for the sake of theoretical discourse, if that graduate student, or someone else in your lab, decides to do the same experiments, submit it to another journal for publication and another granting agency. With, for the sake of theoretical discourse, their name on it," John advanced, charging the cannons full speed ahead atop the galloping horse between his legs. "Or with, for theoretical discourse,---"

"---My name on it?" Smith interjected. "That would be..." he delayed. "Playing around with whose name is associated with what discovery is a practical necessity, since, well.   Here in MY lab, we will do a lot more with that line of investigation than idiots like John Baltimore could ever do. And a lot more than that cowardly, cautious crusader, who I HAD to beat to the press so that science could advance. Of course, I am referring to John 'above all do no harm' Baldino."

Smith ranted on about his former postdoc bud who became his publishing rival, pointing out every one of John Baldino's flaws and failings to Selena. From John Baldino's thinking, the source of all evil is ignorance. To his former competitor's futile experiments to try to develop drugs that turn the worst sinners into the most intelligent (and consequently generous) saints. Baldino is dedicated to fixing people injured in conflict rather than standing up to the aggressors who inflicted it.

Meanwhile, John looked up at the bar graphs and charts on the wall behind Smith, recalling the statistical adage that you can get drowned in a lake with an average depth of two feet. He also recalled how politicians lied to the public all the time with statistics. Elegance and symmetry of form could turn fabricated fiction into fact for the gullible, weak, or poorly informed. Uncle Ross Perot wasn't the first one to pull off that trick, and wouldn't be the last.   And indeed, the graphics, if you ignored what they measured, were impressive.

"It seems that scientists here, and everywhere, are spending more and more money putting their work into convincing presentation than into the work itself," John finally interjected, getting up from the chair designed to keep his eyeline below Smith's, and his ass comfortably placed.

"Yes, Selena," Smith conceded, finally acknowledging his having stooped into becoming a 'commoner' gutter snipe regarding Baldino. A man who was dead, or soon to be dead as a fugitive from justice. Whose scientific studies he did before he went mad and became a taker of life rather than a saver of it, he would destroy on his own terms.   Then Smith turned to the woes in his own daily attempts to become the scientist of the year, or decade.

"You spend one day doing the research and the rest of the week writing up the paper," L. Harvey related, recalling one of the biggest burdens of his glory-seeking, and often glory-getting, life.

"And a month to get the right color graphics," Selena suggested. "I saw the most lovely combinations of colors on the most influential posters along the walls at the last set of science meetings I was sent to report on. They were mathematically chosen, 120 degrees from each other on the color wheel. Very lovely to the eye."

"We learn tricks which we have to use to please and serve the public," Smith related. "Just like your profession, Selena, that lies so much with words."

"Give the impression that you're telling the truth, the whole truth, and nothing but the truth, but never put down anything they can pin you down on?" she related, gazing at and thumbing through the research papers on his desk, with submission dates noted as TBA.

"So, you went to law school, too, Councilor Horowitz?" was his reply.

John smiled through Selena's eyes, "Lawyers are only one brand of liars. They have to tell their fibs within the context of the law."

"Laws which can be bought, and which change, Selena."

"But science doesn't---or does it, Doctor Smith?" John challenged, turning to Smith, gazing into his eyes.

From Smith, the most profound contemplation. The doors to his mind and soul shut closed with a loud thud.

"But, a kiss is just a kiss, a smile is still a smile..." John offered, pulling back his cow and bull horns. "The fundamental things apply, as time goes by," he sang in Selena's voice, his first experience in music as an active participant in three decades. His courage was rewarded.

"For the record, Selena, there are different kinds of scientific lies," Smith related, after which he puffed on his pipe.

"Misdemeanor one?"

"Bias," Smith said, getting up from his chair, and placing the pipe in what looked like a diamond-studded intricately hand-carved holder made in Johannesburg, South Africa. "Say a scientist looks at six pieces of data. Five are clumped together, the other twice as high or low as the bunch," he continued as he demonstrated the point on a fresh graph printed on an easel behind his desk, marking the points boldly with a blood-red Sharpie. "The scientist does an outlier test to see if data point six is of the normal distribution and borderline. The scientist looks at dwindling resources, and an abstract deadline for the meeting, and remembers patients who could benefit from the cure he KNOWS will work. That scientist omits data point six from analysis," he concluded, putting an X on the outlier dot, correlating the rest with three bold circles.

"I see," John challenged walking in a circle of his own, after which he let his padded ass on the edge of L. Harvey's desk, inviting him to continue the game. Be it about understanding how neurobiological science works, or how biology can be enjoyed with endorphins emerging in the anticipation and pleasure centers of the brain. "Misdemeanor two?"

"Our theoretical scientist's intuition says that drug A causes an increase in liver enzyme activity. Only three data points are available for the experimental and control groups." L Harvey advanced after saying 'yes' to whatever Selena was offering. "You need statistics to prove the difference between groups, with n values of four," he continued, showing off his prowess as a scientist and a man, at ease with a fresh graph and bigger Sharpie. "So, the scientist puts in an extra data point or a bar graph, and his hypothesis gets proven. Or you throw out the numbers that look messy. Mendel, or his well-meaning assistant, did this with his pea experiments, but no one picked up on it for another thirty years. Meanwhile, the discipline of genetics was born, and saved many lives, and many crops."

"Felony level 3?" John inquired, continuing the dance of body and mind.

"The head works faster than the hands," L. Harvey smiled back, in the same way, he did when he and John were grad students, desperately in search of an admirer of their work who was endowed with big hair, low cut blouse, and batting oversized eyelashes rather than a tight bun, lab coat, and oversized black framed glasses. "You know the experiment will say that drug A will kill cancer cells, and you saw it once, so you throw in two more pieces of data, maybe four. It makes logical sense, but you can't wait. One day, you'll get around to proving what you already know is true. The gut is seldom wrong, and the data usually tells you that you were right. Or sometimes---not."

"Why do scientists lie?" John asked Harvey, and himself, knowing that his own record for telling the truth to patients and people had no shortage of redacted black lines on it. For reasons, of course, that made practical sense at the time. And some that didn't.

"What if a scientific lie, a felony lie, is passed on?" John, who was lying now with every word from his lipstick-painted mouth, asked Smith and himself. "What if a small lie, an inflated fib, led to promotion, then a bigger lie, a whole body of scientific information based on lies? What do we have then? Could this have happened? Did it? Could it happen here?"

"Of course not," Smith related. "Science cures itself, somehow."

"I'm glad to hear that," Selena said.

Twenty minutes had passed, and it felt like the allotted time was up. Smith had been penetrated deep to the place where few people ever reached---his conscience. His stare was blank, his color pale, and his arms frozen. For the first time, John saw the Asshole of Academia as a victim of evil that was larger than himself. But what was he hiding? And how did it relate to MID?

John knew that thinking about something too hard made too many things happen, way too quickly. Still, he had to keep going... He gazed into the micrographs, let his mind remain open to everything, focused on the silence between, over, and within the Bach Brandenburgs, and then---

"Doctor Smith," a half-breed tech interjected into the tension-infused silence that took over L Harvey's office. He carried a stack of data files high enough to cover his eyes. They were tired eyes, dedicated to the service of a man thought to be a god. "We have fresh data, all the micrographs you asked for, carefully collated and---"

John stuck his foot out just at the right time to trip the exhausted tech, and---

"You fucking idiot!" Smith blasted at the young Indian as the papers, photographs, and graphs spilled all over the floor, covering almost every inch of it. "Give you people a simple job to do and you screw it up. Stumbling into this office, drunk! With valuable data that..."

Smith stopped himself, gave an apologetic smile to Selena, and picked up the photos. Seeing Smith on his knees, desperate, was a picture John and every other scientist in North America would hang on their most precious wall. But it was about other matters now.

John, feeling the weight of the Selena's in every portion of his body, and noting that his male genitalia was beginning to show, bent down, kneeling on the floor. He assisted Smith in gathering the papers together, badly, of course. He pressed the button that put on the hidden cameras in his purse, aiming it at the data while the camera in his own eye absorbed what it could.

"We'll take over from here," a gruff voice echoed from above. It was Smith, talking from a different place, a desperate one, and an angry one.

"I was trying to help," Selena said to Smith.

"When can I see the newspaper article you're writing about me, to check for accuracy, Ms. Horowitz?" Smith asserted.

"As soon as I write it," 'Selena' replied.

"Over dinner tonight?" Smith continued, calm, cool, and very dignified.

"Or maybe breakfast afterward," Selena added, seductively using every part of John's body for her very secret agenda.

Smith's techs, having witnessed the final volley between him and his special guest, released "whooos" in congratulation. Selena Horowitz seemed to be the hottest babe who ever walked into the lab, or for that matter, the Klasen Institute, and she seemed to have a brain to match the body.

"What the hell are you doing?!!" John protested from a mute portion of Broca's area 4. "I know I'm getting a strange sensation between my legs--"

"--Which is only part of the data I've stolen, stuck into YOUR crotch," Selena silently related to John.

"You can get more with honey than vinegar, John," she related as Smith undressed her in his eyes. "We can make it a three-some if you want, Dr. Baldino. I love you, John, and I'm doing this as much for you as for me," Selena 1, merging into the voice of Selena 2, related to John.

"This is very dangerous. And we have other people to see," John replied.

"They can come along, or we can interrogate them tomorrow night?"

"Interrogate, Selena?"

"Lies of the heart are always the most interesting, John, " Selena 1 warned him.

"And dangerous," Selena 2 said, contradicting her 'sister'.

"Who are you?" John demanded to know about Selena 2.

"Someone who has to get out of here, right now," was her reply. "For ALL our sakes. But with style, for the moment anyway. None of what we are trying to do will be done until we both go….home," she said with a prophetic tone which even the most skeptical reductionist had to accept as inevitable Fate.

After an exit from the lab that no one in the lab, and perhaps the Klassen, would ever forget, John felt the presence and frustrations of Selena 2 with even more intensity than before. He would never again be John Baldino until he did what she wanted and needed him to do. Such was the price of getting the truth behind the lie that was MID.

But there was something else that troubled and assured John, both at the same time. Smith had not been on Erica or Leonard's list of 'must see as early as possible' suspects or informants about MID and certainly not that devised by the Director of the Klassen Institute. But, the interception of serendipity, gracious and deceptive lady that she was, John knew that it was time to make his own list of agendas and strategies.

XII

Another call from the smoking balcony of the Klassen to 1-800-FUCKUPS, Erica's 'call only if there is blood, puss, and brain fragments in the streets' hotline, yet again led John to a radio station playing even more Golden Oldies, CNL, ELP and ABBA. What 'Wooden Ships', 'Pictures at an Exhibition', and 'Take a Chance' had to do with MID baffled both John and whatever entities sought to find shelter and solace within his brain. He glanced down three floors to the pavement below, noting that the black asphalt was tinged with blood. He wondered if it was the Dancing Elder's blood, remnants of some other curious soul who 'had accidentally fallen, or perhaps it was Erica's.

"She's hiding," John told the Selenas after smoking another cigarette mandated by Leonard as 'medicine' to modulate the A137 still lingering in his brain. On the way to the next interview down a corridor with a sunroof on top, the Eagle touched down and gazed inside, hoping and flying to keep up with John's progress towards the lab run by the next mark, informant, and/or suspect on Erica's latest list.

"Who is Erica, really?" Selena 2 asked.

"A friend," John answered.

"What kind of friend?" that same Selena inquired.

"An-almost lover, Selena 2, or whoever you are," he replied.

"It beats being an ex-lover, I suppose, John."

"Probably," he surmised.

"It sounds like you loved her, John."

"She had other people, Selena 2. Other commitments, other things to do with her life. I 'bonded' with Erica. I 'met' her on the inside. I don't know about love, but I know about trust, and I can trust her."

"Better not start loving her, John."

"Why, Selena 2?"

"You'll stop trusting her. And you value trust more than love."

"It's a man thing, I think, I remember, I...eh." John looked up to the roof, noting that the Eagle had perched itself on the ledge. And, as all Creatures created by the Creator and/or the Big Bang, did what all biological beings bearing feathers, scales, or hair had to do on occasion. His shit landed on a roving surveillance camera pointed down at John, clouding most of the lens, causing it to short out and blow up in a spark. John mouthed a 'thank you' to the bird, receiving a 'yer welcomed' caw from the avian guide and/or voyeur. After which the avian messenger from places John knew had to be visited eventually wisely buggered off back up into the sky, disappearing behind one of the few clouds available.

"Now it's our turn to visit…hmmm," John said, allowing himself to chuckle when viewing the name of the next appointed interviewee, feeling a joke Selena 2, and probably the now absent Selena 1, did not find funny.

The door to 'Prof. Dr. IM. Morte's' lab in the about-to-be-completely demolished wing of the Klassen with 'Do not enter" signs along the way was halfway open, barely hanging on one rusty hinge. Sneaking a look inside, John noted stacks of books abounded inside, accompanied by data-filled cabinets with locks on them. A slightly-bowed skeleton was set in place as the doorman, 'motioning' with its stationary left hand to 'enter at your own risk', the other hand holding onto a small bucket labeled 'Tax non-deductible contributions to free/Free Science welcomed'. John reached into Selena's purse and, despite feeling a pinch on his fingers saying 'don't do this', pulled out a fistful of change. He placed it into the collection bucket and then found a key at the bottom of the empty bucket. The name scratched on the half-hinged wooden door had to be a misnomer or a private joke shared by someone inside who didn't want his, or her, identity known to outsiders. But in small print, the letters faded, was----E. Regrub- Rehsif.

"We should wait," Selena 1 and 2 warned.

"We've been waiting too long already," John countered, pushing aside the door as gently as possible. Upon entering the room smelling of mold, asbestos, and intensity he was greeted by a further outreaching of the hand of death from another skeleton on duty, this one wearing a blood-stained white lab coat.

"Heeelloo, Doctor Fred," John said to the second gatekeeper's skull, a perfectly preserved skeleton with a pair of Groucho glasses on his nose, a Cuban Revolutionary beret, and a cigar between his teeth. "Where's Erica, Fred?" he inquired of the skeleton, putting together the last name on the door in a reverse, being Fisher-Burger. It was as clear as day and night that Erica was closer than he thought. And as for "Fred", that skeletal anatomy teaching tool and subsequent good luck companion had been the third wheel on every one of John and Erica's dates when they were in medical school, the designated driver when Erica got caught speeding, and when appropriately dressed up, their escort into Physicians for Social Responsibility Meetings and Pathology Rounds. Suddenly, the present started John out of fond memories from the past.

"Do you know this former faculty member, going by the name of Linquist this time, who was recently dismissed from this Institution, and keeps mulling about, illegally, Ms. Horowitz? " Thompson, the ASSISTANT Director of the apparently new Klassen Teaching Hospital according to the nametag on his purple sport jacket and matching grey trousers commented, appearing out of nowhere yet again. With his even more boyish face and middle-aged bubba belly, he reeked even more of 'those who can't do science become administrators, and those who can't administrate become assistant Directors.'.

"Someone like her," John said regarding knowing Linquist, a new player in the game of 'who can figure out what MID really is'. Though he was still using Selena's voice, it was beginning to lose its naturally high pitch and softness. "Or him," he appended, self-observing, too late this time, that he had revealed too much knowledge about Erica, and himself.

"And you knew it was a woman because?" Wilkinson pressed.

"This place has, somehow, a woman's touch to it," John offered.

"Or a demonesses curse," the Assistant Dean's reply, after which he spit on the door and crossed himself. "It's dangerous to be here, Ms. Horowitz, with this wing and room. This and the rest of the rooms in this wing that you accidentally wandered into are, said as a Christian, occupied by demons. And said as a scientist, occupied by rats and termites that we have to exterminate before bringing in the renovation crews. It's very dangerous for anyone to be here."

"Yes, I can see that, now," John replied, turning his head.

"And there is something else," Thomson said, coming back to his Norman Rockwell 'real' self. He turned to John, looking into his face. "Now I know where I know you from, Ms. Horowitz," the exclaimed with glee.

"What do we do now, Selenas?" John silently asked his inter-cerebral female co-pilots.

"Believe it and you will become it," their silent reply to John. "The most effective liar is the one who believes his own bullshit."

"HER bullshit?" John countered.

"Oh, ye of little faith. I'm the Pagan Indian and you're the Gospel-raised Catholic," came from the Millennial Selena which John was never informed about, or anticipated possible.

"I'm an Ex-Catholic," Baldino shot back, answering the accusations he could identify.

"There's no such thing, John," the, finally identified as First Nations Selena noted with deadly accuracy. "You're still just another addicted to guilt and terrified of hell AND heaven

Paleface who apologizes for rain but who, if you have an umbrella, rents it to others instead of donating it."

"New Orleans...: that's where we met!" the old well before his time Thompson interjected, disrupting the dialogue in John's head with that annoying detail of 'the world', appearing out of nowhere as abruptly as 'Fred'. He seemed to be 'Boss Thompson' now, from his newly-shined shoes to the freshly manicured nails on his hands so clean that they had to be very, very dirty on the inside.

John quivered, gazing into Fred's eyes and envisioning what his skull would look like on Thomson's mantelpiece, or slate in the morgue that was never open to the Press or the Pathology Students.

Selena 2, who had already dived into the depths of John's soul, decided to offer him a life jacket. "Pick a lie you can believe in. A lie that's fun...Until you get caught, lying's the most fun you'll ever---"

"The symposium sponsored by Renaldo Pharmaceuticals, at the Star Hotel on Bourbon Street!" Thompson exclaimed, the memories from his foggy black and white youth re-activating his aging libido in living color. "And that room we….".

"Number 54, I think," John interjected, to throw off Thomson's memory. "Or was it Suite 666?" he continued, perking up Selena's lips for the 'fun' of messing with Thomson's mind, and biblical guilt. "It was great fun while it lasted."

"But that hair..." Thomson pointed out, remembering…something.

"I wasn't so blonde then," John replied, twirling the very blonde wig knotted into his sweaty scalp.

Thompson looked, pondered, and reflected. "No, you're not her," he concluded.

"We all look alike to you under the sheets, but we know each one of you, even in the dark," John stoked Thomson's forearm with a gesture that said mother, lover, and even friend.

John watched Thomson sink back into 'respectable' mediocrity, the 'almost-was-alive once' Administator's fate, and secret passion. From the other eye, and side of the brain to which it was very attached, John watched Renkin, who had appeared out of nowhere. "We have some papers that need signing, I've been looking all over God's wondrous creation for you," Professor Pastor Renkin said, presenting his official boss, but in actuality administrative servant, documents to sign.

There seemed to be nothing behind Renkin's agenda, other than getting signatures approving the transfer of supplies, funds, and people from one department to another, He seemed to be, for real, a clean-cut Mormon boy-turned-man who seemed to have no garbage or skeletons in his closet.

Thomson signed the papers given to him by Renkin with the bold enthusiasm that had more energy in his head and face than Trump when he approved an Executive Order for the cameras. Such was probably the only relief the dull-out disease administrator had left in his life.

Meanwhile, Renkin nodded 'hello' to 'Ms. Horowitz with the most G-rated of agendas, with nothing but kindness embroidered into flawless courtesy and professional protocol. John recalled from the Neuropathology Conference held in Salt Lake City so many decades ago, Erica saying to him at that most pleasant of symposiums, "I don't trust any city where I can't see the garbage."

There was another flaw that John had to contend with. Though he had attended Buckminister Fuller's improv-of-the-intellect lectures at Town Hall whenever possible, he was late on the uptake on the short, bald-headed Einstein's most important maxim. "Become a Verb!" A verb which would, when the time is right, and there were more than well-meaning feces-shedding Eagles trying to hide his footsteps, require him to use the key Fred's skeletal assistant's hand to unlock the rusty locks on the cabinets inside Erica's hideout. Where she was apparently known as Linquist for a while. A hideout which, ironically and perhaps smartly at the time, was in the middle of the domain occupied by her enemies.

Putting things into motion, taking his lead from Fred, and his inspiration from Erica, John turned to Renkin.   "Who is, or was, Doctor Linquest?" he asked with a whispery, businesslike tone.

"Someone who threw herself off the balcony," Thomson interjected, having finished signing the documents Renkin had given him.   After handing them back to the full-time scientist and part-time clergyman who, seemingly, he both envied and admired, he turned to John.   "According to the janitors, after they have their weed smoking breaks here, and according to the rambling of Apache patients while they are having Mad Indian Disease hallucinations in the ER, it is said that Doctor Inquist's 'ghost' sneaks into the departmental office to her mail, do a few more experiments here in her laboratory dungeon. She, most probably in the flesh, also sneaks answers to the exams we give the medical and nursing students assigned to us so they pass their exams. Particularly the all-heart and no brain slow-witted C minus ones who somehow wind up getting A's."

John averted his stare. He self-observed and allowed his outer lips to burst into a wide, shit-eating grin, made even more Blissful with Selena 2's enthusiastic blessing.

"What was that, Ms. Horowitz?" Thomson inquired, leaning in towards John with a disapproving frown.

"I didn't hear her say anything," Renkin pointed out. "You're imagination is running away with you again, James."

"It's DOCTOR and soon to be DEAN Thomson!" the administrator trusted with so much power perhaps because he had so little brains, or balls, blasted back at Renkin.

"Of course, Doctor Dean Thomson," Renkin gently offered in return as a pastor rather than a medical professional. "But we have to remember that this contagious brain tumor epidemic going through the Indigenous population and some of us has us all on edge. And…" the scientist turned pastor, or perhaps paster who had become scientist gave Thomson a good looking over from head to toe, then back the other way again.

"What are you looking at?" Thomson bawked, pulling away, buttoning his coat, hiding behind the title on his name tag. His right hand was beginning to shake. His pen, the sword with which he battled all the academic bullies in his world, falls from it. He picked it up with his non-shaking hand, and inserted said appendage into his deep trouser pocket. "What are you looking at!?" he blasted at Renkin, then John.

"Someone who maybe should get a thorough neuro exam?" Renkin proposed, as a question of course. "For the sake of our institution, your family, yourself, and…"

"…all the other families who need you to stay healthy, and who are depending on you?" Selena 2 and John offered as nurturing nurses and dedicated doctors.

"Yeah," Thomson replied after a tense delay, I'll look into it.

With that, Thompson strolled down the corridor towards the exit sign, disappearing behind a door he had to force open with the kick of his mirror-shined Oxfords.

"Time for both of us to attend to our assigned duties I suppose," Renkin said by way of explanation for what had been said, and not said. "Idle hands are the devil's handy work, you know."

"Yes, they are," John's abbreviated reply. He looked at Renkin, allowing himself to see the goodness and innocence in the pastor-scientist's soul. Something that got him through so many difficulties before. And which, when the time was right, would get him and everyone else involved with, or afflicted by MID, 'through the night' and into brighter, healthier, and more importantly Alive big A days ahead. Getting to the bottom of what MID was and forcing Mother Nature, the Heavenly Father, or the Great Spirit to provide a cure for it would serve the living and the dead. And those caught in between, such as Fred and his fellow skeletal doorman bud who winked a 'see ya later, old friend' to John, and Selena 2.

XIII

John left the old abandoned wing of the Klassen, sensing at every turn ghosts of dead but not yet departed tuberculosis victims who frequented it in the past century as well as the ghosts of the many Indian and fewer in number White patients who for some reason decided to linger here rather than go to the Happy Hunting Grounds, or the Pearly Gates. John pondered the idea that perhaps they were still here to guard the abandoned treatment room in which Erica squatted to continue her research on MID, and the well-funded professionals who were supposed to eliminate it.

Upon saying a 'thank you' to the ghosts for haunting the place, so that the renovation crews would put it last on their list to finally demolish, John emerged again into well lit, and, from above, easily observed sunlit hallways in the modern section of the Institute. John reassessed the options as to where he could regain perspective. Perhaps it was the hotel room, which he was able to enter, without being watched, even by Tom the night clerk. Tom was busy drinking brains into mindless contentment in the hotel bar with no less than four deputies. The conversation around the table centered around making jokes about the hallucinations the 'Injuns' and 'wannabe Injun' whites were having with MID. The White Bubba Bellies blamed it on everything from the special brand of peyote only the Elders knew about to ET implants dropped from the sky into the redskins' bird-sized brain boxes. And that the Indians were too stuck in their traditional ways to know that the pre-Columbian golden age 17th buffalo-filled century ended a thousand years ago.

John looked out of the window of his hotel, gazing up at the sky, sensing infinity within and beyond it. He admired the creatures who could soar upward and swoop downward without the aid of propellers, jet engines, or poverty-promoting gurus who claimed, for a hefty $1,000 a day lesson, they could teach you how to levitate. Lots of birds hung out around the Klassen, particularly crows, an observation that was not photographed or spoken about. Baldino remembered how those black-feathered corn-eating 'varments' would tell you more about a town in Upstate New York than any newspaper or even local short-story novelist. He remembered a clinical rotation in Auburn, New York, and the 'park' outside his hotel room, the Prison where the first man was electrocuted to death a stone's throw from the low-budget special. Winter and summer, crows would congregate in that three-treed 'park' sharing something other than meager rations of berries and nuts on their trees. It was like that in every prison town Upstate, particularly near the High-Security lock-up facilities where prisoners went in, but never came out.

"Maybe it's a Teslian electromagnetic homing devise phenomenon," Baldino speculated as he did another much needed, and now wanted, shave on the face that Leonard said would 'grow as much hair as the Arizona desert would sprout palm trees'. He sensed that Senena 2 was equally repulsed by men sporting facial hair as women having such. "This is a high-tech research institution with high-tech equipment and the crows are just interested in weird electrical patterns," Baldino, alone now, in mind and body considered, said to another avian visitor outside the window.

"Yes, and no," the eagle, said as he perched himself on the ledge his two-legged and wingless colleague, friend, and…to be honest about it…provided free food that was NOT filled with chemicals that would kill man and bird alike with a myriad of disorders, most notably including cancers. "Crows are curious about strange electrical signals, and don't shy away from them like my kind do," the Eagle replied between bites of organic bread and presumably non-GMO seeds John fed his uninvited but very much welcomed guest.

"Correct," Dr. J. silently telepathied and gave voice to. "Ghosts give out electrical signals or something we label as such. Particularly when someone dies, or...is killed. The first three days were the most intense, according to scientific observations and some religiously-overvalidated-sort-of-scientific theories. And maybe for some cultures, and ghosts who come from them, three days evolve into three weeks, months, years, or centuries. How the ghosts died and what they experienced during that transition determine the strength and duration of the electrical field. And by tracing where those disembodied electrical fields are, and where they come from, we can..."

Baldino turned his gaze to the flock of blackbirds, taking note of where the crows were congregating. The North Wing of the Klassen Health Center seemed to be the densest in population of sitting crows, the East Complex displaying a lot of traffic of the black-feathered birds, particularly the young ones. But one direction seemed, yet again, to have the most crows 'hanging out' in the sky---the Western horizon. The same Horizon that Baldino's eyes were fixed upon just before coming here to investigate Mad Indian Disease that was in reality decimating more people than the Press or Medical Journals were reporting. The Horizon with nothing behind it except desert hills, and people of the Desert---Apaches.

The eagle confirmed it in a language John could feel, but not quite hear. In words that felt...familiar. The kind of telepathy that allowed you to understand the meaning of the words, but not the words themselves. The kind that enabled Dr John Baldino to understand everything a Chinese, Russian, Albanian, or even Greek patient was saying without knowing a single word of their native tongue. A very private conversation this time with the Eagle, and nobody else, or so John thought to the best of his intuitions, was the most logical protocol for this investigation.

As a researcher, young Baldino had aspired to save populations. As an aging clinician, he was obliged to save people, or a single person, one slow and agonizing step at a time. But there was one more 'patient' who seemed to be speaking to him. Very clearly in a language very closely connected to the distant mountains beyond the blue-tinted window. Selena 2 showed up again, this time projecting a cloudy image of what appeared to be an Apache maiden experimenting with urban goth makeup in a glass situated on the windowsill rather than in his mind. The most certainly NON-AI generated 'hologram' beat out beams of light in tune with John's own heartbeat. She seemed younger than he imagined, but for reasons he could not define. Yet there was one question he felt compelled to ask, besides her age, in ghost or body-containing years.

"What's your Sign, Selena 2?' he inquired. "Astrologically, that is?"

"That is, like, ya know, a real stupid question, Dr. J," Selena 2 scolded in Valley-something-else in a young voice John could now hear as well as feel. "Why are you, like, asking me that at a time like this?"

"I don't know," Baldino pressed on, remembering how group-oriented the Selenas he knew in real life was. And how they were so concerned with appearances. And how their personalities changed with the wind, and the wishes of the group. And how much, no matter how loudly they boasted about being independent, they feared being…alone. "Ya know," he 'said' slowly to Selena 2. "Being alone scares a young person, or Soul, and---"

"---Yes?" she interjected, with youthful impatience.

"For a young soul, you seem more woman than girl," John advanced in 'Einstein'ese. "Your eyes are still wide open to the world. Life, while you were living it, was probably a dance to you, not a war, and not even a timeline. You have to be a Cancer, Virgo, or an Airies or…hmmm, a Scorpio?"

"Okay. I'm a Scorpio, John. How did you know?"

"You just told me." John declared victory with the final sting, but not conquest. Connecting to his own voice, the one he still remembered before all the MID and even A137 'situations', he continued. "And before your seventeen birthday, you experienced more fantasies in men than realities."

"I was only sixteen when...when..." She faded again. Vanishing from 'feel' and inner sight. The eagle cawed, looking for her with desperate futility.

"Selena! Hold on!" John screamed out. "There's still work to do! We'll make it fun! Come on Selena..or whoever you are, or want or need to be! Don't leave me!"

It was just John and the Eagle now. "Man" business that had to be completed between a presumed to be a male bird and a solitary man with a hot ass; red lips and bombshell legs whose Mission was somehow connected to a woman, or Women, inside him.

XIV

The rest of the day went according to the Klassen Agenda. According to numbers. According to the publishable facts about the scientists, and the science, the upper-ups at this isolated 'State of Any Art' Institute needed to be put into print by Selena Horowitz and reported to their funders back home in the Big Apple. At each of the forgettable interviews with even more forgettable 'yes men' White technicians who called themselves scientists, Selena 2 took down the details with charming journalistic professionalism with a special sincerity not shown by Selena 1. Baldino wrote the real facts between the lines. Her account and his would find their way into print in the appropriate newspapers, magazines, and, for those who still knew how to read, novels.

All the while, John's focus was on his new intracranial partner and 'behavior' coach. She and John made a great team, each somehow fulfilling the other's agenda in ways neither of them really could define.

Each lab on the Klassen list involved another dull-out disease-infected technician, another scientific ego, and another set of data having nothing to do with MID. It was about taking photos, taping interviews, and getting raw data for an article that was supposed to be about the Soul of the Scientist but, if the REAL Klassen administrators had anything to do with it, be a soul-less account of how scientists were the new gods of the 21st century and how science itself would be the Godhead, without any element of GodHeart. Still, John persisted, hoping he could figure out who was wearing a white hat, black hat, or no hat.

For John, something 'snapped' into place and out of its pre-designated slot between the ears, and between the legs. This hyper-intense experience of lightness was the chance to step into someone else's life. Selena 2, whoever she was, seemed to be a very interesting young woman. She was energetic, bright, and committed, AND she knew how to have fun, too. Such was a trick Baldino never learned while playing any other role in his nearly half-century on planet Earth having to be someone different for every patient, funder, administrator, or colleague. But there was one individual who John was forced to be his true self with.

"Vinny will be proud of us, Selena," John told himself and her en route to another designated interview, this time led but not controlled by Assistant Dean Thomson's assistant, a by-the-numbers administrator whose gait and bearing, who kept his passions and agendas well hidden. "I can feel that my brother Vincent is alive, too. We'll foil the bad guys here, have a beer together, and then in the next 'place of change' we do good deeds there. And it will be VINCENT who has to wear the dress, me in the Commando Gear."

"OK," Selena 2 said. "But firewater is bad for me, given my biology and periods of dark history with it."

"Sure," John acknowledged, letting that additional piece of intel about Selena 2 find its natural slot in his chronically busy and now overloaded brain.

On the way to the next destination, John wasn't looking at the floor to avoid being seen by any camera attached to the ceiling. Neither was he staring at the walls while another individual walked passed him. His eyes were fixed on one sight--victory! The clicking of his pumps on the floor turned into the clanking of cavalry boots and huff clicks of that horse between his legs. Then, the rousing "Gary Owen", victory and glory song of the Seventh Cavalry, began blasting in his head in time with his power steps.

When John and Vinny played cowboys and Indians, John always wanted to be the Injun. Vinny would put on the cavalry hat and shoot at John while he rode his bicycle around in a circle, shooting rubber bands and throwing dirt balls at General Vinny Armstrong Custard. Once John became old enough to touch the stirrups of a horse, he and Vinny went on a two-week camping expedition in the Adirondacks. It was over 1,500 miles from The Little Big Horn, and most of the mounted time was spent at a controlled walk, but the 'Gary Owen' was always John's favorite tune, the one he couldn't get out of his head, most particularly when he was playing an Indian. Of course when John was playing 'Sword brandishing Ukrainian Cossack Cavalry on the way to destroy Napoleon's cannons or stick a Molotov cocktail into one of Hitler's tanks,' the Gary Owen was even louder. Indeed, John's tongue began to roll with the fife and drum music in his head.

"Stop that!!!" Selena screamed out in her new 'young voice' as John turned the corner and turned the silent hum into an audible whistle. "Stop that!!!!"

She was terrified. But why?

"It's just a song, Selena," John said in the silent conversation between them which was becoming more audible while being both informative and enjoyable. "It's an Irish song, written by someone who never even knew Custer or Sitting Bull."

"With a beat, you danced to, and we died by!!!" she protested. "And you and your people, ya know…"

"No, I don't know, tell me!" John demanded.

From Selena 2, dead silence. The kind that a woman gives a man when he asks 'How are you feeling?' when, according to her, he should know, if he cares about her that is.

Meanwhile, John was escorted past a glass window that covered the whole wall. It advertised a splendid view of two mountain ranges and a valley between them below that redefined the word "open" to anyone East or West of the Continental Divide. His escort got a call on his phone, motioning for John to 'halt, please' in a military voice with a tinge of an Afrikaner accent.

The escort related a plethora of 'yes sir', 'no sir', and 'copy that's' to whoever was at the other end of the phone. John discretely worked his way towards the receiver of the escort's phone to decipher what the caller was asking, relating, or ordering, when he felt a thud in his chest.

"Listen to the silence of the desert and let your Soul see its spirit, without letting the brain blind you again," Selena 2 said by way of explanation, turning John's torso towards the window. "Now, put the Gary Owen back on that tape deck between your ears and tell me what you see."

"I see the enemy ahead," John said from a persona, part Cavalry, part scout, part Indian. "It's a good day to fight!!! Warrior to warrior." Imagination was in full glory. "It's a good day to fight!!!" his inner voice raged as armies of mounted warriors from both sides converged on the middle of the field at full gallop. "The Little Big Horn."

"Wounded Knee," Selena countered as the movie in John's mind obeyed the guidelines of a completely different script. Indian warriors in General John's gunsights seemed more like skeletons, starved to skin and bones, their rifles now spears and single-shot muzzle-loaders. Behind them, the village, defended by women and children, armed with nothing but tenacity against the Gatling guns, repeaters, and steel swords that could cut through tree trunks.

"Now, from our perspective," Selena said, appearing as an orb in the glass that somehow merged into a movie screen.

John saw the horsemen approach, and the tanks, and the railroad. Green and yellow, they were, eating the blood of vanquished men, women, and children. In the demon beast's horns were entrails of the conquered. Stuck to the tips were the heads of those slain, eyes blinded but minds feeling every part of the pain, humiliation, and living death. But there was one place where the demon beast was still vulnerable. One deep black hole in its penetrating spotlight eye could be seen, penetrated, and destroyed if---

"Enough!!!" John said, putting his hands over his ears. "Enough!!!" he cried, hopefully behind tight lips, tears now streaming down his face.

"That's been our ancestral hell," Selena shot back as an orb coming out of a stucco wall. Vibrating even more brightly in synch with every beat of John's pounding heart, with a collective raspy voice which was both old and young, but at its base---terrified. "This is MID. Mad 'Injun' Disease. These are not the visions of the Eagle Clan."

"And what are the visions of the Eagle Clan?" John asked.

"You have to look into the eye of the demons first," she said with a wisdom far beyond her years.

"And...?" Dr J asked.

From the Messenger inside him, nothing.

"I am listening," Baldino went on. "Really. Or at least I'm trying to."

Again, silence. That 'nothing' that patients in the kind of pain doctors can't fix always say as the last thing to their physicians before the time of dying.

"I REALLY want to...no, NEED to know," John pressed, feeling the pain of the patient within, or patients, perhaps. "Please..." He looked in the mirror. No was one there. No Baldino. No Dr. J. Just 'John', sort of.

Selena 2, as she allowed John to call her anyway, finally answered. "You'll find who and what I am when the time comes. It will be the measure of your manhood. And humanhood."

Baldino felt the corners of both lips move upward. The color came back to the cheeks. Blood ushered back into the brain. "We okay?" he asked the reflection.

"Only if we fix that face of ours," the mystery woman replied. "Our mascara is running."

John made the necessary cosmetic adjustments in the make-up mirror in his purse, noting that his 'civilian' escort was indulging in even more military talk on the phone. When defocusing his own eyes, opening them up wide enough to not let his brain define what was coming into the retina. He saw in the orb semi-Mongaloid eyes, then high cheekbones and a strong jaw. The still clouded face was surrounded by coarse black hair light reddish skin not yet wrinkled but somehow ancient, with a large schnozz that would make Jimmy Durante's nose look like a pip-squeak-smelling device. "You seem to be VERY 'Aboriginal' and...lonely," he noted, and related. "You were torn between worlds. And though you could give love, you received so little of it. You look like…a lost soul."

"Until now, John," she said. "And, yes, you have seen my face before. Like so many palefaces. Cops, reporters, and…you, Doctor J. "

"I'm a healer, not just a doctor," John relayed back. "Who…yes!" Finally, the relevant details of the diffuse image came together, sort of, courtesy of the newspaper pictures he saw of her when he was being briefed by Leonard. Selena 2's image in the afterlife was very much like that of the Mexican half-Apache teen who had been taken away by the psych orderlies in New York for doing a duel with demons only she could see, putting her in the morgue somewhere in Flagstaff, Arizona. Then most probably one of the locked 'Do Not Enter' anatomy 'teaching labs' at the Klassen, no doubt. An unidentified 'nobody' Mexican, given the first name of 'Maria' and surname which was a number, in the manner of White unidentified women acquired the name of 'Jane Doe' after their passing. But then again, persons of color, be they living or dead, were always fairly unidentifiable to John due to his being brought up around mostly humanoids whose skin tones were his own. But for the moment, John had to return to his claim about being a healer, rather than a doc to this 'Maria', or too suntanned Jane Doe. "It's my job to care about people. Something I have to do, not what I want to do."

"Whatever you say, Dr. John," she shot back.

"Letting the man win the argument, Maria," he said, recalling her name. "Or letting him think he did? A technique that works in the White, Red, and Yellow world, so I read anyway."

"And so I've experienced," Maria replied. "But at least one of us still dressed to kill and…Will have to do a whole lot of harm to make any mark worth making in the world as it is."

With that, Maria's face vanished back into the orb, which flew into and vanished into the sky. Leaving John on 'solid ground' with an escort who asked him when he finally got off the phone. "Ms. Horowitz. Is any wrong?"

"No," John replied, as another link in the chain of lies was forming an even deadlier spider web around everyone, including the elusive escort.

XV

The next item on the Klassen Agenda, and Leonard's, was 'M' to his friends and enemies, Doctor Hans Manheim to the rest of the world. A 'careful and precise' investigator was his MO, with numerous articles in all the top journals to validate his persistence and/or luck. He had been one of that 40-papers-on-the-resume kind of junior investigators who then became a 100-plus-paper-man, not one of those biochemical investigations bearing his name alone as an author. Manheim was one of those people who never said or did anything, but always seemed to know what you were doing.

Baldino caught a glimpse of 'Dr M' from his open lab door. The generic face, the set-in eyes, the hairline that receded just enough to say 'aging' but not enough to say 'Elder', the ultra-trimmed mustache that seemed British Oxford from the left, and Hitlerian when you looked straight into him straight on.

Manheim's lab was spotless, his paperwork organized in perfectly arranged right angles. He had the reputation of being and was the kind of perfectionist whose anal droppings had to be as geometrically symmetrical as his life perspectives and moral bookkeeping. After John was escorted into Manheim's lab, his ears were blasted with not the sound of silence, but the sound of 'dead'. It was given voice by Doc M himself. "Ms. Horowitz, I'm Doctor Manheim. Dr. Thompson said you wanted to write an article about my work."

"An article about YOU," John said, using Selena's professional charm and Maria's understated wit. Of course, also threw in the mix a potent dose of Baldinoesce Jungian 'shrink' to break through the super nerd walls enveloping the most revered researcher at the Klassen. "I'm writing about the soul of the scientist, the man behind the work, the human 'whys' behind all those mind-boggling 'whats'."

"Very nice subtext, girls," John said inside his own head to his female co-pilots for having suggested those words for him, grateful for a ringing of Manheim's phone that he answered without excusing himself. "You used the tools of a bitch, whore, and slut, all at the same time, and made my bullshit schtick smell like a rose," John said to 'the girls'.

"Your schtick is no bullshit, John. You've been lying so long, that you don't know when you're telling the truth," Maria related. "But your logic and my passion aren't going to break this guy. He's not an idiot or an asshole."

"Then what is he?" John silently inquired, taking a look around the spotless, staff-less lab, then the stack of research papers on the table next to him, arranged in the fashion of display so that the viewer could see the authors and titles of each of them.

"'He's a real nowhere man, sitting in his nowhere land, making all his nowhere plans, for nobody,'" Maria sang to John from the "Yellow Submarine" soundtrack.

John treated himself to a subtle chuckle between closed cheeks as Selena 1 continued the serenade. "'Doesn't have a point of view, knows not where he's going to, isn't he a bit like you and me,'".

"Nowhere man, won't you listen," John added, addressing himself as someone who once was and still could becoma a Manheim. "You don't know what you're missing."

"Nowhere man, the world is at your command!" Selena and John sang in perfect harmony and enough real-world volume to be heard by a deaf man.

Dr. Manheim's reaction to the contorted face of his interviewer while he was still on the phone, and his pain-wrecked face was passionless, and emotionless were defined best as---

"Nothing!" Maria noted to Dr J. "We jump into this guy's brain and we find nothing!"

"The glasses are academic, the cranial capacity wide, but the forehead is still sloping, Maria"

"I don't see the lobotomy scar, John."

"More is the pity," Baldino said in conclusion of the matter. "And the opportunity!"

Taking advantage of his host's indifference, John perused the plethora of research papers. Manheim had his name on more papers than any other investigator at the Klassen, but it was always somewhere in the middle of the multi-authored publications. "He probably did the proofreading, or checked the statistics," John said to Maria, and, if she was still hanging around, Selena 1. "There's nothing political or social in this office. Even if those three kids on the desk photo are his own, he's still probably a virgin. Okay with you if I dissect him like a pithed frog?"

"Go ahead, it's our funeral," from the 'girls' in unison.

Manheim said an uneventful and very professional goodbye to his caller and hung up the phone. Getting back to the 'real' world, John took the helm, addressing 'M' in the kind of language he could understand best. "Doctor Manheim, you look familiar," John said in pleasant Selena-ese.

"My facial structure is very common," Manheim smiled back, sort of. "Most reporters recognize me from somewhere else, particularly most female journalists."

"Monotone," speed-said Maria noted to John. "Not even Vulcanian. No beat, rhythm, or meter to the verbiage. Stiff and stilted extensor-flexor tone. Eye movements which are hardly noteworthy, which when taken together clearly indicate and display the unmistakable aspect of---Oh My God!!!"

"Yes, Maria?" John inquired regarding the three seconds of silence that followed. "You sound more flatlined than usual. Slow, too. He's paced even you down to his sublight speed and earthbound perspective. And yes, boredom and mental deadness ARE contagious. Weren't you trying to tell ME that?"

"Okay, okay, go on...Manheim's too boring to lie, Doctor J."

"But smart enough to know the whats, and maybe a few of the why's," John said as the final word with his inner voice. "MID, what exactly is it, today, biologically speaking?" John asked Manheim with his biological mouth.

"It's an interesting disease, verified to date in approximately 670 patients of mostly Aboriginal extraction, in the advanced stages," Manheim replied in a tempo and tone more worthy of a printed research report than spoken words to an actual person, or patient.. "The number of afflicted individuals harboring the vector that causes it is probably 4.7 times that. Current research says that it's caused by a viral in an unidentified plant, yet to be identified. Most probably a retrovirus, which moves from the oral cavity through the trigeminal nerve into the cerebral cortex. Inducing a wide range of neurological defects. They included cerebral tumors releasing abnormal quantities of serotonin, impaired motor dysfunction, memory deficits, and a strangely stereotypical distorted sensory perception."

"Based on the fear of the people afflicted," John delivered, logic from the mouth, compassion from his baby blues, greens, browns, or whatever other color his eyes were becoming. "Genetic memories are unraveled, awakening the most painful memory of death, so scary even the most iron-willed people give up the will to live."

"That is one theory, seen in approximately 84.5% of our patients, Ms. Horowitz," the accurate and dispassionate reply.

John never used the word 'patient', even as a Doctor. It implied a loss of control and surrender of dignity. He was appalled when 'health consumer' came into vogue, chastising every nurse, physician, or student who said it, irrespective of their professional position or emotional vulnerability. But right now, it was all he could do to hold on to his patience and not strangle Manheim's lily-white neck until his face turned beet red. And his sunken eyes would see and feel the agony that healthy people did when they become dying patients...

"Go for the jugular, General, Hetman, Chief John!" Maria exclaimed.

"That's exactly what I plan on doing, Maria!" John felt the sharpness of the elongated vampiress nails Leonard had so skillfully cemented onto his hand.

"I mean the jugular veins INSIDE his head!" Maria screamed at Doctor-turned-Ball-Buster Baldino. "Everybody cares about something. Selective compassion isn't universal compassion, but sometimes it's a useful place to start."

"Yes," John pondered, feeling that Selena's cerebrally expressed heartfelt insight would answer another question down the road not yet posed. " And regarding Selective compassion."

"Are you married?" John asked Manheim, snapping back to 'reality' before his 'mark' could detect his absence from it...

"Yes, Ms. Horowitz." the businesslike reply.

"Kids?"

"Three," informationally related.

"Their ages?"

"Five, seven, and eight," in mathematic rhythm.

"Their names?"

Manheim gazed over at the photos. His lips turned up, slightly. "Tom, Dick, and Harry," he said, without any appreciation that it was a generic set of names given only by generic dull-out disease-inflicting parents to offspring who would share that comfort-laden pathology.

John and Selena turned their 'inner' lips upward, letting out a polite, and respectful giggle at the stereotypic names too real to be true. But then another thought....maybe Manheim did have a sense of humor after all. Which became evident when he said---

"Thomas Alva, Richard James, and Harrold William, to be accurate," Manheim related regarding his three offspring, but--- without a trace of irreverence or even levity.

"You seem to care about them a lot," John replied, noting Manheim's face in the wilderness photo with the boys, his fatherly arms protecting and feeding off of the lads.

"They're good boys," Manheim related with a smile so proud and wide that it pushed every hair of his mustache upward towards his oversized nostrils.

"Happy ones, Professor Doctor Manheim?" J   asked, noting the communicable deadness in the faces of the two oldest boys, the youngest least afflicted---so far.

"Yes," Manheim's reply. "They're all now contented in their chosen careers. Tom is a pharmacist, Dick is a dentist and Harry became a research dermatologist with a rather thick skin." Manheim's voice reeked of even more pride.

The smart-assed quips raced through John's mind, along with projected things that so often happened to well-taken-care-of and sheltered offspring of accomplished hard-working parents. Was Tom one of those by-the-numbers pharmacists whose knowledge of medications didn't take into account how happy rather than merely healthy what he was dispensing was? Would Dick die by his own hand due to the primary reason for the high suicide rate in dentists being boredom?   And was the reason why Harry became a dermatologist because he wanted to find a cure for baldness which was afflicting his father and which would afflict him one day? But, to be fair, Manheim enjoyed order and passionless harmony and wanted to pass that on to his sons. That was human. That was family. But what of issues larger than family, and far more human?

"With the way MID is going, do you think it will affect any non-Aboriginal populations? More than it already has, that is," John, as Selena-Maria of course, asked. "My children, your technician's children...your children?"

"No," Manheim replied after a defiant silence. He then leaned in towards John, not once letting his eyes wander to the exposed cleavage between his well-formed 'breasts'. "Mad Indian Disease is a genetic, and an environmental, disease. Tom, Dick, and Harry have no Apache genes in them and even less interest in Aboriginal cults and herbs." Then, a small smile came over his face. "Unless they become anthropologists studying ancient cult religions or environmental botanists who sample the rare plants they are paid to study."

John politely chuckled at Manheim's failed attempt at witticism. Selena protested the action. "Don't move those lips into a smile and think I'm going to be happy in here, Professor Baldino! Making lips smile so the brain is directed to happy thoughts works on normal people, but neither of us is normal--not anymore!"

"Tell me something I don't know, Maria," John said, doing his utmost to maintain the front of pleasant to Professor Nowhere Man who now seemed so repugnant. "What do you want me to ask him? Give me YOUR lists of questions."

"Details again, John, details," came from the younger advisor.

"A good place to start, Maria.":

"That's not what I meant! You're dwelling on the details! Listen to what I mean, not what I say!... John...John John!!!!" Maria volleyed back.

John took over the helm once more, cognisant that if Manheim noticed that he was talking more with voices inside his head than people in the real world outside of it, it would mean the rubber room in a locked ward...John took in a deep breath, then prepared to crash through the walls Manheim was hiding behind. Part of the attack plan was speculation, part fact, and the rest improvised along the way---John always said that any lecturer who didn't discover three new insights every half hour, and relate them to his students, should be sued for failure to deliver goods for payment rendered. Several times in John Baldino's career he did have one-new-idea-a-lecture days, after which he'd pay every student in the room ten dollars as partial compensation.

John knew fully well that intelligence was contagious, as was the lack of it. And this blitzkrieg interrogation had no room for dullness of spirit, nor narrowness of mind. He opened all the cerebral portholes and let the waters come in from wherever they might, letting everything find its natural slot, nature always giving you a problem to any solution---as long as you were bold enough to redefine EVERYthing you thought you knew and look at the answer straight in the eye. And the delivery was----

"There is a theory, Doctor Manheim, that MID is a virus originating from the walls of this institution," John advanced, his claim based strictly on intuition, supported by historical accounts of smallpox epidemics wiping out Native populations in the Americas and Australia being due to intensional distribution of infected blankets. "Could it be that the retrovirus is carried by liposomes? Could it be that the carrier is astrocytic specific, causing swelling, breakdown of the blood-brain barrier, and filaments arranged in bundles of nine connected to one tubule, with altered potassium levels in the milieu of the synapse but...also, maybe as a separate action---disrupting the normal degeneration-regeneration equilibrium, the one where RNA is released from cells degenerating in just the right amounts to stimulate growth of cell processes in neighboring neurites. And...as the fundamental action---affecting the communication between the front line stimulus secretion coupling at the cell membrane and the nucleus, where genetic expression is most tightly--and racially--determined.

"By the types of tumors seen, the distribution of the lesions, and the prediction of Native PEOPLE to be either spiritually centuries ahead of the White man or the first ones to start a fight after a beer, I'd say it would have to involve limbic structures that we know are defective in alcoholics, and as for the transmitters...it's the ratio of serotonin, dopamine, and norepinephrine, not the absolute amounts.

"And as for stress or religious fervor for an Ancient Religion making it worse--adrenaline from the adrenals getting through the blood-brain barrier, or even the intracranial space, activating beta two vasodilatory receptors in the brain, and most specifically in the defect areas afflicted with said virus, that spread the cachexic factor, first to the visual occipital lobes, then to...association cortex, where the whole picture is so...."

John stopped himself. He had stumbled upon, and stated, five new insights into MID and three into basic neurobiology. A new record performance, but at the wrong stage. Still, the hand had to be played as all of his cards were on the table. "But this whole mystery disease problem, the whole picture is so---"

"Interesting," Manheim said. He looked aroused, maybe even enlightened.

"Nice work, John," Maria said.

"Old trick, Maria. The most effective way to break through a brick wall is to run through it. It has something to do with mass becoming energy. Which, according to the lightness of this body we're sharing, seems to be happening right now...Or is it right 'later'? Time passes strangely when you're communicating with----"

"--Outside exploration first," Maria reminded John.

"You pose some interesting questions, Ms. Horowitz," Manheim said to John.

"About the 'whats', or the 'whos'?" John and Maria pressed.

"The 'who' question behind the MID problem, and the propositions you are implying is...."

"Yes." John took out a notepad. He wouldn't trust any camera inside an earring or microphone inside a padded bra for this one. "The 'whos'"

"The theory about co-regulation of degeneration and regeneration was proposed as early as 1975, but polyamines were suspected, not nucleic acid," Manheim explained, more fascinated with the laws of pathophysiology than people who became its victims. But still, passionate about something. "It was Klein et al, Brain Research volume 23, page 134, I believe. As for the neurotransmitter ratio you spoke about, Nakamura and Schwartz worked out something like that in Heidelberg, 1986 in The New England Journal, October, as I remember, but I don't think anyone considered incorporating vasoactive dilators into the story, with the possible exception of Wilson and colleagues at the Rockefeller, but they never talked about beta receptors as the mechanism of action..."

John slumped back in his chair as Manheim spouted out names and references for research papers that had nothing to do with MID. Like those musicologists who knew every Beethoven Opus number and Mozart Kirshal listing, but who never played a note, nor even felt the music. One of John's breasts sagged down as well, but Manaheim didn't seem to notice, or if he did, probably didn't care.

"This is getting us nowhere, John," Maria lamented.

"We still have one more person to see today, Maria."

"And my people will have to bury another three of us by tomorrow morning, John," the young yet prematurely intelligent and embittered ghost related by way of reminder as John heard the clock ticking on the Manheim wall.

John was clear about everything except one word. 'My'. Could it be that Maria was a Universal Compassionate activist? Or maybe something more…?

"Is there any chance you can grab a knife and give this Paleface a haircut, two inches below the scalp, Dr. J?" the dead Native teen who seemed to be experiencing adulthood in the 'afterlife' pressed on regarding Manheim?

"I'd love to," John replied, listening to the words with his ears, their real meaning with his mind. "But Dr M probably would never notice anything. How can you kill the dead?"

"Yes, dead is dead," Maria said, hauntingly...

"Yes," John conceded.

"And dead is also contagious," she added, fading away again.

"Yes," John noted, opening up as many circuits as possible so that the REAL answer could be found by the part of the brain that thinks, intuits, and feels. Somehow, identifying the elusive 'empathy' center of the brain was more vital than ever, even if such a task was deemed undoable by modern technology, human will, or Divine plan.

XVI

Something disturbing went through John's head, again. It had something to do with Erica. If she was undercover as Doctor Linquest here, why didn't she have the down-and-dirty scoop about Mad Indian Disease?   'Strange', 'weird', and a very solitary investigator' was all John, Selena, or even Maria could get out of Klasen researchers, graduate students, or even janitors about Erica. 'Doctor Who?' was the most common response to any question regarding Linquist, or Erica.

Taking another opportunity to get 'lost' in the appointed rounds from point A to B, John snuck back to Erica's lab, opening it up with the key he had stolen from Fred the skeleton's blood-stained assistant skeleton... It was absent of the vintage microscopes, surplus asset mold-covered jars of elixirs, glassware, and pizza boxes with biological notes on them that John had seen on his previous visit there. His gaze was held hostage by skeleton Fred's face, a special message in his mouth.

"Great job, Selena. Signed, 'V'," John read.

"It feels like your brother is still alive," said Selena, known now as Selena 1, making an unscheduled appearance.

"Yeah. And so is Erica. She has to be," John said and hoped.

John walked around the lab, avoiding spiders, loose lab rats, and a few bear traps under pizza boxes on which the scribbled notes he saw earlier were removed. "So," he gently asked Fred. "Where's your skeletal assistant, Erica or Doctor Linquist?"

From Fred came nothing, driving John to listen to and work with his lowest and most powerful instinct. "Tell me what the fuck is going on!" he demanded of Fred, shaking him by the shoulders. Possessed and driven by primal rage.

The reply was a buzz coming into his ears from a motor inside the skeleton's spine. A key fell from the inside of Fred's skull, crashing to the floor onto John's foot. Upon retrieving it, another motor elevated Fred's right arm, the fingers on it pointing to a set of locked cabinets with 'do not open' signs on them warning anyone tempted to open them that they contained contagious microbes, radioactive material, or corrosive chemicals. All except for one which bore a likeness of a walrus on it, with the number 42. 'A projectile from Fred's radial bone shot a dart that landed on that cabinet.

"Ok, ok, Fred," John said to the skeletal friend he bought from the Halloween store three decades ago with Erica, who appeared in his dreams as a dancing and singing troubador in more than one nightmare, or wet dream. "I get it already."

Upon opening cabinet 42, the door to what was inside opened, along with openings to the four larger cabinets above him. A torrent of research notes fell down on John with the intensity of downpours from the black skies that occurred every day at 2 pm sharp when he was doing an independent study at the University of Miami.

"Unreadable", Selena 1 commented, burrowing John's eyes when he perused the plethora of data. "I can't make sense out of this. Neither can Maria, who's indisposed right now."

"But I think I can," John said speed reading the files, notebooks, and formulas scribbled on pizza boxes. "Erica has been doing her own research on MID here, with, I'd bet, more answers about what it is, and isn't than anyone else in this fucking, goddamn, mother fucking---"

The opening to the floodgates of John's finally released primal rage shut down when he heard footsteps in the hallway. Then conversations between ultra pale-skinned Thomson and three Darryls in a language in Africa. With a sense of urgency he never acted on as quickly, John pushed the notes into his Selena handbag, ramming the rest into the complimentary tote bags proudly bearing the Klassen Institute logo of an old-fashioned stethoscope.

He frenetically reinserted the cabinet doors in place with duct tape as best as he could. "Fred, Maria, Selena, I'm open to suggestions as to what we do from here, but for the moment…" Seeing that everything was as much in place as when he arrived, John removed his heels, so as not to be heard, and tip-toed to the door. He looked to the right, hearing that men were still talking around the corner. "Ok, so we go left," John muttered, sneaking out of the lab, and making his way to an exit sign, when he bumped into Tompson, carrying a tray of coffee cups.

"Ah….we, eh, I got lost again," John said to Tompson's consternating face.

"'" We', Ms, Horowitz?" he replied, tilting his head.

"I mean, me, and my, alter egos," John said in his best Ms. Horowitz voice.

"And…" Tompson continued, pointing to John's shoeless feet.

"Yeah," he replied, referring to his stiletto heels. "Walking around in these all day…not so easy."

"As maybe you know?" one of Daryl one said to his superior, taking one of the coffee cups into his hand.

"He's kidding, Bill," Daryl two assured his insulted superior, taking the second cup of java.

"It's Doctor Thomson to both of you!" the Assistant Director said to his inferiors, in accentless American English. He then turned to John. "And as for you, Ms. Horowitz."

"I know, I know, give a girl a map and she'll get lost, but in the meantime," John said, after which he felt and everyone else heard a rumbling in his stomach.

"You're hungry, and so am I," Tompson said. "And so are NOT these 'gentlemen'" he asserted, dismissing the Daryls.

"Yeah, I could eat," John replied.

"And will!" he insisted. "And eat well!" he continued, taking a sharp left turn towards the cafeteria.

The eatery had two sets of tables, with an empty row in the middle. One for Red and Brown skinned glass cleaners, janitors, and junior researchers, and one for masked Palefaces. "It's not what you think, Ms. Horowitz," Thomson said, noting the disapproving frown on John's face. "It started as CDC orders. A precaution which was wise to follow. Then it became a habit, embraced by them, and us."

"And the food that they and us are served?" John inquired, noting that the waiters serving the Indians and Indian-looking Mexicans had bigger smiles on their faces than the servers delivering tables to the White tables. Most of the latter were from L. Harvey Smith's army of affirmative action medical students, postdocs, glasswashers, and floor cleaners, all of who were there to find cures for the cancer-killing their families and friends, and themselves.

"The food is cooked in the same kitchen, and served hotter and faster to our darker-skinned workers and staff, Ms. Horowitz," Tompson assured John, anticipating her bringing up issues about Jim Crow heading West. "And with a better selection, more suited to traditional Native tastes and, according to some recent research reports, biological needs," he continued, handing her a menu. "Bannuk, sort of a fried bread. And inside of course, agrove hearts, Emory oak acorns, Saskatoon berries, sunflower seeds, corn, pinon nuts, and fresh wild grass-fed elk, deer, and rabbit," he boasted.

"Which sound like…" John halted a server carrying a tray to a group of Indians which included some of Smith's affirmative action promoted medical students, and life tired glass washers and janitors from other labs. All of them shared jokes in broken English and Apache. "Yes," John said as he smelled the bannock biscuits fresh out of the oven. "It smells…. indefinably delicious," he said, sensing something very familiar and appealing about them. With ladylike grace and alacrity of motion, he picked up one of the bannuck mini-sandwiches, to have it pulled away by Tompson.

"No!" Thomson said, stopping all conversation in the room from those of every skin color. "It's for the customers who ordered them. And…" he pulled John aside, motioning for people on all of the tables to continue their banter, rants, and pleasant chit-chat. "An Apache superstition from THIS century and THIS decade is that toxins from a White man, or woman's hand on their food will poison their bodies and souls. Which, of course, is not true."

"No, of course it isn't," John said.

"And, I think you'd enjoy the cuisine from the other part of the menu even more, though admittedly it isn't as healthy as what our Aboriginal brothers and sisters eat," he said, turning the page on the menu.

John gazed at the menu, noting that it contained more fun than nutritious food. Pizza, cheeseburgers, fries, pork chops, and for the exotic diner, fried fish. The latter is something that no health and culture-conscious Apache would, according to John's research, never eat.

After a meal that admittedly John's belly, and Tompson's, needed to have, it was time to prepare for a scheduled dinner date. Something that apparently Tompson was seldom able to get in his youth as a socially shy geeky biology student en route to becoming a boring and dull disease-infected administrator nerd,

John said a cordial goodbye to his host. When Thompson moved in to kiss him, John gently refused, noting that it would have to be after the second dinner they shared, which would be the next night they were both available. And that it would have to be when any other woman who he was involved, or interested, with was out of town. It bought John some more time to effectively be Selena with a man who, so it seemed, knew more about what was going on in the Klassen than anyone else he had stumbled upon or was directed to.

The walk to the parking lot offered yet another panoramic view of the sun setting over the Western horizon on an ugly day, medically speaking. Still, John allowed himself to be treated to a view of the desert few White men ever had. For the first time, he saw colors in the rocks and mesas he never imagined, so magnificent that they had no names in English. Maria, having deposed or relieved Selena 1, whispered what they were in Apache.

It was a magnificent solo ride back to the hotel in a luxury cab which Tompson had arranged, until John saw the Eagle Clan dancer doing his dance outside the University Hospital entrance. This time, a documentary was being shot for PBS by a professional crew. But, that dancer perhaps knew as much about Eagle Clan dance as the Apache Elder knew about the Country Line dancing. Both were solidly entrenched in their own world, as was Tompson.

"I'm glad you've met some of our researchers, Ms. Horowitz," the nameless and unidentified driver related in a cordially friendly tone, a revolver concealed under his coat, a semi-military haircut between his perked-up ears, a watchful eye on the road. "They're the cream of the crop, East and West of the Mississippi, aye?"

"And maybe back home, North of the Canadian line as well?" John inquired, noting the tinge of Kanuk's diction under his Western American diction.

"I miss Canada, " he confided. "Particularly in winter. The Snowbirds come down south to avoid the snow and get a little cultural spice to fill in their golden years. But, as the bumper stickers say, Thirty Below keeps the Riff Raff Out."

John smiled, then stroked his face. He noted that there wasn't ANY five o'clock shadow coming through the rouge. "Good thing," he thought. "And strange thing," he pondered. It had been a day of hard sweating, and John's beard always grew thickest when the going got tougher. Was something happening biologically? Mentally? Or, spiritually?

In mid-thought, John was interrupted by something more feared than the driver's gun, or the ER staff's lethal doses of ketamine, and Roman awaiting anyone who asked the wrong questions about MID or accidentally voiced the right answers. Along the side of the road where the limo stopped for a red light sat an Apache Elder clad in rags complimented by the semi-circular Eagle Clan insignia on the back of his coat. His eyes met John's, after which he yelled out "Thilkoki hy linko, kimosavi!"

"Maria? What's he saying?" John inquired with closed lips and averted eyes. "I mean besides kimosavi, which I know, very accurately, means shit face"

"Loosely translated...' later', Dr. J," her reply.

"Later for what?"

"Something he doesn't want you or me to know about yet," she said. "Great Spirit help him, and us."

XVII

Tom the hotel clerk made all the calls he could to the appropriate head offices after 'account closed' came up on John's escalating hotel tab. Selena Horowitz's credit cards were all mysteriously expired, the only money to her name was in her purse. However, she was the woman of the hour in the realm of local credit. Every researcher she interviewed at the Klassen sent the seductively spunky journalist something. Everything from flowers to fruit baskets, to vintage leather books of old West folklore, which had as much accuracy as the medical facts related to John, as her, during the interviews.

"But not one dollar I can spend the way I want to," John noted in the privacy of the hotel room, having just emerged from the shower, without any of Selena's clothing or makeup on his still penile-bearing body. "I guess this means I'm a kept WOMAN for the next few days."

"Or maybe longer," Selena 1 said from the back of John's mind. She pointed him to a plain wrapped bag amongst the gifts dropped off from her white-coated admirers. Inside lay more news clippings of rapist Baldino, on the run from the law, having ravaged children now after faking his own death. Also inside, more assignments for Selena Horowitz in places of change ever further away from home, signed with a "V" in Erica's handwriting.

"Afghanistan, Angola and....no, say it's not so...Newfoundland AND Labrador," John said. Then he looked at the dates and bawked. "In six months!"

"I'll stay with you as long as you need me, John," Selena 1 said. "After you dump that underaged Apache groupie of yours. And besides, this is a golden opportunity for you to--- "

"----To do what?" John yelled back at the wall, on which Selena refused to show herself, even as a faceless orb. "To lose ALL contact with my past? To give up football, hockey, hunting, and..." He felt the pair of spherical jewels within his shriveled-up scrotum. "They feel smaller than they were this morning."

"You have harder balls instead of bigger ones. It's a matter of belief and perception."

"And maybe reality!"

John looked into the mirror, touched his face, and his chest, and confirmed it. His skin was getting darker, and smoother. His face stopped growing hair today, and the enlarging nipples were... He flashed on something. "Someone is giving me pills I don't know about."

"Which are probably temporary..." Selena assured Dr J. "AND necessary. For six months. That's not a long time. Healers in Native cultures spend three YEARS living as the opposite gender to know what their patients think, feel, and need."

"So how did it feel when you grew a mustache in maybe YOUR last lifetime?" John asked in mocking speculation.

"We're talking about you, John. And a world that needs saving. But ultimately, it's you who has to decide how to save it."

"This won't work." John looked out the window. More crows appeared on the horizon, but no eagles, or even river seagulls or urban pigeons.

"The plans assigned to you beyond this assignment, which will end soon, are logical, reasonable, and make perfect sense, John."

"Yes, except to one man, maybe" John pointed out seeing something else.

"You, Dr J?"

"Him". John walked to the window with feet gone sore from excess walking as well as tight-fitting footwear. Another Eagle Dancer was making his rounds, around the dumpster. His face seemed familiar, both old and young. His feet stumbled more than danced. His arms and hands shook with painful tremors each time he tried to wield his fringe leather feather-loaded talking stick. The rotation of the eyes was in a pattern that wasn't any pattern at all, clearly indicating that he was living in another world, one whose primary emotion was terror.   His skin-over-bones walking skeleton was more than halfway to the Other Side.   But somehow, he remained in control of his soul as his body was deteriorating. "I can hear his death rattle from up here, even through his chanting and victoriously defiant smile," John noted. "I also KNOW that I'm a doctor. And…" the flash of an idea seemed very real. "If I save, diagnose, and cure HIM, I save the world."

Maria, using Eagle caws as her auditory voice, replied, "He's seen you, and me, at that research think tank, with his very real-world eyes, I think."

"He's seen Selena Horowitz with the white devils who are killing his people," Dr J stated as he saw the disease get worse The Old Man picked up a stick, wielding it against an invisible foe that John's inner eye couldn't see, but certainly feel.. "And I have to help HIM. NOW!".

"With what?" Maria challenged as John looked around for his medical kit and bag of medicinal tricks.

"I don't know!" John protested. "Maybe I, we, you can get us into the hospital and steal a lab coat, some diazepam, one of those portable CAT scan units that---"

"---will get us arrested and him thrown in the psych ward, or worse," Selena pointed out. Indeed, she was right. The Old Man's 'battle dance' against the Demon was about to be witnessed by a Police Car. First one, then two, then a green sedan with men in bioprotection suits that sat there and waited for him to faint. And waiting for him to, apparently, become 'harmless'. To cease being, as the excuse to put outlier humans into locked boxes, 'a danger to himself and others.'

"I'm going out there!" John screamed out to Selena, feeling Maria being notably somewhere else. "With or without you or Maria, wherever she went to." He grabbed the first aid kit from the hotel bathroom and rummaged through the bag full of jeans, boots, and cowboy shirts left in the room by Tom if Selena wanted to experience the REAL West with a ride on his horses and put them on. He ran to the door, stumbling onto the floor, tripping on what felt like an invisible ghost's leg, or a suitcase said the ghost, or ghosts', had 'accidentally' moved.

"John, think of the big picture," Selena 1 said. "Selena Horowitz can save millions of lives with her writing. John Baldino can only get himself killed. And if you go out there as you, John Baldino, MD, now Most Wanted for---"

"---it will be quick, fast, and to the point," John pushed out of gritted teeth. "If I can be alone with that man, as me, man to man, as a Man who hears the Eagle. A member of its Clan who allegedly is made delusionary and Visionary with this virus containing peyote no White man can find...A clan that maybe only allows men in it? Which explains why you, Maria, or Erica, or even you, Selena, can't tell me who's in it. Or what this Apache Good ole boy's club is about?"

"So, you know the first secret, John," Maria interjected upon her arrival said. "Or you guessed it. Which is it?"

The Old Man outside screamed a blood-curdling battle cry. The Police Cars approached from every side street. Dark silhouettes of gloved men armed with rifles, their faces covered with surgical masks, approached on foot. "Come on, with me, up there," John said to the Elder in English, Spanish, and his best Apache pointing to the dimly lit fire escape leading to his hotel room. "I'm a healer, not a doctor, who can heal you," he continued, showing him his medical kit containing what he intuited would at least halt the progression of the seizures associated with MID. The Old Man shook his head with a defiant 'no'. Then he seemed to see something attack from above, 'Demon birds!" he exclaimed. After they landed on the ground below he pulled himself back. "Demon bison", is the next descriptor. He motioned for John to get behind him with the utmost urgency. And 'Demon locomotive,' he screamed out next, commanding John to go behind him using his talking stick to protect the perhaps transgender and certainly transcultural Doc from the advancing train like a bullfighter against a mad steer that would turn his butcher into hamburger.

"Ok, you can protect heal me, and I can treat you," John continued, recognizing and finally confirming the rumors about stage 2 of Mad Indian Disease, noting the remnants of a hospital ID on the Elder's wrist. "But we have to move fast, Okay? To a hospital I control," he went on, approaching the Old Man with a steady gait and outstretched hands.

The Elder, whose face seemed to be that of a young man who had aged prematurely, nodded with approval to the gesture as his eyes rotated in his sockets. But just as the Elder's hands were about to grab hold of the young-turned-old man's shaking appendages, more vehicles arrived. This time, they were military ambulances, from which emerged men in white bioprotection suits, armed with syringes and semi-automatic weapons, working their way past the stetson-wearing Cops. The Old Indian looked at them, spit in their direction, and then pulled out three rocks from under his coat. He threw one of them in front of the contingent approaching from the East, another to the 'doctors' to the West, then pushed John into the wall of the alley, throwing the third rock in front of his feet. All three stones emitted a cloud of blinding aromatic black smoke.

Upon gaining his eyesight and breath, John saw that the Old Man had fled, leaving his Eagle Clan buckskin jacket, bearing the semi-circle and stem brand on John's hand, behind. Seeing the advancing horde of doctors and Cops coming towards him, John grabbed hold of the stick, wielding it like a spear to keep them at bay. He imitated to the best of his ability the Old Man's chanting. But the head man in the White Protection suit motioned for his men to ignore the paleface decoy. They pushed John into the wall of the alleyway. The medical hunting party pursued its originally intended prey.

John could hear screams of agony and defeat from the old man somewhere to the North of the building, then several car doors closing. Then, clicking of cameras from balconies above him. When he looked up, the amateur photographers or perhaps professional intel gathers, retreated back into their hotel rooms.

"So, what do we do now?" Baldino asked a bird he heard behind him as it landed, noting that the last spray of feminizing vocal cord adjustment Elixor was as ineffective in altering his voice as Banoca Mouth freshener. Upon turning, he noted that it was not his Eagle friend but a plain black crow, hopping its way to an eyeball of an Indian corpse hidden inside a dumpster, helping himself to the left eyeball after some other bird, or two-legged varments, had taken out the right.

John could have prayed to Jesus, Allah, or Buddha for an answer, but instead, he sought the help of his two vagina-owning angels. But neither Maria nor Selena 1 answered him this time.

XVIII

Tom the hotel clerk made all the calls he could to the appropriate head offices after 'account closed' came up on John's escalating hotel tab. Selena Horowitz's credit cards were all mysteriously expired, the only money to her name was in her purse. However, she was the woman of the hour in the realm of local credit. Every researcher she interviewed at the Klassen sent the seductively spunky journalist something. Everything from flowers to fruit baskets, to vintage leather books of old West folklore, which had as much accuracy as the medical facts related to John, as her, during the interviews.

"But not one dollar I can spend the way I want to," John noted in the privacy of the hotel room, having just emerged from the shower, without any of Selena's clothing or makeup on his still penile-bearing body. "I guess this means I'm a kept WOMAN for the next few days."

"Or maybe longer," Selena 1 said from the back of John's mind. She pointed him to a plain wrapped bag amongst the gifts dropped off from her white-coated admirers. Inside lay more news clippings of rapist Baldino, on the run from the law, having ravaged children now after faking his own death. Also inside, more assignments for Selena Horowitz in places of change ever further away from home, signed with a "V" in Erica's handwriting.

"Afghanistan, Angola and....no, say it's not so...Newfoundland AND Labrador," John said. Then he looked at the dates and bawked. "In six months!"

"I'll stay with you as long as you need me, John," Selena 1 said. "After you dump that underaged Apache groupie of yours. And besides, this is a golden opportunity for you to--- "

"----To do what?" John yelled back at the wall, on which Selena refused to show herself, even as a faceless orb. "To lose ALL contact with my past? To give up football, hockey, hunting, and..." He felt the pair of spherical jewels within his shriveled-up scrotum. "They feel smaller than they were this morning."

"You have harder balls instead of bigger ones. It's a matter of belief and perception."

"And maybe reality!"

John looked into the mirror, touched his face, and his chest, and confirmed it. His skin was getting darker, and smoother. His face stopped growing hair today, and the enlarging nipples were... He flashed on something. "Someone is giving me pills I don't know about."

"Which are probably temporary..." Selena assured Dr J. "AND necessary. For six months. That's not a long time. Healers in Native cultures spend three YEARS living as the opposite gender to know what their patients think, feel, and need."

"So how did it feel when you grew a mustache in maybe YOUR last lifetime?" John asked in mocking speculation.

"We're talking about you, John. And a world that needs saving. But ultimately, it's you who has to decide how to save it."

"This won't work." John looked out the window. More crows appeared on the horizon, but no eagles, or even river seagulls or urban pigeons.

"The plans assigned to you beyond this assignment, which will end soon, are logical, reasonable, and make perfect sense, John."

"Yes, except to one man, maybe" John pointed out seeing something else.

"You, Dr J?"

"Him". John walked to the window with feet gone sore from excess walking as well as tight-fitting footwear. Another Eagle Dancer was making his rounds, around the dumpster. His face seemed familiar, both old and young.   His feet stumbled more than danced. His arms and hands shook with painful tremors each time he tried to wield his fringe leather feather-loaded talking stick. The rotation of the eyes was in a pattern that wasn't any pattern at all, clearly indicating that he was living in another world, one whose primary emotion was terror.   His skin-over-bones walking skeleton was more than halfway to the Other Side.   But somehow, he remained in control of his soul as his body was deteriorating. "I can hear his death rattle from up here, even through his chanting and victoriously defiant smile," John noted. "I also KNOW that I'm a doctor. And…" the flash of an idea seemed very real. "If I save, diagnose, and cure HIM, I save the world."

Maria, using Eagle caws as her auditory voice, replied, "He's seen you, and me, at that research think tank, with his very real-world eyes, I think."

"He's seen Selena Horowitz with the white devils who are killing his people," Dr J stated as he saw the disease get worse The Old Man picked up a stick, wielding it against an invisible foe that John's inner eye couldn't see, but certainly feel.. "And I have to help HIM. NOW!".

"With what?" Maria challenged as John looked around for his medical kit and bag of medicinal tricks.

"I don't know!" John protested. "Maybe I, we, you can get us into the hospital and steal a lab coat, some diazepam, one of those portable CAT scan units that---"

"---will get us arrested and him thrown in the psych ward, or worse," Selena pointed out. Indeed, she was right. The Old Man's 'battle dance' against the Demon was about to be witnessed by a Police Car. First one, then two, then a green sedan with men in bioprotection suits that sat there and waited for him to faint.   And waiting for him to, apparently, become 'harmless'. To cease being, as the excuse to put outlier humans into locked boxes, 'a danger to himself and others.'

"I'm going out there!" John screamed out to Selena, feeling Maria being notably somewhere else. "With or without you or Maria, wherever she went to." He grabbed the first aid kit from the hotel bathroom and rummaged through the bag full of jeans, boots, and cowboy shirts left in the room by Tom if Selena wanted to experience the REAL West with a ride on his horses and put them on. He ran to the door, stumbling onto the floor, tripping on what felt like an invisible ghost's leg, or a suitcase said the ghost, or ghosts', had 'accidentally' moved.

"John, think of the big picture," Selena 1 said. "Selena Horowitz can save millions of lives with her writing. John Baldino can only get himself killed. And if you go out there as you, John Baldino, MD, now Most Wanted for---"

"---it will be quick, fast, and to the point," John pushed out of gritted teeth. "If I can be alone with that man, as me, man to man, as a Man who hears the Eagle. A member of its Clan who allegedly is made delusionary and Visionary with this virus containing peyote no White man can find...A clan that maybe only allows men in it? Which explains why you, Maria, or Erica, or even you, Selena, can't tell me who's in it. Or what this Apache Good ole boy's club is about?"

"So, you know the first secret, John," Maria interjected upon her arrival said. "Or you guessed it. Which is it?"

The Old Man outside screamed a blood-curdling battle cry. The Police Cars approached from every side street. Dark silhouettes of gloved men armed with rifles, their faces covered with surgical masks, approached on foot. "Come on, with me, up there," John said to the Elder in English, Spanish, and his best Apache pointing to the dimly lit fire escape leading to his hotel room. "I'm a healer, not a doctor, who can heal you," he continued, showing him his medical kit containing what he intuited would at least halt the progression of the seizures associated with MID. The Old Man shook his head with a defiant 'no'. Then he seemed to see something attack from above, 'Demon birds!" he exclaimed. After they landed on the ground below he pulled himself back. "Demon bison", is the next descriptor. He motioned for John to get behind him with the utmost urgency. And 'Demon locomotive,' he screamed out next, commanding John to go behind him using his talking stick to protect the perhaps transgender and certainly transcultural Doc from the advancing train like a bullfighter against a mad steer that would turn his butcher into hamburger.

"Ok, you can protect heal me, and I can treat you," John continued, recognizing and finally confirming the rumors about stage 2 of Mad Indian Disease, noting the remnants of a hospital ID on the Elder's wrist. "But we have to move fast, Okay? To a hospital I control," he went on, approaching the Old Man with a steady gait and outstretched hands.

The Elder, whose face seemed to be that of a young man who had aged prematurely, nodded with approval to the gesture as his eyes rotated in his sockets. But just as the Elder's hands were about to grab hold of the young-turned-old man's shaking appendages, more vehicles arrived. This time, they were military ambulances, from which emerged men in white bioprotection suits, armed with syringes and semi-automatic weapons, working their way past the stetson-wearing Cops. The Old Indian looked at them, spit in their direction, and then pulled out three rocks from under his coat. He threw one of them in front of the contingent approaching from the East, another to the 'doctors' to the West, then pushed John into the wall of the alley, throwing the third rock in front of his feet. All three stones emitted a cloud of blinding aromatic black smoke.

Upon gaining his eyesight and breath, John saw that the Old Man had fled, leaving his Eagle Clan buckskin jacket, bearing the semi-circle and stem brand on John's hand, behind. Seeing the advancing horde of doctors and Cops coming towards him, John grabbed hold of the stick, wielding it like a spear to keep them at bay. He imitated to the best of his ability the Old Man's chanting. But the head man in the White Protection suit motioned for his men to ignore the paleface decoy. They pushed John into the wall of the alleyway. The medical hunting party pursued its originally intended prey.

John could hear screams of agony and defeat from the old man somewhere to the North of the building, then several car doors closing. Then, clicking of cameras from balconies above him. When he looked up, the amateur photographers or perhaps professional intel gathers, retreated back into their hotel rooms.

"So, what do we do now?" Baldino asked a bird he heard behind him as it landed, noting that the last spray of feminizing vocal cord adjustment Elixor was as ineffective in altering his voice as Banoca Mouth freshener. Upon turning, he noted that it was not his Eagle friend but a plain black crow, hopping its way to an eyeball of an Indian corpse hidden inside a dumpster, helping himself to the left eyeball after some other bird, or two-legged varment, had taken out the right.

John could have prayed to Jesus, Allah, or Buddha for an answer, but instead, he sought the help of his two vagina-owning angels. But neither Maria nor Selena 1 answered him this time.

XIX

Upon climbing up the staircase, carrying the buckskin coat bearing the Eagle Clan logo, and finally making it back to his hotel room, John quickly opened the door and locked it behind him. A quick look around the room indicated that there had been guests from the real world who had entered it in his absence, re-decorating it. Selena's clothing was neatly packed into three suitcases. The notes, cameras, and pictures he had taken had been packed into a large blue bin marked 'radioactive'. On the dresser, in an envelope marked 'tips for housekeepers', he noted two one hundred dollar bills and two tickets to the Rocky Horror Picture show at the Phoenix Repertory Theatre. As for the gift baskets of sweets, fruit, and cheese, they were being gobbled up by a very real humanoid sporting a jean jacket and military paratrooper pants.

"So, Vincent," John said. "Long time no see?" he advanced.

"And there's no free lunch," the unexpected intruder said, upon which he turned around indicating it was no other than Erica. "Take off that shirt," she said to John regarding the denim cowboy shirt donated by the hotel clerk, a request that he complied with both eagerly and cautiously. "And that buckskin coat," she said of the oversized leather garment left by the once muscular Eagle dancer. "It's too big for you," she said, snatching it from his tight grasp. "But this one does," she continued, retrieving another Apache coat, smelling of elk, horse, and an herbal aroma John had never encountered, along with the odor and stain of fresh blood. "Especially around the eyes," she said with a smile as she placed it on his chest, then insisted on putting it on his arms.

"I'm a big boy, Erica," John protested as Erica forced the coat on him. "You, Leonard, Vinny, Erica, all want to dress me up and show me off, but---"

----Erica punched John in the belly, silencing his next criticism. "It belonged to someone very special to me," she said, gazing at a turquoise Native wedding ring still on her left fourth digit. Who told me nothing about what 'this' was really about," she continued pointing to the Eagle Clan emblem. "By the name of Tom, Tom-Tom as he wanted to call me when we got into drumming together," she said with a sorrowful smile and sardonic chuckle. "Who, well---" Her assertive arrogance turned into grief, then helpless vulnerability. She turned her back, doing her best to not let John see the tears that eventually forced their way out of her bloodshot and tired eyes.

"Tom died of an 'accident'?" John gently said, extending his hand towards than eventually onto her shaking shoulder. "Like Jack, your husband, died back in New York years ago when his research into what his colleagues were doing for BITE got too accurate?"

"And other terrorist organizations, some legal some not," Erica added, after which she turned around. "But you and I are officially dead and have to do something to keep the world and the people in it Alive. Particularly the 'outliers'. And the potential outliers who, if they survive, can make a big difference in the world, while doing…well…as little harm as possible."

"How?" John asked. "Who do we have to work with now to stop all of this? To dispel all the lies about this tumor epidemic, and find this so-called Satanic virus containing ceremonial peyote that is supposed to be causing it? And, we have to find out who exactly is, or was, in this Clan that, officially anyway, started and is perpetuating the disease. Who is their leader who is SAID to be spreading the Mad Indian Disease?"

"Jake Cuthand," Erica replied, showing John a picture of an Apache in Eagle Clan attire armed with the latest in semi-automatic weapons, the most Ancient of spears, and fire-breathing eyes ignited with passion and commitment. "Who doesn't trust me anymore."

"Why?" John inquired. "Something you did?"

"Something I am," her reply. "Under here," she said, pointing to the genitalia between her legs. "And the complexion I was born with," she continued, pinching the white skin on her arm.

"Which I also have," John replied. "Under this 'temporary tan' that Leonard gave me," he said. "And hairless face that...."

"----We hope doesn't sprout any hair," Erica interjected, stroking his cheek, and lips. "And if he does decide to give you a Yul Brenner head shave," she continued, running her fingers through the long brownish hair on John's machine head made such by the extensions that were still holding. "I've asked Jake Cuthand to not give you heads three inches below the scalp." She put up her hands, as a boy scout. "Honest Injun!"

The sign outside of the Apache Reservation warned White intruders to stay out, along with new signs from the White world reading 'Epidemic Inside'. They were appended by the signs put up by the Apache saying 'want a haircut, just try coming in, Whitey', nailed to bloody blond and brown haired wigs that were perhaps weaved in China, or perhaps taken from real people. A truck arrived from Amazone Delivery Service, swerving its way along the road to the Rez, somehow avoiding the metal spikes hidden in the grass and the mini-land mines that had been planted there... An arrow landed in front of it, halting its progress. The archer walked to the truck, pulling his arrow out of the ground. The archer, Jake Cuthand in full regalia including his Eagle Clan buckskin coat, approached the driver. "What do you get in the truck?" he asked, pulling out the US Army pistol he somehow got past customs after completing his last tour abroad to defend the God-given right of America to remain a Capitalist, racist, and of course Christian country.

"Food, medicine, laptops, healing roots," the half-breed driver replied pointing to two overloaded bins next to him, after which he pulled out a leather pouch from his pocket, showing it to Jake. "And sacred herbs and ceremonial identification beads, from ....surviving Hopi, Navajo, Yaqui...not like our ancient, and accordin' to what I heard, still enemies, the Commanche."

"And you?" Jake replied while confirming the contents of the bin, then the leather pouch. Looking up, he noted that the driver had more Commanche than Apache features.   He abruptly pointed his pistol at the driver's head. "Why should we let you or any of this in here?".

"'Cause I got shot up by the Sheriff's deputies in town, just like you and the rest of your people who wandered in for supplies, to visit the sick, or attend that protest against this quarantine without permission," the Driver related showing Jake a bloody stitched up wound in his right arm. "So did my truck," he continued, pointing to the evidence of such.

"Hmmm," Jake said, still harboring suspicions. "And you are,,,,?"

The driver produced a wanted poster bearing his likeness, with a price on his head that nearly matched the one on Jake. Jake's frown turned into a welcoming smile.   "You are welcomed!" he said, in Apache, waving in the fellow rebel, rabble-rouser, and, as he saw it anyway, revolutionary. He cawed like an eagle to the brush in the East and the West. Five mounted Eagle Clan men emerged from the former, twice as man from the latter. All were armed with the most regal weapons of past centuries and functional ones from the present one. They got off their horses and loaded the supplies onto their horses, welcoming the driver into the group. But the driver gracefully refused, getting back into his truck. "Gotta get more supplies for the Cause. Maybe in the next round, I can bring back more people," he said. Jake stopped him offering him meat and money. The former was accepted, the latter refused.   With that, the driver turned around and headed back down the mountain into the valley below, doing as much bumping as forward motion, littering the road with plastic packages of junk food, condoms, and skeletal remains of assorted chickens and rabbits. Jake checked the traps and mines leading to the gate, locked it shut, then mounted his horse, joining the others as they rode up into the hills, disappearing into the thick bush as the trees closed the door behind them.

John, clad in Tom's Eagle Clan shirt with enough warp paint on his face to make him look 'Indian' but not unrecognizable, saw it all from a tree-covered overlook with high power field glasses made even more so by adjustment of the lenses by Erica. With a high-tech hearing device implanted into his aching ears and the translations of the chitter chatter in Apache she provided with her lip reading skills, he heard it all as well. There was one thing that seemed strange, though, that John had to give voice to. "I'm hungry," he said.

"For the truth about this epidemic and yourself, I assume," Erica replied.

"No," John replied rubbing his belly as a whiff of wind blew up towards him an odor that came from one of the open bins of supplies that fell out of the delivery truck after it made its way into the Rez. "Something smells."

"Fishy?" Erica said.

"No," John replied. "Familiar, somehow."

"You're seeing ghosts with your nose now? Smelling them?" she said. "You never told me if ghosts ever have to take a shit or piss, or if after a hangover, they barf."

"I don't know," his reply. "I never thought to ask them about…"

The discourse about the physiology of the ghost GI tract was delayed by the proud cut gelding Erica had found for John opening up his mouth to call out the mares being ridden by the Eagle Clan members. She put an apple into his yapper to keep him from escalating anything. John held him back from bashing through the barbed and electrified wire fence built by the barbed wire fence built by CDC in town, and the wooden fence which the Apache had constructed. Armed with thick gloves, she connected the wire fence to an alternative circuit, then cut the fence in three places, pulling it open just wide enough for the horse and its terrified rider to enter. Then she dismantled the wooden fence.

"Ok, go!" she said. "And ride under the tree, so the crop dusters can't spot you. Your Eagle friend can find you once you get to the plateau where the medicine wheels are. And maybe the peyote that, according to Tom-Tom, only a male member of the Eagle Clan can find," Erica informed John. "Because 'his eyes have been open to it.',", she continued with raised eyebrows pushed to the top of her head by a frustrated limited brain behind it. "You head East to where the trees end, then West till you see where grass grows, then North till the sand becomes rock."

"But," John said, looking at the map she had provided him. "Tom's map says that I head West, then East, then South," he pointed out.

"Tom's directions led me to a swamp a year ago, where he was waiting to 'rescue' me, from 'finding out truths that only approved of MEN are supposed to know;" her reply.

"So, I'm a man. But if I'm not approved by Jake Cuthand and a jury of HIS peers?" John inquired.

"Then you'll wind up in the swamp. Dead," she replied as she packed up her supplies. "As someone who died trying to do something important, which is more than how most people die. Which, as the ghosts you are talking to say, according to your 'fact-based novel' and real experience, is a better life than the existence we call living on this side of the veil."

"But this horse!" John said as he tried to mount the animal, who was sidestepping each attempt he made to get into the saddle. "He doesn't look like he wants to go anywhere."

"Neither do you," she said, after which she gently said and then yelled something in a language John didn't recognize at the gelding, scaring him into submission. "He was Tom's favorite horse, who he never named," she related by way of explanation. "A proud-cut and prouder-minded Arab Quarterhorse cross who will do whatever you need him to do if you ask rather than tell him to do. Who always knows the way home."

John mounted the steed, not finding any problems with him, while standing still anyway. "And if I, and he, get lost? Or if he doesn't know where 'home' is today? Because he wants to stay a night or two with some of those Apache mares first?"

"That avian friend of yours will probably find you," Erica replied. "Of if he can't, the underaged female companion inside of you who, maybe you are getting sweet on, can help," she said with more than a twinge of jealousy.

"Maria," John said, confirming Erica's speculation. "Who…"

"Is right here, and will be eighteen tomorrow," he heard from his inner voice from the optimistic Apache teen who was deprived of the experience of a disappointing adulthood due to Mad Indian Disease. "I think I know the way home," she said, seemingly from a 'force field' arching its way into the small of John's back. "And if I don't he does, probably," he heard from his finally reactivated inner ear as he noticed the horse moving forward at a brisk walk, without him having given the gelding any request to do so.

"The list of every member of the Eagle Clan, a sample of the peyote I can test in the lab, and.…" Erica yelled out to the duo atop the horse she loved more than herself or even John. "You will come back alive, please," she whispered. "Please!" she begged of the Christian Deity above who she had just re-opened cordial conversations after a twenty-year hiatus in their embittered relationship.

John, while consulting Tom's map and taking the opposite way to go, rode through hills, and argued with Maria en route on a multitude of topics to pass the time. It served to avoid being paralyzed by the fear of being spotted by crop dusters, mauled by bears, or becoming the recipients of arrows from Eagle Clan members who didn't take kindly to uninvited guests to their sacred sagebrush temples. Such topics discussed with Maria included the values of popular vs. esoteric music, the conspiracy theory that tattoos contained ink that made you inappropriately happy then stupid, the contention that blonde hair dye DID contain ingredients that infiltrated the brain, converting dark-haired warrior women into shopping mall dwelling Barbies and why God the Father decided to make life easier for men than women when Adam was just as 'guilty' for eating the forbidden apple from the tree of Knowledge as Eve, and whether there were vegans now in charge of the happy hunting grounds who Maria would have to educate about the nutritional necessity of eating meat. But there was something else of more immediate importance as the air got thinner, and the ground more rocky, with no shortage of goffer holes, particularly to the left.

"Ok, horse," John told the steed as it made a left turn on what seemed to be a fork in the 'road' upward. We turn right here," John said following Maria's adjustment of the map, having noted that for the last several miles, the sky seemed darker, and devoid of any avian life.

"No…eh.,..left," Maria said, seeming to have changed her mind. "And let that horse have his head!"

"But all of these goffer holes, and Erica's alternative map," said the Doc who had in his sheltered and accomplished past, was infamous for planning his adventures before experiencing them. "And you, Maria, said that we're supposed to go right," John pointed out. "Because if we go left---"

"---We'll get there faster," Maria's reply. "Before everybody else does."

"And 'there' is, and 'everybody else' is?" John pressed, holding the horse back.

"You'll find out when you get there, Doctor John,".

It was the first time Maria had called John by his former title, and function in life. A Doctor who was careful to above all do no harm to his patients. And who also knew how to listen to his inner intuition rather than established and published logic. Or accept as gospel truth the popular opinion in the hospital conference or symposium lecture hall when trying to determine what would work for said patients. Listening as hard as he could to that inner voice, he concluded that maybe Maria was right. And that the right thing to do was something that kept changing.

"OK, then, to the left," John said. "At a walk!" he commanded the horse, who burst into a trot, then a lope, then a flat-out gallop. It resulted in John losing control of the horse, then the map but, as far as he could tell, not his bladder. After being a passenger rather than a driver, over big magnificently virgin terrain that excited and scared him, John finally brought the horse to a halt. He sniffed something in the air. And it wasn't his own urine or feces. The horse seemed to see something with his nostrils as well.

"To the right, then, straight ahead, forward?" John asked the horse and Maria.

"Agreed," she replied. "But at a…trot this time."

"Agreed," John said, nudging the steed onward at a controlled ground covering wide stridden trot which required no rein contact to maintain. It merged into a 'think it and the horse does it' zen experience which was suddenly interrupted when the horse decided to run away from something behind him or rush towards something ahead.   John held on till Tom's favorite steed halted abruptly at the entrance of a flat, grassy meadow, where the horse dined on the flowery green botanical offerings the earth had spring up there. The steed was in horse heaven. John lay on the ground, in a pile of manure. Upon wiping the brown off his face, discovering that he really was more White than Wannabe Red skinned, he saw skulls of animals and people around him, some with intact skeletons. He broke into mad laughter.

"Yeah…I know," John said to the skulls surrounding him. "The dead sometimes bullshitted me. But never shit on me. And…."

As John cleaned the manure from his mouth, he noted bits of red flakes that found their way into his mouth. It was pleasing and exciting to his tongue and nostrils. He noted that the red flakes had come from pedals sprouted from mini cactus plants growing between clumps of thick, green grass. He carefully pulled out a pinch of the red-flowered 'leaves' towards his nose, then mouth, and broke into a smile. The unexpected light lunch break was interrupted by a jolt rammed into his left temple.

"Ya don't pay yer dues, ya don't eat in this Alpine café, Doctor John," Jake Cuthand said from behind the pistol crammed into the skull covering Baldino's favorite body part.

"You know who I am?" the good Doctor said to them, as some called him and with good reason, bad-assed Indian. "How?" he continued, turning his eyes to see his executioner face to face.

"The question you and us have to find out is do you know who YOU really are?" Jake blasted at him. "And what your REAL intentions are," he repeated, pulling back his gun, but keeping it aimed at John's head.

"And if I guess the right answer, or give you the wrong answer?" John challenged, overtaken with something he identified as 'courage', taking the opportunity to look straight into Jake's eyes.

With his non-gun holding hand, Jake pointed to the dead skulls.

"Point taken," John noted. His mind was a lot calmer than he anticipated it would be the first time someone pulled a gun on him. "But I need to save you, me, and according to Erica, the world who doesn't give a shit about either of us…"

John looked at and into Jake. Apparently, by mechanisms none of the textbooks anyone, including himself, had written, Jake's rage turned into applied intelligence and then, albeit cautious, compassion. He lowered his gun, then grabbed John's right wrist, taking note of the scratches on his forearm. "The Eagle Clan insignia," he said. "That was put on you by who?"

"An Avian friend," John replied, after which he looked upward at the birdless sky. "Who, well, I'm afraid isn't here to verify that claim."

"You came all the way up here, on Tom's horse, to me. Expecting me to tell you the names of the members of the Eagle Clan?" Jake said letting go of John's arm, leaving it in considerable discomfort bordering on mind-distracting pain. "And get a sample of what your people call 'Satan's peyote'" He gently pulled out one of the red pedal-bearing plants from the ground. "A demonic plant that your people say is giving us cancer. And your people say we're planning to spread around towns and cities to kill off your people."

"They aren't my people," John asserted.

After putting the plant into his medicine pouch, Jake scratched his chiseled hairless, and scarred chin. "We'll see about that," he said as a threat, and wish.

Jake said something in Apache to trees around the meadow, his speech interrupted by some kind of answer from their talking branches. "So, this guy is just as wicked and enlightened in the soul as I am," John thought. Until armed warriors in full regalia, with makeup that hides their faces, emerged from the brush, some sick, most not sick. Each of them knelt on the ground, gave a prayer to the Four Directions, then gently picked no more than a single red pedal from the mini-cacti amongst the thick grasses, placing them on their tongues. The 'meal' seemed to revive them.

Jake turned to John, "Ya see, Doc, no cancer. And no devil coming into our brains, which all of us still have."

"I don't suppose you gentlemen would give me your names," John said to the Indians whose faces were covered with white, red, and black makeup which made their eyes seem all the more firey, and Alive. "Or the names of the other members of your, I know, and accept, Sacred Clan," he continued to Jake, the only one of them who did not have warpaint covering his facial features. "So I can cross reference them with the cancer patients in town. Or who are buried here after you snuck them out of the investigative morgue."

Jake shook his head in a 'no', as did each of the other Clan members. Three of them pulled out their arrows, and placed them inside their bows. Then aimed them at John's head. Jake looked at the angry dissenters, motioning for them to put down their weapons with words in Apache that John, nor Maria, when John silently asked her, understood.

"NATIVE American democracy and philosopher king rule at work, Doc," Jake said. "But as a scientist, I know that you have to prove to yourself and others that this herb is NOT what's causing my people and your people to get sick and die. And to test in on Erica's lab rats…"

"Of which I seem to be now," John said. He gobbled down the herb, a large portion of it. A handful of red pedals which he swallowed with a large gulp. The Clan members consulted with each other, disturbed at what John had done. Jake looked at the doctor with….concern.

"What? I did something wrong?" John asked Jake and the congregation.

"Something…potentially enlightening, given the White disease of greed regarding knowledge, and other things," Chief Cuthand's reply.

Jake said something to his people. They scattered into the woods, then rode away. Jake laughed, his mind sharing a myriad of jokes with his soul, Then he muttered the setups and punchlines in Apache.

"OK…so what is he saying, Maria?" John muttered to himself.

"That the location for the ceremony is somewhere else today," Jake said as he walked towards his horse, taking the reins of Tom's steed as well.

"Huh?" John blurted out, standing up, wondering how he would get back home on his tired and lost feet.

"You read hearts, according to your book," Jake said, pulling out a copy of 'Heart of the Healer' from his saddle bag. "I read eyes," he continued. "But not as well as you do, and she does," he said, motioning to the air behind him, which to John was nothing more than a pile of windblown dust. "Right, Maria it is?" he asked a cloud of dust that appeared out of nowhere…

"Yeah, Maria," John said as the cloud of dust disappeared, turning into Maria, in the flesh, to the good and shocked Doctor's eyes anyway. With long thick hair not made thin and absent by futile chemotherapy. With a flush, full face not emaciated into thin skin covering painful bone caused by radiation 'therapy'. With legs under her fringe leather skirt that were shapely enough to be shown off on a fashion runway as well as capable of carrying her into first place in a marathon held in Arizona, New York, or Paris. But she seemed angry, due to her allowing herself to be so visible. She folded her arms as if she was bracing for a punishment from Jake for coming to this spot, uninvited. "That is Maria," John stated, as fact.

"Who, IF that's really her, should know that she is…" Cuthand said, after which he turned around. "….home now," he continued, warmly. And with more gratitude than any sick patient John had ever turned into a healthy person. "And has to let Mister Baldino find his way home, though another route than the one he took here, right?"

Maria, in John's eyes, nodded yes. "She mounted Tom's horse, then pointed John to a small meadow just below the one he was standing on. It was a collection of rocks in a circle.

"It's called a medicine wheel," Jake explained mounting his horse. "A porthole to…well…you'll find out in three days if you enter it."

"Maria put up her fingers in 'two', then punched Jake in the belly. He seemed to feel it.

"Or…yeah, sooner than two days," Jake related to John. "That is IF you can eat from the tree of TRUE knowledge and not fall into a goffer hole, or an abyss leading to…" As for the destination of such, Jake motioned 'cookoo' with his fingers, which John smiled at. "Or," Cuthand continued, putting his fingers across his throat, indicating death, which John seemed to embrace.

With that Jake and Maria gleefully galloped into the Western horizon with a victorious hoop and holler. John limped his way to the medicine wheel to the East, under a birdless sky getting darker with each painful step. "No pain, no gain. No fear, no discovery, No risk, no accomplishment," John told himself, hoping that those three credos he championed were actually true, and not a setup for a joke with him as the blown-up punchline.

XXI

John observed himself walking into the medicine wheel without any hesitation. Unlike his expectations, he didn't feel anything different upon sitting on the ground in the middle of the collection of rocks. No pulsing in the third eye above his nose. No throbbing of the vibration-sensing Pacinian corpuscles below his navel. No electrifying thunderbolts coming out of the ground electrifying his ass and zooming up his spine. No, the only sensations he felt were those of 'commoners'. The coldness of the air was amplified by the wind blowing into his face and under-covered chest as it kept changing direction each time he adjusted his body to keep his back to it. The howling of wolves who did eat human flesh, or if they were satiated enough, gave you a warning bite with teeth coated with rabies virus. And the feeling of being….alone in Mother Nature's arena, with nothing man-made visible in any direction. Such was something as terrifying to an urban born and bred New Yorker as open seas were to a cruise line passenger who, upon the ship running out of fuel in mid-passage from port to port, recalled he couldn't swim. Then there was the growling of John's emptying stomach, knowing that there were no Domino Pizza Delivery trucks coming by with a late-night snack to keep him going till the next morning, or the one or two after that.

But a moon bright replaced the setting sun, laying a generous blanket of light upon the hard ground. It enabled John's eyes to see what was going on in the outside world, which did become inhabited by visitors from the inner realm. John's watch decided to stop ticking. Then, to his eyes anyway, its hands moved backward.   "What time is it?" Doctor John asked the first visitor to his 'office', a well-muscled grey-haired man with more battle scars than the skin on his face in a weather-beaten black Stetson, sporting a large handlebar mustache with an even bigger six gun and machete secured under a 'belt rope' around his this waist thin waist.

Great, in more ways than one, Grandpa Baldino, an Italian immigrant who had fled poverty, obscurity, and the long arm of the law wielded by Mussolini rather than paid off Sicilian Cops, removed a pocket watch from his vest pocket, saying in his native diction, "It's eight pm, nineteen twenty-five, you idiot."

"Why are you calling me an idiot, Grandpa?" John inquired.

"Because you never figured out I was an asshole!" Grandpa Josepi replied.

"Who fought against the Federalis in Mexico to defend Yaqui Indians and dirt poor peasants, and before that, worked his way up to owning and renovating slums in Manhattan that had housed three families in one room," John pointed out. "Who landed in Ellis Island…"

"With ten cents in his pocket," Grandpa said half a second before the words came out of John's parched mouth. "Yes, and also this," the inspiration for every admonishment John's parents threw at him when he was a lazy or selfish underachiever said. He pulled out a leather pouch from his hole-ridden pants pocket, then showed John the contents.

The glitter from the diamonds inside was so bright that it blinded John's eyes.

"Those are what you found when you were on a pilgrimage to Spain to visit the cave where Saint Anne was martyred when you went to Spain to fight against Franco and Fascism," John said, recalling the stories passed down to him as to why the Baldino's kept themselves and many Mexican families alive through the Great Depression.

"I had many agendas to attend to in Spain and special assignments when I got there. There were many Fascist banks we robbed and put the money in, under different names of course, when...." Josepi pulled out a comfortable pillow-bearing chair from behind his back, laying his backside against it. He then pulled a blanket out of nowhere, placing it over his shoulders. Shaking his hands, he produced a hot dog out of thin air, proceeding to eat it with small satisfied bites. John, with chattering teeth brought in by a cold North wind and a rumbling stomach that screamed out to be filled by something, noted the back pocket of his peasant revolutionary Grandpa's pants filled with hundred dollar bills, British Pound Sterling notes, and gold nuggets the size of marbles. "And Saint Anne was a whore," Grandpa Josepi related with a chuckle pushed through a proud grin, revealing gold coatings on his teeth. "Who stole it from French gypsies, who stole it from...Well...no one who'd miss it. Which is why I came here."

"Here being?" John inquired, sensing that indeed he was in another universe.

"Senora, Mexico....Where I disappeared. Into the Huya Aniya for a while," Josepi explained.

"The Yaque dream world....from which you can change the real world....Which."

"Changed the course of the Yaqui Indian revolt?" Josepi scoffed. "Like a lot of other white misfits, fortune seekers and...Yaqui Injuns, set out to do anyway." The Old Man patted the head of the younger one like the younger one was a child, then snapped his fingers, commanding to elements to produce a chair which he sat on. "But after the revolutions were over, the smart ones got back to...business. And being...sensible for the sake and welfare of....the family. "

Grandpa's pocketwatch alarm rang out 'The Godfather' theme. He checked the time. "Well," he said, after which he folded up the chair, converting it into a cloud of sawdust, whipped the blanket in the wind, causing it to be blown away as bits of irretrievable cloth, then threw the rest of his hot dog down his throat. "Time for me to go." he smiled at John as a luxury vintage cab materialized outside the medicine wheel, the chaufer opening the door for him to enter. "And it is time for for you to…stay!" he informed John as his grandson tried to get up to follow him.

Grandpa Josepi entered the cab, the vehicle and its inhabitants driving off towards then dissolving into a rock wall. John was left alone, with his first dose of 'truth'. A medicine he underestimated about its nature and potency. He looked down at his hands, where he saw a scorpion nibbling on his cold and now fragile flesh. He felt woozy, then faded into a trance.

He woke up, several moments, minutes hours, or perhaps eons later, feeling something else enveloping his skin as well as body and mind underneath it. This time it wasn't the wind. Indeed, John was clad as a Selena, very attractive by even Selena 1's standards, in a sexy First Nations-themed outfit that could double as something chic enough to be the recipient of an award at an art show in Cannes, or a Pulitzer Prize in Manhattan. He smiled with delight as he felt his shaved legs. His C-cup breasts were REAL this time with an absence of a disturbing set of testicles between his legs. After running his fingers over his ultra-thin swooping eyebrows, he saw a middle-aged woman in Army fatigues to his left, her strong, muscular arms folded.

"All these years of schooling, training, and education for THIS, John 'girl'," Doctor Baldino's mother sneered with disgust and shame.

"Mom?" John blurted out, not knowing, or caring, if she was here from the land of the living or the dead. Or if indeed it was her at all. He rose up to get a better look. He tried to touch the image in front of him to affirm her real existence or lack of it.

She pulled back from John, just as he was about to get an answer, then pulled out her rifle, cleaning it. "You look disgustingly 'lovely' and 'silly'," Mary Baldino pushed out a set of angry gritted teeth while cleaning the barrel of her man-sized rifle.

"It was…and…maybe still is a cover," John replied by way of explanation. "Which worked for me. And the Mission I'm still on. Also part of me may be becoming sort of a 'Shamen' who can understand and heal patients of both genders. Like the Shamen of more than one Native tribe North of the Rio Grande."

"Yeah, right," she replies. "Of course, a SHEman' should enjoy his, or her 'work'," the ex-intel-gathering Pacifist Nun and spy turned super soldier, in this presentation anyway, volleyed back.

"We do what we have to do," John asserted.

"And enjoy doing maybe too much?" she said. "Like your father said when he went on 'special' assignments?"

John felt a burst of wind and a flash of light emerging from his right side. Turning to rather than against it, he saw his father, legendary super soldier 'Iron Mike' Baldino, in a perfectly ironed skirt, blouse, and blazer, complimented with a long blonde wig sending curls down to his breasts.

"Which I was, enjoying it as I was being effective," he related to his wife. "With this!" he continued, pulling a super-sized machine gun from under the belt of his left hip. "And this," he went on, retrieving a pen from the middle of his ample cleavage. "Yes, Mary, I was very effective as and with all of this."

"And still am?" Mary pressed. "Or are you preparing yourself for your next life assignment in your afterlife?"

"My next reincarnation, Mary. Maybe as a lioness instead of a lion?" he related, placing his weaponry back into their slots under his skirt. He stroked his now hairless but, for most of his time when he was at home, lightly bearded chin. "Who…Well. Maybe can get back together with you, who….?" He reached into his small weapon-containing purse, pulling out a list. "You who, well…"

John sprang his head back to his mother, curious and afraid of her comeback. He recalled how hot and 'interesting' the parental disagreements were between them during the rare times when they were home.

"Well, what?" John's mother replied, her focus completely on the 'man' she had the mixed fortune to marry rather than the son she was blessed to conceive.

"According to the intel I got from up there," Iron Mike said, pointing to the sky. "There's a double occupancy womb where two fetuses are open to be inhabited by two souls in…"

He put away the list and then pulled out a map. "Yeah….Arkansas, Mary!"

"Where we can pretend to be more than brother and sister?" she pondered, after which she spit a wad of tobacco into John's face, ordering him with the flick of her dirt-soaked hand to look at his father. "Well, we're waiting for an answer, John" she demanded, folding her arms even tighter than before.

John's traditionally stoic, pathologically responsible father, whose only two experiences with dancing or singing were his wedding night and, at his wife's insistence, John's wedding to his first, only, and deceased wife, broke into blissful laughter. After which he said by way of explanation to a puzzled son and frustrated spouse, "Sibling rivalry is a lot more fun than being rival superspy spouses….What do ya say, Mario?"

Mary considered the offer, wavering between choices. John nodded his head in the affirmative.

Maybe it was something in her 'son's' eyes, or something in her now less than masculine husbands, but Mary's hard-edged yang personal edged over the yin side of things. "It's worth a shot, Michelle," she said to John's father. Her hardened face broke into an inviting smile. After which she walked towards her husband.

Michelle and Mario hugged each other and then kissed. Then broke into a dance in which they took turns as to who was leading.

John thought about singing a tune to keep the dance going. But he had learned that he loved humanity too much to subject anyone to his off-key singing voice. Still, he quietly hummed the happy, to-be-united-again-as-different-genders, couple in song as, perhaps because of his own courage to be expressive, they whirled and twirled themselves into a blissful frenzy. It lightened their hearts, making their mass convert into energy that vanished in a flash of light which seemed to warm the air as well as illuminate John's post.

John surrendered to the unknown dimension otherwise known as sleep. The next morning, or perhaps many next mornings afterward, he awoke to find that his hair had grown long, and white. Most of it fell into his hands when he stroked his fingers through it, leaving in its wake a crown of head devoid of any hair. Or, as he had to check as it was in 'Injun territory' where White assholes were still scalped, blood. "Either I incarnated into being Rip Van Winkle or…maybe I got a bad case of uranium toxicity?" John said to an American Army officer in combat fatigues with an arsenal of weapons strapped to his torso standing in front of him just outside the circle of rock. His combat-ready face was covered with mud. The bright sun silhouetted his giant-sized Herculean frame. "This ground, when it isn't shaking under my feet, does feel 'hot' to the touch," John said to him, feeling the bald crown on his head. "Which could explain the source of MID,… but as we know---".

"---No grass grows on busy streets," the uniformed visitor interjected in a voice John recalled all too well. "A fact that you avoided when you had that mop of a long, hippie. And, according to Mom AND me, girly looking hair when you were in college, then medical school, then…" he continued as he strolled around the medicine wheel, the sunlight on his face revealing his identity.

"--_Vincent!' John said, recognizing his brother. He reached his hand across the border of the medicine wheel to touch him, to confirm if he was from the realm of the living, dead, or imagination. But Vincent pulled back every time John tried to confirm his existence. "Erica said you were still alive in the real world. Are you?"

"To be answered...." Vincent replied. "On a need-to-know basis," he continued, John, said those words not only along with but before they came out of his brother's mouth.

"Yes," Vincent said by way of finality. "On a need-to-know basis." He sat down on one of the rocks illuminating the medicine wheel. He retrieved two cigars from his pocket, placing them in his mouth. He lit them both, being careful to not ignite his overgrown jet-black mustache and bushy beard, then offered one to John.

"No thanks," John said.

"You wanna know what kind of herbs, tobacco or pharmaceuticals are in these, because as you said before, again and again, while all your Hippie friends and my military comrades were enjoying great weed, booze, and women, 'creative madness is best enjoyed straight'. I understand," Vincent said, after which he pulled out from his breast pocket the package they came from, and took a generous puff from the stoggie. "They're Cuban...Illegal down below, but here, well."

"Vincent!" John yelled out through a throat that emitted a voice twenty years older than it was a day or two earlier. "What are you doing here, besides looking a whole lot younger than I do?"

"Oh yeah," Vincent replied, pulling out a ziplock bag filled with pastry.

"I'm supposed to give you this..." he said, throwing it to John. "For you to analyze. With Erica if you have to."

"Bannock," John, noted with his eyes and confirmed with his nostrils. "Flavored with....an indescribably delicious aroma which..." He pulled the authentic Apache delight food up to his mouth, informing his growling stomach that it would be filled very soon. He assured his woozy brain that his ultra-low blood glucose levels would return so that it could function clearly and objectively again. The promises to both organs were negated when Vincent grabbed John's arm, grabbing the pastry and putting it back into his pocket immediately after John was able to sample a small nibble of it.

"So," John said with a victorious grin, having felt Vincent's hand as something real to the touch. "Either you are alive, like I am, or we're both ethereal ghosts in some universe no one in the physics department in any University knows about."

"This is a biological sample, you idiot!" Vincent grunted at his brother. "That you have to test on lab animals, in Erica's lab. From the bakery in town owned by a more Mexican Greek than Apache healthier and richer than he should be sleezebag who…"

"Is the caterer at the Klassen that serves authentic Native food to authentic Natives in the dining room and Whites who want to eat, think, and maybe be Native?" John interjected regarding the 'indescribably delicious' he nearly swallowed before testing. "That was in the food bin delivered by the Amazone driver in the shot-up vehicle who somehow knew where the mines and traps leading to the Rez were? Delivered by someone whose features were…."

"Maybe more Commanche than Apache?" Vincent asked. "Who maybe, as a paid-off Commanche, still had a vendetta against the Apaches for scalping his great great granddad in 1886, and the Apache nation for being at war with his Commanche ancestors since 1710?"

John could feel a third brain sprouting up between himself and his brother, that entity that was a whole lot smarter and wiser than either of them. But, as John's mind knew, and his stomach reminded him, a human brain without food can't think clearly. Anticipating such, Vincent pulled out another cellophane-wrapped pastry.

"Toxins which you can handle," he said, after which he read the long list of artificial ingredients in the Hostess Cupcakes. "They give you cancer a lot more slowly than the peyote growing in these hills is said to do. Or the authentic Apache cuisine probably being delivered to specific people on the Rez and to selected Indians in town, who become…"

"Interesting patients, or n values?" John surmised. "In an experiment that…."

"…has to end with me fading away, and you coming back from whatever universe you're in now, and that I migrated into," Vincent said. "Because I was ordered to…"

The eagle landed next to Vincent, squawking at him, pecking at his feet like a rooster defending his favorite henhouse. "Alright, I'm leaving!" Vincent said as he backed up away from the bird.

John self observed himself smiling with delight, but not knowing why. He tore open the pack, so his hands said anyway cupcakes. Opened his mouth, and then proceeded to eat one of them. The Eagle snatched the other one from his hand.

"Hey!" John said, as a Doctor, trying to pull it away from his avian friend. "Chocolate is no good for birds. It contains theobromine, processed sugar, and all sorts of other ingredients that give cats, dogs, and birds and…"

The Eagle, in no mood for a lesson in biochemistry from John's universe, but John's hand, then scattered the cupcake his human companion was in the process of eating into the dirt. After which he, or she (as John never had figured out this Messenger's gender) flew up into the sky, disappearing behind the rocks above him.

"Okay, got it," John's replied to the bird, and whatever spirits inhabited this strange yet somehow familiar place. "But," he said to the Fates in all of the Four directions, his eyes seeing three trees when his mind knew there was only one, and cliffs above him wobbling back and forth to the tune, the wind singing the first two measure of 'I'm Henry the Eight I am' repeatedly. "My blood glucose is going down, I'm thirsty, and my potassium levels are probably low, which means….well…ok. I know, man, woman or anyone in between doesn't live by bread alone, or…" Something flashed into John's head. "Die with some kind of carcinogen delivered by truck to the Rez and well-groomed, tastefully dressed smiling waiters in town, especially to L. Harvey Smith's crew of…"

John felt himself getting woozy, much like the cancer patients he was trying to find, and help. It was then that the bird returned, dropping a branch loaded with a plethora of ping pong ball-sized berries, which it ate. Then offered another portion to John. "Sure, why not?" John said tasting the berries. "Gotta die of something." The berries tasted delicious. And were plentiful. So much so that John's belly felt at the very least fed, putting him into a restful sleep.

XXII

A wet snow that ended as warm rain poured onto John Baldino's face. It washed away the foundation that Leonard had sprayed him within New York that made him seem more 'exotic' than Selena. When it rain stopped, John awoke not as Selena. Not as Maria. Not as a balding old man. And not as a young half-bird-half man.   He was himself again. The same self that he presented to the world when he illegally entered the Rez, still wearing Tom's Eagle Clan shirt and attached to the long locks of dark hair Leonard had sewn into his own.

"So," John said with blurry eyes, thankful that there indeed was a visible reflection of himself in the mirrored surface of a puddle that had materialized in the middle of the medicine wheel. "This is me," he continued, disappointed and relieved regarding the details of that image.

"Yes," he heard behind him from an Old Man's voice who cast a large shadow. "Just like this is you too," he said, picking up a rock from the ground outside of the circle. Turning around, John noted that this visitor was a small short-framed man with defiant intensity beaming out of his defiant eyes. He was clad in torn jeans, knee-high fringed mocassins, and a blood-stained Eagle Clan leather shirt.   It was none other than the epileptic 'stage two' Shamen who 'by coincidence' had been doing his death dance below John's window in town.   "And this rock, John," the Old Man with more intensity than any ten young warriors said of the plain grey common stone in his firm hand as he boldly stepped into the circle of 'interesting' ones that did seem to change color and occasionally sparkled depending on how the sun or moonlight hit them. "This plain rock was and still is you, Doctor Baldino. Stagnant. Dull. Boring. Nice. And most of all predictable," he said with pity and disappointment to the plain man sitting in his, as John intuited by the way he sat down, private power spot.

"It's called being responsible, Sir," John replied with a respectful bow.

"Sir! You call me Sir?!" the Old Man barked back to the younger one, scaring John into backing up. His ass hit the sharp stones making up the circle in which he found himself defiantly remaining.

"So...What do I call a Native Elder?" John asked, after regaining his composure, and noting that he luckily had not soiled his White drawers with feces or urine. "Who...was respected by his people in life. And should be remembered with respect in death? What should I call you?"

The Apache warrior broke into a warm smile which allowed a self-realizing chuckle to emerge from his parched, thin lips. "Asshole! Idiot! Wacko cocoa puff! Or maybe...SOUL doctor!" he yelled out without any restraint on his expression of emotion or commitment.

"Who wants me to do...what?" John inquired, edging his way closer to the man, and the inner core of the power circle.

"For starters," the Old Shamen considered. He nodded his head, considering several thoughts, hypotheses, and options. Then, after feeling which ones the moment demanded most, he sprang up to his feet, feeling as much strength as pain in them. He looked to the sky, then each of the four directions, saying something in Apache to all of them. Then he commenced to dance in a 'jig' that was as strange to John's ever-investigative eyes as it was boldly free and gleeful to anyone else's. It was accompanied by the humming of a song that had no melody, no one key, and no structure allowing you to detect what notes would happen next.

"Yeah," John said, fondly recalling a happy memory of the past which he knew could never be experienced in the present, as part of the 'deal' he had made with Spirit Big S so that others could experience 'happiness' and bliss. "I did the Zorba dance for Athena Theodoris and five other ex-girlfriends who said it would make them happy and make me fulfilled. And for my wife Jennifer. At our wedding."

"And what did you experience at the wedding?" the Shamen asked between 'stanzas' of the song and yet another acrobatic leap which nearly knocked John's logically thinking noggin into a trance.

"Pain," John replied. "From broke their toes when I got too close to the other dancers, including my wife. And a twisted back when I tripped over myself that kept me on muscle relaxants and chiropractic visits every day of my honeymoon. I dance with these now," he went on wiggling his fingers. "In print when I'm holding a pen when putting together a fact and truth-based tale, and with a scalpel when putting together schmucked up flesh, and with the tips blessed or cursed with vibration, pressure, and electricity detecting Pacinian corpuscles when palpating an abdomen for masses or limbs when diagnosing Western diseases with Eastern acupuncture points which…"

John's medical discourse with the accompanying movement of his digits was interrupted by Kurt Thundercloud's fists grabbing them on both of his hands. Upon the Old Man let go of his firm yet somehow warm hold on them, John discovered that all of his fingers had shriveled down to limp strands of bony flesh which oscillated in the wind beyond his control.

"Ya want them back, Doctor John," the confident Old Man proposed to the terrified younger one. "Get up and do a Zorba Redskin Greek Dance."

"Bbbut..I can't!" John studdered back.

"Why!?" the Shamen blasted into John's eyes, at close range.

"Because!" John yelled back. "Ya gotta have a table to do the Zorba dance on."

"Got a point there," the Shamen replied, stroking his chin. With that, he snapped his fingers and commanded the ground in the middle of the medicine wheel to do the rest. The ground sprouted up a wooden table top that folded its short legs into place in front of John.

"And you need the right music," John countered.

"Sure," the Shamen conceded. After which he pulled a flute from under his shirt, and a mandolin from his back. After a few trials of dissonant sounds, he was able to turn the noise from the instruments into music. Magnificent music.

How the Shamen was able to churn out a version of the Zorba theme that was also authentic to his own Native music, John did not know. But he was sure that there was an important 'why' to taking to the table and letting his feet provide the choreography to the dance. And it was not just about getting his fingers back. Or to provide any birds flying above with entertainment they could give their approval of with caws and screeches. Or their disapproval of a shower of avian fecal material.

John's feet, to his amazement, did have musicality in them. And brains too, as the left and right foot worked with rather than against each other. As to what the steps were, John let his hindlimb appendages keep deciding that. He soon felt a sensation in his fingers and felt no droppings from above. But no caws of applause.

"Now, sing with me," the Shamen requested and commanded, dropping his instruments, using the most ancient and still most expressive of channels for great music---the human voice. In a song that John felt more than understood.

John joined in the Shamen's emotion-inspiring and intellectually opening 'tune', then heard himself leading the 'song'. Then sing it, alone. Then ending it with a finale worthy of anything voiced at La Scala, or the Met. The Shamen smiled with delight, and pride, giving John a thumbs up. The strands of limp flesh on John's hands were pumped up with an electrified jolt of warm blood, converting them into strong, functional, and controllable fingers. The Eagle landed outside of the circle, screeching an expression of delight. The birds above, representing no less than five species of avians, voiced their approval. John gave his air, then his grounded audience a 'thank you' bow, after which he felt a thud of warm, wet fall on the top of his head. He ran his fingers through his thick mop of long dark brown, bordering now on jet black, hair, retrieving into his hands the contents of that unexpected rain. Then smelling something in his fingers that had landed on his now open-to-everything head...

"Well," he said of the bird shit that had landed on his head. "There's always a critic and if you're pleasing everyone you're not serving anyone," he self-discovered, yet again.

"Indeed yes," the Shamen replied, in...badly accented Italian.

"Yes, indeed," John replied, noting that it was in...yes...Apache. Shocking him and assuring the Shaman.

"So I guess this means that you want something from me?" the Shamen said. "The members of the Brown Ghost, or as some call it, the Eagle Clan, I am assuming."

"So I can cross reference their names with the Apache who are dying, or dead in town?... And dispel the false rumor that MID is caused by peyote, so Erica, the woman who sent me here, can figure out what is causing it. " John's next inquiry.

The Shamen pondered the issue carefully. He walked around the inner perimeter of the medicine wheel at least three times, pausing at each of the four directions. Finally, he stopped, then turned to John. "You've heard of the Free Masons."

"A white society that has secret rituals and an impressive list of members past and....some say...present," John replied, standing up on his tired feet, finding that the ground had turned....earthy, with no special messages coming up into his spine via Pacinian corpuscles on the soles of his mocassined feet. "Yeah, the Free Masons."

"Who are free because no one knows those rituals..or has a real membership list? Which doesn't include women," the

Shamen answered. "Because of reasons that…well…we don't understand but have had to accept."

"And what about women who wanted, needed, or deserved to become members, for reasons they didn't understand, but had to accept," John challenged. "Like---"

"Maria ran away from her home here for the wrong reasons, and returned for the right ones," the reply. "Thanks to you."

"And Erica?" John enquired. "Whose intensity and dedication to her work against bad people and bad ideas scares not only me but probably herself?"

"Yeah," the Shamen replied. "As her husband Tom said, she's is a necessary evil. Who our council said was not a needed evil, for us anyway."

"Until now," John said. "Which I suggest, and recommend….Very fucking goddamn strongly!!!"

The Shamen contemplated the matter, consulting the four directions, then turned to John relating with a calm, assertive tone. "This is a sacred secret place that…"

"---I came to voluntarily!" John said. "Where I risked my life and sanity! And maybe lost them both. And where do I need to get the list of ALL of your Clan members, alive and dead? And prove that the demon root that's causing MID comes from….somewhere else. Testing this peyote and proving that whatever it does, causing brain tumors is not one of them. Peyote which"

"---I still can't give you, John. But which you, and only you, will get," the Old Indian said. "In its own time and from the right place." He repeated those profound words in Apache. With that, the Shamen disappeared, from John's view anyway.

"What the fuck is happening here?" Doctor J asked whoever would answer him, feeling himself again transported to another universe. And not just the kind that happens after an intense writing session down below where his fingers channeled truths his brain didn't know, and mind couldn't easily handle.

The Old Shaman appeared again, his stoic face beamed with illuminating satisfaction.   He laid his hand on top of John's shaking shoulder, confirming that he was real. Real enough to be believed in anyway. "In its time and from the right place, brother," he said, after which he walked out of the circle towards then into the rocky cliffs protecting the mini meadow from wind, sleet, and uninformed intruders.

John looked to his left, finding in the wake of the Shaman's departure more berries, along with a package of intact, uneaten chocolate-covered cream-filled cupcakes. As it was getting cold again, John buttoned the Eagle Clan shirt that had belonged to Tom, adjusting it around his chest, finding that it indeed did fit him, and not just around the eyes. Figuring that there were more angels offering help and opportunity here than demons presenting toxic and comfortable temptations, he indulged in a much-needed snack of wild natural berries and anything but natural cupcakes then fell asleep.

After waking up, on his own terms to another sunrise, John looked around him. The stones demarking the medicine wheel did not change color or go sparkly in tune with his heartbeat. The ground did not vibrate. And the mild gusts blew through the trees relating to his ears nothing but wind.

He heard horse hoofs approaching, then saw two equines coming his way. The rider on one of them was clad in clothing made and designed for the current century.

A man atop the lead horse with clean, white Texan Stetson, a paramilitary park ranger shirt with faded jeans, and reflective sunglasses over his eyes and a badge over his heart trotted into the meadow. Strapped to his back was a vinyl made-in-China backpack bearing a US Army emblem. On his right hip, an authentic Colt revolver in a leather engraved Texas Ranger holster.

John held his ground as the visitor got off the horse, then approached at a slow, steady, confident walk.

"So, 'kimosavi'," he grumbled in an unnatural feeling baritone voice, whipping out his pistol, the business end of it not three inches from John's forehead. "Wanna tell me why yer so brave all up here alone, Tonto, having Visions that'll give you cancer that can spread to others?"

"And can you tell me why, when you decided to not be spotted by the Cops below or the probable toxin dropping Crop Dusters above or the surveillance cameras from the 'Forestry Management' choppers that came by this morning, you forgot to buy a pair of cowboy boots to go with that outfit," John said with a confident and proud smile, pointing to the Deputy's fringed mocassins.

"We do what we gotta go, sometimes with a little bit of deception," Jake Cuthand said as he pulled off his Stetson and the short-haired wig underneath it, his long mane of thick jet-black hair flowing in the wind. "Which, I suppose ain't my strong suit. Lying about what and who I am, something new to me,"

"Me too," John related and confessed, inviting Jake to sit next to him. The unmasked 'Tonto' helped himself to a few of John's leftover berries and then gently caressed a peyote plant. "So, what kind of visions did you have this 'toxic cancerous peyote', that you took an overdose of?" he inquired.

"No eight-winged flying reptiles," John related. "No white buffalos turning into railroad cars chasing me and taking away my family to Florida in 1885, to Auschwitz in 1944, or Hoboken, New Jersey on the hottest, smelliest day of any year. Which---"

"How did you know that the people who got brain cancer had these demonic visions?" Jake asked the only white man who found and would be allowed to survive after seeing the Medicine Wheel.

"Maria," John said by way of explanation. "Who I was able to talk to a lot more clearly than the shrinks in Manhattan after she was picked up for disturbing the peace. Or the neurologists out here when she was transferred here by, well I don't know who, yet. Thanks to A137, a very real herb given to me by international terrorists who DO have the ability to kill the mind, body, and soul of humanity that drove ME mad with neurological disorders that nearly killed me till Erica came along. So I'd spill the beans about…my secret and best-kept hidden medical research, international political activities, family, and people."

"Those beans bein'?" Jake asked.

"Something irrelevant to you and your people, and most of mine, but maybe to another Eagle Clan dancer who I ran into, or who ran into me yesterday," John related with averted eyes after a pensive delay. With alacrity and skill his head never knew his hands had, John drew a quick sketch of the Death dancer he tried to rescue from being arrested in town. "You know him?" he asked Jake. "Or know where he is now?"

"Critical condition in the civilian and now military hospital in town," Jake replied. "The best intel I could get while wearing this outfit from the nursing station yesterday evening, manned by nurses I didn't recognize or like. "A trusted friend, who…well…" tears came to the hardened Warrior Red Power activist's eyes. "In real bad shape. But still livin', if you could call it that. Did any of them visit you last night?"

"With this 'special condition,' I got in MY head, as Erica may have mentioned to you, only dead people come to visit me," John related to Cuthand, whose hopeful eyes catapulted into the depths of grief and helplessness….

"Or, on occasion," John added, hoping he wasn't exaggerating a few freak cases about his clairvoyant 'gifts'. "I can talk from a distance to the dying too," Doctor B related, laying his palm on Jake's shaking shoulder. As desperate to know that Vincent's appearance was from the land of the still living as Jake was about the Old Shamen still being on this side of the veil.

"Which means, that there's hope for him?" Jake inquired.

"If I, we, have anything to do with it," John asserted, "And do what we have to do. In its right time and from the right place." He repeated the phase in Apache.

"The password of the Eagle Clan," Jake exclaimed, his hope restored. "Only known and told to trusted members of…." Cuthand pulled up the sleeve of Tom's clan shirt which was still on John. "Yes," he said, smiling at seeing the semi-circle with the stem in the middle decal embedded into John's forearm.

"Which, I know, I mispronounced badly," John said, apologetically on the outside but with a sense of pride bordering on arrogance on the inside. He heard a squeak of an eagle, which landed in front of him. "Right?" John asked the bird, to which he, or she, cawed back a, as he allowed himself to believe, a 'yeah, Right bro'.

"Yeah," Jake replied, shocked and awed. He grabbed hold of the notepad in John's pocket. "The names of the members of the Eagle Clan. The men and, yeah it has happened, women who for a time during our special peyote ceremonies, passed themselves off as men. For your eyes only and…Erica's and…anyone one of YOUR trusted friends, if indeed you still have any. And if anyone, no matter what color skin the Great Spirit and their parental units made them carry around their tired bones, asks where you got this list---"

"---My lips are sealed," John said, raising his right hand up in the air like the Boy Scout he never was. "Honest…well…wannabe and if you let me be…adopted Injun?" he advanced, braving a politically incorrect and no doubt culturally offensive joke. All the while, hiding from Jake the fact that he baited the bird to come down by bringing out a portion of the Hostess Cupcake as bait. "I'm just…ya know…"

"Someone who has to go back to your world, to save ours, and your own," Jake said, pulling out a cowboy shirt and jeans from his backpack. "

"I know," John said, with true regret, as he rose to his feet, and then stepped out of the medicine wheel. "Someone who also needs to test and analyze…"

"Special peyote which you got from someone else," Jake said as he exited the security of the wheel, and went to his saddlebag, pulling out a large cellophane bag loaded with a bag of peyote plants into John's pockets and Tom's horse, an animal which now chose a White Man as its new caretaker, and student. "That has as much potency as the person taking it wants or wishes it to have. With as many brain-altering effects as a glass of Koolaid made so thick that you have to eat it with a spoon."

"That idiot mom in my world says it's more addictive than heroin, and more carcinogenic than asbestos," John mused.

"Which, maybe they're more right than wrong about?" Jake shot back. "But, let Erica's rats tell you how toxic or carcinogenic this brand of sacred peyote really is. And by that, I don't mean pale-faced humans that she intoxicates with them without them knowing it. An experiment which---"

"---she would never do," John assured Jake as he walked to his horse, finding it to be welcoming to a rider this time.

"We'll see," Jake's reply as he mounted. "And for the moment, I head West and you head straight East which is…"

"….I do know where the four directions are," John said. "Now anyway."

With that, Jake headed upward to destinations he had to keep secret from John with the knowledge that he had at least one completely trustable friend in the White world. While John headed down the valley where what his Soul had learned at the Rez would find its way to his Mind and Brain, and eventually hands, 'in it's right time and from the right place.'

With the aid of Tom's horse, who 'found' John after Jake left him, his journey down the many hills led him to a location where his cell finally got a signal. He called Erica, who said she would 'be there shortly'. Shortly took three hours, which John used to resecure the fence that Erica had opened up for him, and teach himself how to be a horse rider rather than a human passenger. It led him to tire tracks at the main gate, where he dismounted, finally feeling the firm ground under his feet. The gate where the Amazone truck driven by the Commanche driver had hit a rut and accidentally dumped kitchen waste and mini packages of expired junk from town onto Apache land. Beyond the gate, there were tracks from trucks that DID enter the reserve, lined with skeletons of small creatures. Still having a stomach that needed feeding, John opened one of the packages of food, assuming that Jake, Fate, or the Great Spirit was providing him with a 'free' lunch. The aroma from the 'authentically bannock and nothing but bannock' biscuit smelled familiar. It brought back, this time, RECENT memories. Recollections of the deserts are being served in the Indian side of the café at the Klassen. And at the mini snack bars in L. Harvey Smith's lab.

Prior to John taking a bite from the much-needed infusion of glucose into his most probably hypoglycemic body, the horse nickered. "Yeah," John said to the horse that have finally become a friend rather than a vector for making his butt sore. "You probably are hungry too." He offered the steed the lion's share of the 'authentically bannock and nothing but bannock' treat, being sure to not let his fingers come between the crushing teeth of the horse and the most probably overloaded with sweet irresistible preservatives to keep it fresh dessert. But the horse pushed it away. "Yeah," John said, "Maybe too much of what we like is exactly what we don't need." The question of where that would lead was answered by a honk of a truck that was more rust than metal pulling a horse trailer. "Tempus Fugit, John," Erica shouted out from the driver's seat, more so with her eyes than her parched mouth.

XXIII

Not much was known by the scientific community about how quickly the toxin that caused MID worked. The popular, and therefore only accepted, belief amongst the most funded and high profile biomedical investigators was still that it was the carcinogenic virus containing peyote that was being used on the Rez by Indians or taken by Vision-seeking Whites to 'resurrect the spirit' acted quickly. But two investigators didn't buy into the party line. Their laboratory was self-funded and falling apart.

"It's just a little rain coming through the roof," Erica said to John as the roof of her cabin nestled in the woods gave way to another splash of water on his head. "The important thing is that nothing spills into the beds occupied by the n values here," she said, looking to the rats in cage number one, who were given a hefty dose of Eagle Clan peyote. "Normal behavior," she said of the rodents she had been breeding for research of many toxins, and antidotes, for many diseases, the identity of which she did not share with any researcher at the Klassen, NYU, the CDC, or John. "And these rats have normal brains unless you see something in those slides with those multi-talented and multi-modality ocular portholes of yours," she said to John. "Or hear anything 'the tissue is telling you'."

"No. All seems…normal," John said looking yet again at the slides, comparing them to the slides taken from rats exposed to nothing but stolen rodent feed pellets from the pet store in town and the animal breeding facility at the Klassen. Erica had made friends with the ignored, underappreciated managers of the staff who cleaned cages, watched lab animals mate and, after a year or two, developed allergies to the the creatures they took care of better than they cared for themselves. "The peyote I got from the Apaches, even in the ultra-high dose groups, is doing nothing to their brain cells…" John said by way of conclusion. He turned around, noting Erica feeding the rodents the lion's share of carrots, lettuce, and sunflower seed salad that was intended to be her lunch. "But maybe the peyote is affecting your brain?" he continued, noting something on Erica's face he had seldom seen---a carefree and loving smile. "You're looking very maternal today. Maybe you want to have kids?"

"Thankfully, I won't have any kids with anyone, for their sakes," she shared and related to the rodents who, though they looked alike to the cold, objective, scientific observer, all had names.

John pondered the question of whether Erica would want to have a family with him. A son to pass on his scientific knowledge and investigative instincts to. Or a daughter to be given Erica's firey torch to continue the Cause of understanding and curing human pathology outside of the lab or the hospital. But there were other matters more pressing now. They pulled John's attention to the large cages of rodents to the far right of the warmed wooden shelves on where there was another experimental group. "And them?" John said of the animals undergoing shakes and seizures, attacking some kind of beast in their midst that wasn't there. The ones who were still living anyway. "The ones gave 'special spice'. L. Harvey Smith's 'special pantry' that you said you 'borrowed' from him without his knowing it. That does smell like…" He took in a whiff of the powder added to the salad given to the rats unfortunate enough to be in the carcinogenic eating group. "The 'indescribably delicious' cookie-biscuits you said and I smelled which was fed to selected members of his staff, the Klassen fed to 'Injun' tables in the cafeteria. And which…hmmm…. the Amazone delivery truck brought to the Rez. And the expired that accidentally dropped out of the truck which I picked up on the way back to the pickup location after leaving the Rez."

"Made, so I think anyway, from the same 'special flour' from Smith's safe. Which, well, decided to open itself when I snuck into his private office and listened to it secretly tell me the combination," Erica related. "Which you led me to after figuring out that the closest 'who' behind MID was him. A glory-seeking, money-hungry, and more clever than wise investigator who told Selena about a special pesticide he was investigating for Monsanto et al as a possible replacement for Round-Up. Which produces the same kind of tumors in mice as MID causes in people."

John looked yet again at the slides obtained from the last batch of healthy rat brains that turned into pain and death conferring tumors after eating the 'bannuck and nothing but bannuck powder'. They displayed the same key features present in tumors of human MID-afflicted patients which Erica was able to somehow take pictures of. They all displayed astrocytes that were a hybrid between a classic astrocytoma and a rapidly growing reactive astrocyte that occurs normally after neurons are schmucked and shriveled up by disease or trauma. A unique pattern of nine filaments connected by a single microtubule which, when broken down to its molecular element contained a major building block protein of 42,000 daltons. "But…why didn't you tell me you were going to Smith's lab to do a midnight raid of his safe?" John inquired of the woman who he always felt was his soulmate or ultimate executioner, or perhaps both. "How did you get in, and out?"

"Because unlike Selena, or you," she said proudly. "I know how to be in like the wind and out like a silent banshee. Making it look like I wasn't there. A ghost who…"

"…Could have gotten caught, or told me about what you were doing!" John blasted back with both anger and concern.

"Yes, I could have been caught," she said, after which she stared him down. "But wasn't."

Erica had that 'on a need-to-know basis' look on her face, the same that Vincent threw at and into John every time life allowed the good doctor to be united with his 'necessary evil' Black Ops brother. As to the reason why Erica didn't tell John what she had done for the three days and nights when he was investigating his Inner Soul at the Medicine Wheel and she was courting death by spying around in the high-security labs in the Klassen, that would have to wait. For, as John intuited, and said in Apache. 'the right time and in the right place'.

But for the moment, Erica grabbed hold of a blood-stained axe, handing it to John. She sent him out to chop up firewood and gather berries, the 'red ones' which she claimed were the reason for the red tinge on the sharp edge of the axe. "And after you're done with that, take Tom's horse around the perimeter of the fort, scaring away any four or two-legged varments with this." She threw John a Winchester rifle. "And if the warning shots to their feet don't scare them away, above all DO harm to the fuckers before they do a whole lot more to you, me, and everyone else we care about. Or should care about," her final statement on the matter. But there was one fact about Smith and his lab that she did reveal to John. "Our once friend and scientific rival wasn't in his lab when I broke in," she said. "He put a 'gone fishing for bigger fish to fry' on his door. And said that the reason for his absence was that 'Holloween is coming'."

"Which means he's at…" John flashed something in his head.

"At where?" Erica asked, demanding to know.

John turned to Erica after a tense and reminiscent pause. "The Yale Club, where…every year at Halloween, he…becomes someone different than he has to be."

"Who is?" Erica pressed.

"Someone who fortunately is not in the lab now, Erica," John replied, wondering if that indeed was her real name. A question which he would deal with later. "Which we both have to break into. To get what you forgot to bring as evidence for what I intuit is going on here."

"What evidence?" Erica blasted it to John's ears as he chuckled. "And what do you think is going on?"

"As for the evidence, which we need more of," John said, taking a pair of scissors and cutting his hair back to pre-Selena and pre-Flagstaff Doctor Baldino length.

"What are you doing?" Erica blasted at him.

"Becoming a ghost, Doctor Linquist," his reply as he gazed at his old persona in the mirror, with assurance and regret.

"Or maybe, a necessary evil?" Erica suggested. With an invitation to become a member of HER secret cult that he could not, but so wanted to refuse.

XXIV

Why the First Nations Bakery and Herb Emporium was still standing in a town in which Native inhabitants and visitors were banned, and establishments owned by anyone with First Nations blood or political sympathies had been looted or burned was about to be found out by John as he entered the one-story store boasting its contents in English and a variety of what seemed to be Indian languages. Tongues which, interestingly, John seemed to be able to read with a sense of familiarity.

But this was about the business of the world, not the nature and intentions of Spirit. John was dressed for the occasion, clad in a blue suit with the top and bottom machine, a white shirt, and a red tie. Upon entry into the establishment he, as always, kept his eyes so wide open that the light coming in could set fire to the brain so that the visual data entering his retina would fit into what was there rather than what his occipital cortex put together as the most understandable image. For when he advised his students when looking at slides made from diseased organs, 'let the tissue tell you what it wants to'. But this time it was his nose that sent impulses to his Mind before his eyes did.

Indeed it was that 'indescribably delicious' aroma that he smelled in the food at the Klassen cafeteria only at the Indian and Indian lovers' tables. And in Smith's lab. And from the samples Erica had stolen from his safe. But the main questions were, which one of the many pastries behind the glass contained them? And who were those pastries were slated to go to? And…how much more 'special spice' was in the back? And…

"Yes, sir," a brown-skinned man who could be Mexican, Greek, South American Indian, or all of the above, said with a big, wide grin showing off a mouth of blindingly white teeth. "What can I do ya for?"

"This," John replied, sticking a document containing the most threatening font possible in his face, then whipping out an ID badge bearing his new 'look', ramming it into his face.

"Another health inspection?" the clerk, who by his mannerisms seemed to be the boss, scoffed. "The last inspector gave me a clean bill of health," he boasted, pointing to a certificate on the wall. Signed by none other than Harry R. Wentworth, the name of Doctor-Major who tried to pick up John on the plane when he was Selena.

"But, Harry said we need more verification to keep business going on as usual in, well, unusual times," John said, recalling Wentworth's first name from the airline flight. Yes, Harry, which when formalized to Harrold was the name Dakota Stone used to name his favorite male robot, and when feminized, to his even more favorite female computer.

The clerk scratched his chin, nodded his head, then looked back up to John. "Well, Jesus did say that one should 'render unto Caesar what is Caesar's'" he said, ignoring by intent or neglect the 'and render unto God that which is God's' part.

"Indeed," John replied as an inspector who was 'just doing his job' just as those he was charged to inspect were 'doing their job' by cutting corners where they could elevate the bottom line. "Our new boss's orders. I have to certify every shop on the block. Which I know they are but first…"

"First what?" the clerk asked.

"Can I use the can?" John inquired.

"Just behind the kitchen," the Clerk said, handing him a roll of fresh toilet paper, in which there was a hundred dollar bill in the middle. "Ya know what Frank Zappa said. Nothing more overrated than a good poke, and nothing more underrated than a great shit."

"Indeed," John replied as he took the roll of asswipe into the back. With peripheral vision rivaling that of a horse, verified by a straight look into a mirror, John noted a look of caution in the formerly smiling clerk's eyes as he, after putting a pair of gloves on his hands, reached into his crotch then opened a metal box under the counter. He placed into it a recently arrived package, locking it afterward and returning the key to its former place.

A drunk, brain-challenged Native woman in a custom-made Pancho-like deerskin blouse with fringe on the side and half-circle designs on the front and back complemented with a long loose weatherbeaten faux leather skirt that seemed to be on its way to the ready-to-toss-out bin in the second-hand store stumbled into the shop. Atop her head was a long main of jet black hair, half of it covering her dirt-covered face. She grabbed fistfuls of pastries, then stuffed them into her oversized pockets.

"What the fuck are you doing?" the Clerk blasted at her.

"Getting me some of that super-powered red power pastry ya makes here," the female slurred out of her mouth. "For me and my red-skinned kid. Yeah…Red Power. Red Power. Red…"

The six-foot-three Clerk grabbed her by the collar and the ass, preparing to toss her out like a super-trained bouncer or specially trained MP. But the five foot-five customer's strength, determination, and training she never talked about was greater. She flung him off, tossed him into the wall, and stuffed into his fat face chocolate eclairs and Saskatoon berry bannock that reeked of the 'indescribably delicious' powder Erica had stolen from Smith's lab, and John had almost eaten when requesting to sample the food served to Native diners at the Klassen. As quickly as she layered more culinary gags into his yapper, keeping him on the floor with her knee, he spit them back out.

"Hey!" the Clerk yelled at the mad squaw given the strength of ten men due to the firewater or whatever illegal herbs she had ingested, or stage of cancer she was in. "You stay on the OTHER side of the counter," he yelled out rapidly in English, then slowly, as if it was not his first, second, or third language, in Apache, which John somehow was able to understand. Frustrated with his inability to restrain the squaw who had become a minion of the Red Devil, the Clerk grabbed hold of a gun from under his shirt, aiming it at her.

With quickness of thought and strength of fist, the small woman snatched the gun away from the large Clerk, then his phone. "Gimme everything ya got in that register too," she demanded of the owner of the establishment. "Now!"

"I don't think so," John said as he calmly emerged from the back room, putting his firm grip on her neck, causing her to faint. "Vulcan stun grip," he explained to the relieved Clerk. "Which is taught to paramedics in dangerous locations, the places of change, who…"

Before Doctor John could boast about him being in war zones that Vincent had visited but kept preventing his genius doctor from entering, the woman emerged from the floor, lashing out with her walking stick like a spear, keeping the Clerk and John at bay.

"Red Power," Erica blasted out in her best 'drunk/drugged Injun' dialect. "Death to whites! Life to the Eagle Clan!" She babbled in Apache, words that neither John nor the Clerk seemed to understand. After which her threatening fists started to shake, her head going dizzy, her legs not seeming to be connected to her torso. She yelled threatening battle cries to a creature in the middle of John and the Clerk. Classic stage II Mad Indian Disease.

"I'll call an ambulance," John assured the terrified Clerk as the latter grabbed hold of two bottles of water, flushing his mouth out from whatever he had swallowed. When wiping off his pastry-caked face, John noted that his red complexion was a covering over very white skin.

Meanwhile, John reached for his phone that had 'accidentally' fallen to the floor, perusing the calling log. "Darn it!" he blasted out. "No tower service here!" he exclaimed in well-fabricated frustration.

As an unexpected part of the staged event, the Clerk grabbed back his phone and dialed it. "We got another one," he told the party at the other end, ducking from the talking stick that Erica, faining all too well being stage II MID, was using to yell at, and perhaps hit him. "Another contagious hurting unit," the Clerk said. "Who we can't shoot…not yet anyway."

"Who…looks like she belongs to another century," John added, in character as one of the Clerk's REAL tribe.

"A dead century and dying race," the fellow Caucassion said to John. "That…well…"

"Has to adapt or die," John added. "As we both know. Me being who I am, you being…"

Frustrated by John's chronic addiction to using brain rather than brawn, Erica rammed her walking (and when with the right people, talking) stick into the Clerk's belly, then wiped the rest of his face off, revealing a pure white complexion. While he was doubled over, she grabbed hold of his family jewels, retrieving the key to the box, and throwing it to John. She then treated herself to a twist and pull of his scrotum.

"Give me a name….ONE name!" she blasted into his face, while John opened the metal box next to the overfilled cash register.

"L. H…." the Clerk's reply.

"L H who?" she screamed into his terrified eyes, grabbing the gun and ramming it into his forehead.

"L H Smith?" John inquired, stuck in the habit of using reason rather than rage as his method to get intel from deplorable people who make big money by cheating people and more by inflicting deadly diseases on them. With gloved hands, John placed each of the shop owner's pastries and the bags of powder in the metal box into his oversized 'health inspector' briefcase.

"And who else is a 'silent owner' of this store that hands out pastry 'that you could die for' to selected customers!?" Erica demanded. She was unable to hide the shock on her face at confirming that Smith was this idiot and asshole's boss. Something even more terrifying shot holes into the walls housing her ever-confident 'I win every battle I fight or blow up the battlefield' world when she looked at the call record on the Clerk's phone.

"You two are way over your head," the Clerk, whose real name was now irrelevant, said, either having sensed his interrogators backing off or sensing that they were of an inferior race that would fuck up something else very soon. "My people will be here in three minutes…Or…maybe…less than that?" His white face became even paler. The brain behind it lost connection with the torso below his neck. He fainted, hitting the ground with a loud thud that triggered convulsions.

"Too many sweets containing secret yummy 'to die for' spices that he swallowed?" Erica commented. "Bad for your health."

"That you have an antidote for, Erica?" John asked. "The one you said would probably work, for a while anyway?"

"Must have forgotten it at home, but…" she smirked, followed by a breath of realization. She looked into her authentic Apache purse, which really was a medicine bag. "Maybe I do have something here but.." Her brain stopped in mid-journey on the dark road she could not get off of "No…I don't," she said, looking at a fine layer of dust on the floor. "In that fight with this asshole, the idiot made me lose it. So….we're left with…." Erica grabbed hold of her gun with one hand, a coin with the other which she flung into the air. "Call it. Heads or tails. The winner gets to put this piece of shit out of his, and our, misery. Which---"

Before the coin hit the floor, or Erica was able to relate her next 'you need to know this now' intel memo to John, sirens from the Eastern sky blasted into the air, getting closer by the second. Erica, for the first time in decades, as John remembered anyway, could not hide her emotions or agenda. Her shaking hands grabbed hold of John's unexpectedly firm arms.

"And…our Starship and ET buds are scheduled to be here in soon to bring us back to Om planet?" he proposed, seeing something ghostlike behind the Clerk. Perhaps it was Selena, perhaps Maria, or perhaps a transportable hologram his brother Vincent was able to send over to look after his too-too-smart-and-kind-to-be-dangerously-brave younger sibling. Whatever it was, a real arrow penetrated the Clerk's chest. As the well-paid vendor of deadly carcinogens fell to the ground, John's eyes confirmed what his mind could sense.

"John, let's go!" said Jake Cuthand, in full warpaint, bow in hand, two submachine guns strapped to his back. He threw one of them to Erica.

"For you to hold them off, Erica," he commanded. "The getaway pony I got outside requested you to ride him, John."

"She's a better rider than me," John said, grabbing the submachine gun from Erica as another three plain green sedans approached from the West and the South.

"You and her make a getaway, I stay here," John found himself asserting.

"No, you fucking don't, you pathetically noble idiot," Jake asserted. "And probably lousy shot."

Before John could show off his skill in using firearms, which he learned from his mother, father, and Vincent when shooting up cans rather than people when on 'vacation' in the Catskills, he lost control of his feet and hands, courtesy of a Vulcan grip on his neck. And a self-defense course for Residents, Nurses, and Interns working ER in the South Bronx. Erica carried John away as Jake remained behind, setting himself up to provide cover.

"Go get the goods on the Doctor Professor Smith and bring him back here. To MY laboratory on the Rez," Jake commanded. "Alive if possible, so we can give him an overdose of his own medicine. And for you, Erica, and your new love and hate interest, the special meds we gave to the eleven braves who made the last stand with Geronimo against…"

Machine gun fire interrupted the historical lessons, as John and Erica went on their way to make history. Hopefully with a future that benefited the living rather than the rich and powerful, whose identity still had to be ascertained.

XXV

The answer to how Erica was able to get through the exit-only doors at the Klassen without sounding an alarm at midnight was, for John, another 'on a need-to-know basis'. As to what was in the locked rusty cabinets in the storage room she had converted into a lab as 'Doctor Linquist', her reply was…"Shit, the kind that comes out of the ass. Super stinky shit, mixed with glue that will make it stick to the boots and fingernails on the shitheads who opened them," her reply with a vengeful smirk. "But let's concentrate on what we're doing now, and recall what we did back at NYU which…"

"…Yeah, I was stuck taking the credit for after you disappeared without a forwarding address," John replied. He reached for a photo on the wall showing him getting an award from the President of the United States at the Klassen auditorium, with Jenkins, Thompson, and a very jealous (and resentful for being proved 'biologically mistaken' by Baldino on more than one occasion) L. H. Smith. "I just stumbled into figuring out how the dopamine-more circuits interacted with each other and the GABA inhibitory systems in the thalamus," he said. "And wrote out a medical fairy tale as to how the intermodality interactions possibly worked."

"You mean a mechanism of action which, when you or anyone else considered it true, enabled you to do right by 98 percent of your Parkinson's patients," Erica pointed out.

"But not 100 percent in a Calling where 100 percent is the only passing grade," the hard-working, and some say just lucky, and some say sheltered, biomedical researcher replied. John found himself abruptly missing the simple days in the lab where all he had to do was to cajole Mother Nature to give up her biological secrets rather than having to uncover political, psychological, and romantic clandestine agendas from people. "Ever wonder what it would be for both of us to work in a lab again," he voiced. "And not worry about being----"

"Doctor Baldino!" came from one of Smith's white lab-coated Redskinned post-docs, his most trusted protegee. He shared a story-sized joint with sharing a joint with his scantily clad, barely legal-aged girlfriend. "But you're supposed to be---"

"---Dead?" John replied his back still turned to the intruder, imitating Smith's voice and Boston's blue blood accent. "Yeah, maybe I am."

"He does look sort of…, like, ya know," uttered the seductive female stoner who probably couldn't even spell 'biology', uttered, particularly in her present stone face.

"Ghostly!" Erica blasted into the young woman's confused, then shocked face. "And if you take another puff from that joint which has special herbs in it from the Rez or the Chairman of Pharmacology's secret stash, Professor Smith's ghost can do tricks for you, like wave his hands up in the air and say with three different voices…"

"Boo!" John, the metaphysically expansive anti-drug ex-physician, who always shot out of his mouth. He couldn't recall the last time he enjoyed indulging in mischief, or when it served rather than took away from the effectiveness of the Revolution.

Both intruders fled, running down the hallway at full speed. John allowed himself a smirk of satisfaction, which did indeed flow over into arrogance.

"So, are we through here?" Erica said. "We still have withdrawals to make from that post-docs lab," she continued, pointing to three backpacks on her back, and two on John's. "And with this, that fell out of Smith's most trusted assistant and probably favorite and somehow spared from the MID disease inside of him progressing 'n value', it should be easier than I expected!" she boasted, showing John a key she had stolen from the Post-Doc's pocket before he fled.

XXVI

Once inside Smith's office, Erica made a bee-line for the safe, ignoring John's recommendation to put on gloves. "I burnt my fingertips on the stove before all of this started, but you need your hands, and your neck intact," she related by way of explanation. "Your job is to----"

"---deal with the paperwork," John said, noticing new piles of research reports and data files, neatly stacked on Smith's usually messy desk. He took out his camera, shooting pictures of the cover but…something in that 'picture taking micro machine' didn't work. "What the fuck is happening?"

"Maybe Selena got the batteries to that phone in the divorce, after she found out about you and Maria, or you and---"

"---You?" John interjected, using his fingers as stabbing knives to ram the camera phone into obedience. "Just like my wife Jennifer was jealous of what she thought was going on between us."

"And was, on the inside?" Erica reminded John about his wife, who died in a traffic accident during his Residency when hit by a driver who disappeared or was burnt to a crisp just before the Cops arrived. "We're both masochistic workaholics. Sharing the work rather than the play, in the lab and elsewhere, may connect us as more than research colleagues."

"Until your research became less about medicine," John said. "And more about----"

"Shit!" Erica pushed out of her gritted teeth, followed by eight more expletives. Some of them John had never heard, even when doing his internship in the Hell's Kitchen ER where gunshot wounds outnumbered every other kind of malady or traffic accident. "Someone changed the combination!" she grunted, ramming her fist against the closed metal door. "Which…"

"---You could figure out better with this than your fists," John said, throwing her a stethoscope attached to Smith's wall.

"Yeah," Erica said, the fire in her angry soul directed into getting the job done, and putting off bashing her fist into oblivion later. "Get that camera working again or give that photographic memory of yours a kick in the ass," she commanded him as she proceeded to find the correct first number on the tumblers.

His back turned to Erica, the camera phone spit out 'fuck you, human, I'll work when I want to' signals back at him. John tended to his assigned job and talent of reading the research papers first, as he could speed read and absorb the details far better than most mortals who let their eyes scan the page at normal rates… "More data on more human 'subjects', enough to make even more 'n values' statistically sound by anyone's standards….and more research reports," he related by way of the most relevant summary.

"On how he cured those values?" Erica asked. "From Mad Indian disease, or other kinds of cancer?"

"Yeah….to be published…in a date he penciled on the top page…In…Greek," John noted. "Poorly grammared Greek that is. With handwriting that shows a personality that's…"

"What date?" Erica pressed, pushing John away so she could get a ring-side view of the publications. "Four months from today, on the original discovery research report…Updated to two months from today. The rodent studies that he told 'Selena' were 'in progress with a slow, careful timetable' to be sent to the Editor of Brain Science in three days. And post-dated rat studies which show dose responses for cures and vaccines for MID, and 'most other varieties of astrocytomas' and 'with further investigations, other forms of brain tumors' which, taken together may relate to…"

John's eyes, which were often smarter than the brain behind them, let his focused and expansive stare to stock reports, yellow highlights on one company. "He's working for and funded by Manheim Pharmaceuticals," he noted. "Which, we recall, but the world has forgotten, made a killing in discovering new money-making and often effective medications back in 1946. After, so my father and mother said, files from human experimentation labs in Auschwitz and Buchenwald were transferred to their bosses at the Pentagon."

"Where they were classified or redacted, of course?" Erica said, heading back to the safe, and reaching the second number on the new safe combination. "And your mother and father were told to keep the whole thing quiet or their kids would become 'n values' or worse?"

"Yeah," John replied, quickly consulting Google for the most recent stock reports available. "And as for today, the value of Manheim Pharmaceutical stock is still on the overall downward decline that started in 1975, and today is at rock bottom. But projected in three months, by of course, by some kind of creative mathematics, Smith projected would go up by---"

"---A thousand percent?" Erica said.

"Four thousand, at least, according to the mathematics on this chart," John said, finding even more damning support for the hypothesis developing in his head under the blotter of his desk. "Written by Smith, with calculus that the mathematically declined biomedical researcher all of a sudden got right. Accurate anyway."

"And those maps next to the stock reports?" Erica said, pointing with her fingers to a stack of neatly arranged paperwork in the most easily forced open drawer in his desk. "With black, red, and yellow markers on what locations?"

"As predicted, or as I should have predicted anyway, countries that have mostly black, red, or yellow-skinned people in them. With double markers in small countries that…" John noted "…Are, according to my knowledge anyway, experimenting with independence, democracy, and socialism. Santa Smith took on the job of punishing the 'bad boys and girls' at home, and abroad, or withholding the cure or vaccine after giving them the disease."

"Particularly in China?" Erica asked. "Where, most of us round eyes forget, a fifth of the population of humanity lives, or rather exists."

"Along with Russia, with triple marks on it," John said.

Erica helped herself to a chuckle, then a belly laugh. "Hey, finally someone here who figured out how to get back at China for making it possible for money-saving Americans to buy cans of peaches which cost 2 bucks to make here for fifty cents each at the dollar store. Maybe Smith or one of his buds are running for President. Conquer your enemies without firing any bullets, dropping any bombs, or…" Her jaw dropped as the door of the mini-vault finally gave way to her safe cracking skills, and forceful fist.

"Or…?" John asked, hearing something ominous in Erica's silence.

"Someone put more shit in here!" she grunted.

"What kind of shit?" John enquired, his eyes spotting vials in the safe labeled 'pathogen', 'treatment' or 'vaccines', in Greek, with Bavarian-looking font.

Erica asked what the words meant. John translated, confirming that the spelling was both inaccurate and in street rather than academic Greek. "So, what do we do about it?" John said. "L. Harvey is not smart enough to be doing this alone. He's too arrogant, and as we know, or should know, the real brains behind every terrorist organization in service to evil, greed, and institutionalized cruelty is the man, or woman, or, as gender has nothing to do with intelligence, trans maniac. Who…"

John heard something outside the office. As did Erica. They hear with the same ears, connected to the same third brain. Yet again, they ducked, in unison, shutting the lights off en route to their hiding places behind any furnishings available to them. Erica threw John a submachine gun, keeping a pistol for herself. Both weapons had attached silencers. "Shoot to kill," she commanded. "You can talk to the dead, and they can confess the sins they did when they were in the land of the living, Father John."

"Not so easy anymore, 'Sister' Erica," John replied.

"Then shoot to maim," Erica conceded. "And put this around their mouth." She threw John a gag. "OK…no problem, but…."

Ahead of the projected schedule, Smith's First Nations head Postdoc knocked on the door. I

"Doctor Smith…Professor L Harvey?" he asked, as a subordinate. "Laurie?" he went on, as a colleague, and friend.

"So that's what the L stands for!" Erica grunted out to John. "Why didn't you tell me!"

"He asked me to promise to not tell anyone," John informed Erica. "In confidence. A promise is a promise. And, as we both know, sometimes the best way to keep a friendship is to NOT let the other person have full access to your vault of secrets…"

"---I lost my keys, after getting, yeah, indisposed, Sir, stoned, but not while on duty," the intruder, still outside the office, confessed, more in the manner of a military junior officer than a long-haired, never to be drafted or be subjected to a crew cut ardent Pacifist. "The Janitor let me into the lab. "But, given an offer, I got from my girlfriend's Nashville Music producer stepdad. And she said that I should take care of my mental and physical health before it's too late. I just wanted and needed to give you this."

The intruder, who John recalled was the Post-Doc Smith had assigned the task of finding faults in his competitor's research paper so it would be denied publication, enabling Smith to repeat the study so he could get to press first, pushed a letter under the door. After hearing his footsteps go out of the lab and into the hallway, John put it under his flashlight. "His resignation," John noted, reading it. "'Taking a year off. Need to experience life before going back to studying it.'" He reflected on the wisdom of such, recalling that he didn't have a girlfriend to pull him out of the lab before he became owned by one. "Good a reason as any to take a break from all of this," John noted.

"And with that, we're out of here," he heard Erica say. He turned his stare from his own past and the projected future of the thankfully rescued from dull-out disease and dehumanization that would have killed the PostDoc's soul and body. Then to Erica as she, with back turned to John, dealt with the abundance of vials and bottles in the safe. She examined the powders and fluids, transferring portions to vials in her backpack. Then she placed the originals back into the vault, topping the fluid materials with water, and the vials with powder with appropriately colored sand from her backpack. "We gotta go! Now!"

"Or maybe a little later?" John said as he noted his camera phone saying 'hello', inviting him to take pictures. "I'll make it quick," he said as he moved with alacrity, photographing the key pages in the research papers, stock reports, and maps.

"Make it quicker!" Erica screamed out, out of arrogance then fear. "Come on…Come on…Come.."

In mid picture snapping, Erica pushed John down onto the floor and shut the lights again. "Someone else is coming," she whispered to him, her body closely next to his. Such awakened his heart as well as perking up his reproductive machinery. "And….well"

John and Erica both got the same idea, about the world as it was rather than the one they imagined as possible in their most hopeful dreams. John put on Smith's fedora and lab coat. Thinking with the same thankfully fast-moving third brain between them. Erica slapped the 'Negotiating with God, so fuck off mortal.' sign Smith on John's back, motioning for him to sit at the desk, in front of a laptop with the post-dated research reports beside him.

Another intruder entered the office, having opened the door with a credit card, then flicked on the lights. He was young, eager, and ominously familiar. "Hey Doc!" Dakota Stone said as he waltzed-boggied into the room, to the arythmic tune coming through his earbuds. "Your door was open, and I finished downloading those video games you wanted," he said showing off a hard drive to John's back, ignoring of course the 'Fuck off, am negotiating with God' sign on it. "I uploaded those fake AI videos of your competitors having the conversations you wanted me to 'record' talking about how they fabricated their dats so they would be tossed out of science and medicine. And so you could get more grant money and that Nobel prize which….well we will share…Right? And if you have other ideas, remember that I can still make videos of you doing anything I want you to do or say. They aren't in any Best Buy or Staples store, yet…that is…But, we're state-beyond-the-art partners, Right?"

John endured Dakota's continued boasting about the complexities of computer technology while taking more mental notes and projections about the research reports Smith was going to save the world from MID, the part worth saving anyway, on HIS timetable. Meanwhile, Dakota glanced at the papers still lingering on Smith's desk, focusing on the most important aspects of those articles.

"Hey! Impressive shit!" Dakota exclaimed as he thumbed through the post-dated articles to be published regarding discovering the cause, treatment, and prevention of MID, in that order. "With my name on it! And when all I did was put your data into my statistical computer programs, which didn't make sense to me, through my software programs to do bitching graphics. And that data says, wow…"

Erica pushed a mirror into John's view, allowing him a full view of Dakota Stone's confused and confounded face as he thumbed through the article that had his name on it for credit, as well as responsibility, for its content. "But, hey!" the Millennial 'genius' said. "A publication is a publication."

With that, Dakota took his leave of Smith's office and the work that was being done from it. Erica and John emerged from their hiding places, the former dealing with bottles and vials. The latter took pictures with his camera and mind of Smith's research reports and stock value predictions. Neither finished their self-assigned tasks, and the session was called to an end by the trumpets between their ears and a fire alarm somewhere down the hallway.

Erica and John, clad in lab coats from Smith's lab and whatever hats they could grab, walked as fast as they could without breaking into a run-down hallway. They were joined by the janitors, glassware washers as well as an assortment of post-docs and grad students hiding out from their girlfriends, boyfriends, or spouses by taking work on the night shift.

Erica and John's backpacks and pockets were all filled the the brim, John was still not completely clear as to what they contained. But he trusted, for real this time, that Erica had gathered what they would need by way of biological samples. He spotted two military men around the corner through a mirror, strolling towards him slowly and deliberately. He pulled Erica in towards him, enclosing her into a hug, which evolved into a passionate kiss that he forced on her, hiding her face and his. Wentworth and Tompson, both in military uniforms, halted in front of them. Tompson extended his long arm to grab John by the shoulder. Erica reached for her hidden revolver.

"People," Tompson said in the same tone as a high school vice principal who actively enjoyed being burdened with that task by his superiors. "This is a place of scientific inquiry, not Recreational romance. Some professionalism here!"

Before the Administrator whose job it was to put rebellious geniuses in their place was, with one shot from Erica's silencer-containing piston, assigned a permanent office in the morgue, Major Doctor Wentworth placed his fatherly and kind hand on Tompson's tense shoulder.

"No, Captain," Wentworth said to Tompson. "And you two," he said to John and Erica, their backs turned to him. "Carry on with your inter-relational discourse. And that's an order!"

Erica and John hugged each other even closer, for keeps this time. "This, Captain Tompson, is how new scientists are produced," Wentworth reminded his enraged subordinate. "White scientists that is," he continued. "And romance is a healthy thing, love between a man and woman that is. Isn't it?"

"Yes Sir, it is," Tompson acknowledged. By his tone, John was not sure if his reluctance to agree was about the White part. The human love over scientific logic part. Or the man and woman part. But whatever it was, the duo who seemed to be doing their inspections of the facility moved on to others displaying inappropriate behavior or harboring wrong agendas.

John and Erica worked their way out of the building, heading in the opposite direction, finally figuring out the best exit door to use. Upon leaving the labyrinth of hallways which were built like a maze intended to trap rats into running around in circles, much like the roads in small Upstate New York towns where people who were born there never leave, and visitors, even Indians, lose orientation of the Four Directions, they stood on a darkened sidewalk. "So, are you sure this is where we parked?" John asked Erica.

"Yeah, it is," Erica admitted, unable to hide the anger at herself for the parking spot she had chosen. One that was reserved for Faculty Members. Which she wasn't anymore. "And I don't know anyone anymore in this town who can fix a parking ticket," she continued, as one large Meter Menches, armed with a submachine gun, ticketed her five-and-a-half cylinder just mobile. His subordinate, having picked the easily opened lock on the driver's side, threw the contents of such out onto the concrete. His boss called in the plates to Headquarters.

"So, we need to get ourselves a cab," Erica said, after which she led John through a series of shadows cast by lampposts to an even more exclusive parking lot. To a car with tires that had trodden, paint on the fenders rather than rust, and a license plate that was a military issue, USMC666. After texting someone on the phone whose identity she didn't share with John, she hotwired the vehicle. The engine was quiet. The exit away from the Klassen went undetected.

Erica gave John her phone, requesting that he call the number the 'Honest Injun' Banuk baker had patched a line to during the encounter with him at the shop just before his exit from life stage left and right, due to ingesting too much of his own carcinogenic containing 'goodies'.

"And that area code here is…" John inquired.

"928," Erica said.

The machine at the other end proudly announced with a painfully authentic Arkansauce accent, "You've reached the Happy Emporer's Emporium. Featuring the latest in All-American tattoos. The newest brand of cannabis. And the best tasting barely legal moonshine this side of Hazard Country"

"Three things no Apache, or any other Indian I know, here anyway, want or need," Erica replied as the vehicle's wheels found their way to the backroads and then to the interstate. They were followed by an Eagle above them illuminated by the moonlight and two vehicles behind her. A quick turn to the left into an unlabeled and barely visible logging road freed them from the pursuers. "Try 202 Area code for Washington DC," she commanded John… "A hunch from Three Days of the Condor. And since art imitated life back then, and life imitates art in THIS century, and…"

Before Erica could go into another rant, or intentionally incomplete 'half-truth', John's ears and Erica's beheld a voice on the speaker saying 'Central Intelligence Agency. If you know your extension, please…"

Erica grabbed hold of the phone, tossing it down into a deep ravine. It landed in a fast-running river where no wreck would ever be found. And no one would look for one. So she and John hoped anyway. She took in a deep breath and then proceeded onward. "So, have you read or written any good books lately?" she asked John. "Besides the one you're living and writing now of course."

XXVII

The black car with the license plate USMC666 proceeded Northeastward, at rapid speed. With each turn, it was followed by another vehicle manned by drivers who knew enough to not tailgate. Any bird above it was replaced by one helicopter, then two, then three. One of them landed in front of the car, joining an armada of blue and white Cops cars, and green US Army vehicles. Along with a very large military ambulance bearing, ironically, a red cross which was supposed to confer a non-combat agenda.

With no escape forward, backward, or to the side, the car carrying the heroes and goods that would save the world if get to the right hands or destroy it if into the wrong paws screeched to a halt. Leading the way to the vehicle were none other than Captain Tompson and Major Doctor Wentworth. Behind them, men pointed assault weapons that even psycho serial killers and wacko preppers with friends working for the NRA didn't have access to. On top of their heads were badges containing stetsons, MAGA baseball caps, and bioprotection suites with visors that hid their faces.

"Get out of the car, slowly!" Tompson commanded as he approached with two hands on his pistol, as scared as he was empowered. "Pervert Commie Terrorist Pagan bastards who...."

"Are people," Wentworth reminded Tompson, placing his hand over the barrel of the Captain-Dean's revolver. "Who do we want and need to talk with," he yelled out with reason, control, and, perhaps because of such, practical cooperative compassion. "We are on the same side, Doctor Baldino. And Professor Linquist."

Wentworth's welcoming smile was turned into an angry frown when he saw a third finger extended out of the driver's and passenger's window. His restrained rage burst open when the driver turned on the engine, then floored the accelerator to make a getaway through the bush. Wentworth pulled out his own pistol, shooting holes into all four tires and then into the radiator, bringing the car to a screeching halt. Tompson's gun flung bullets into the windshield. Before they could find their way into the humans behind it, Wentworth grabbed hold of the Captain's revolver. "I said, CAPTAIN, and we hope not Seargent Tompson, we and I need them ALIVE!" he commanded. "And that goes for all of you too!" the Major-Doctor yelled back to the military and police muscle he brought to the late-night party. "We will proceed cautiously and courteously to the enemy!" he asserted, after which he and Thomson walked towards the car. The doors opened up just as they approached. "Hands up, on top of the car! Face down on the vehicle!" He commanded.

The order was obeyed. Wentworth grabbed hold of the driver. "So, Doctor Baldino. It's time we…"

"So, Major and maybe, accordin' ta some folks anyway, Doctor Wentworth," Jake Cuthand said. "I finally get to see yer face. And…" he continued, running his fingers through his recently trimmed Baldino-length hair, then down his artificially lightened face. "Didn't know it was a felony for a Red Man ta do white face….Or get a haircut without permission."

Tompson pulled the hastily and legally dismissed Doctor Linquist around to his angry eyes. He was shocked to see that she had changed genders. "And you, you pervert!" he yelled at the male Indian who had donned a blonde wig with lipstick on his face rather than warpaint. "You are in deep shit!"

"Fer not shavin' before going out for the night as one of the girls?" the Eagle Clan member said as he stroked his upper lip and chin. It had been sprouting hair since he was 12 due to 'some White Nigger in the woodpile' three generations ago. "Suppose so."

The two Indians laughed with unbridled relief as the Cops, soldiers, and assistant docs went through the coolers and backpacks in the stolen vehicle with the re-painted license plate. They found Barbie dolls with Trump heads on them. Along with mini-statutes of General Custer with a lobotomy scar on his forehead, and a dumb look on his face.

XXVIII

The bright light of dawn felt hard and cold when it penetrated through the window of the plane.   It nearly blinded John, sitting in the 'expensive seats' next to Erica, obtained by another one of her scams. Or most probably (the way her face looked when she purchased the tickets) the last four-figure purchase she could make on her remaining credit card as 'Caroline Linquist'.

"Welcome to New York, where the time is 6 AM and the temperature is already a balmy 78 degrees," 'Captain Joe' announced to his impatient and road-weary passengers as the plane meandered its way to the gate. "Sorry, Climate change, folks."

"Including the gap between the lazy rich and struggling poor," John said to Erica. And to the 'appropriately dressed' passengers in Business Class as they, yet again. They upturned their snobby noses at the 'aged hippies' who were mistaken onto their way to the plane as homeless, jobless, and professionally useless off-White 'outliers'. "Don't be scared," John said to his fellow passenger. "We are nothin' but struggling and Passion rich poor."

"We're economically challenged and broke," Erica reminded John, as well as the rich in the pocket but most probably poor in self-taught talent passengers around them. "Poor is a state of mind, broke is a state of,…temporary economics…" she reminded everyone around her.

The plane came to a stop. Finally. The pilot requested everyone to stay in their seats till 'the ground crew and special offloading staff are prepared for us.' A delay and wording that John had never heard before.

The flight attendant who served Selena with such grace and respect barely two weeks ago eyed John with suspicion and condescension. But with some flirtatiousness in the mix. "Sir…You look very familiar," she said emanating gaydar to whoever had an antenna tuned in to that signal…

"They all do," Erica interjected, grabbing hold of John's bent elbow, with a tighter grip than any 'he's mine and not yours' date he could remember. The Attendant's attention shifted from whatever was or wasn't between John's legs to Erica. She stood up to retrieve the many carry-ons she was somehow able to sneak on board.

"M'am…The next time you travel, you'll have to check those bags," the 25 thousand dollar-a-year flight attendant shot down to Erica as if she was a welfare passenger who should have been boarded in coach.

"If this trip works, there won't be any next time…or times," Erica replied as she retrieved all of the toxins, drugs, vaccines, and research paper-packed backpacks from the overhead bins, with John's help. As for who he belonged to, and what he was doing, John gave the Attendant a 'hey, just like you, I gotta obey what the boss says' shrug of the shoulders.

The exit door finally opened. Erica exited the plane. As did John, but not before looking back at the rest of the customers rushing to get their belongings and scurrying off to their appointed rounds with maximal speed, intensity, and a sense of frenetic urgency. One of the few things that didn't change in New York since it became a city for the comfortably rich, and was maintained by the hard-working poor. The former were still mostly white, and the latter for the most part had darker and more interesting skin colors.

But there was one grey area that John had to inquire about. "Tell me again why we're visiting Smith," he asked Erica.

"Because Selena said that there was still part of him that wanted to do the right rather than the profitable thing," Erica replied from the sides of her mouth while the sound of airport passengers and departure announcements competed for attention in John's still plugged-up ears.

John didn't recall consciously saying that, but he seemed to recall that Selena, or perhaps Maria, had planted that suggestion in his head. One that he now had to keep focused on the world outside of it, and inside of such.

The Yale Club was always a place where John Baldino listened to tall tales about hookers and mistresses with his Ivy League colleagues, discourses about potential medical miracles with heads of Pharmaceutical Companies or biomedical breakthroughs that governments would use to topple economic prosperity as well as compromise the health of other countries in the cause of 'national defense'. Most of the intel, information, and insights obtained by him over the decades were obtained after the other party was sufficiently inebriated on the best booze the exclusive club could provide. Or, on certain occasions, the aide of experimental truth serums Baldino had concocted in his non-glamorous laboratory in 'second class' (relative to Manhattan anyway) upstate New York.

Though John's Ph.D. was from the New Jersey School of Medicine and Dentistry in Newark, and his M.D. from Albert Einstein Medical School in the Bronx, he was always welcomed in the Yale Club. Erica wasn't. Maybe because she was an independent woman who called power-bitch Hillary Clinton feminists on their bullshit as much as she did to chauvinist men. Or maybe it was because she insisted on wearing jeans, a 'commoner' piece of clothing that was disallowed in that prestigious institution.

But, in the City that boasted itself as one that never sleeps, and closed all of the public transit stations between 1 AM and 5 AM to ANYONE, portraits of men smart enough to not be presidents, such as Benjamen Franklin, were still the golden passport. Such was slipped to the sternly faced 'greeters' at the Yale Club by Erica with her hand. More effective was the wiggle of her 'we'll talk later' ass. Convincing the underpaid (and mostly non-White) consigliere, doormen, clerks, and elevator operators to put aside the rules about who got past the lobby. John spoke to them with respect. He listened to their real-world problems with real empathy, recognizing their unique brand of intelligence. Such was instrumental in finding out L. Harvey Smith's room number and the fastest route to it.

John and Erica finally got to the right narrow, red-carpeted hallway to Smith's room, carting coolers and backpacks they claimed were refreshments and birthday presents and badly needed medicine Smith had forgotten to bring with him. No amount of greasing of palms, promises of pleasure, or blackmail could open the door.

It was one of the rooms where an electronic key was required for entry. Erica pulled out the master key she had stolen from a Janitor, relating to John who thought the probably illegal Latino immigrant would lose her job for losing the master key. But, such was unavoidable collateral damage, to Erica anyway.

Upon opening the door, John and Erica encountered L Harvey Smith in a white robe, with his back turned to them, the sign on it reading 'investigating other perspectives'. Keeping the man's man eye captive and blasting into John and Erica's ears was Martin Scorce's Last Temptation of Christ on the big TV screen, featuring William DeFoe in the lead.

"I thought you said he was an atheist," Erica whispered to John.

"I did also…but we all have our secrets, I suppose," John replied. "And as to what we believe in…Maybe we never know until "

"---the last breath, fart, or self-induced bloodletting?" Erica said, pointing to Smith's left hand on the side of the lounge chair. A pool of blood covered his hand as well as all but a few letters on the latest edition of Trans magazine, featuring Kaitlin Jenner as the latest spokesperson for changing genders. Upon circling the motionless Smith, Erica's cautious frown turned into a playful smirk. "He looks better than Jenner does, or you probably did. A Halloween exploration into wanting to be Mary Magdalene, married to Jesus?"

"Smith did say, after getting drunk on two bottles of Manischewitz Sabbath blessed wine spiked with some LSD by an angry Israeli ex-girlfriend, that he wanted to one day spawn children who would change the world, and bring God and man together in a final agreement that worked for heaven and earth," John recalled as he beheld a motionless, pale-skinned Smith in a vintage sexy Nurse's outfit that would awaken any brain damaged patient from a coma. "And as for dying with his boots on, like his hero George Armstrong Custer, I never thought that footwear would feature 4-inch stiletto heels," he continued, looking at Smith's dangling and blood-soaked feet.

"Neither did we," came a voice from a man in a grey business suit featuring a clergyman's collar with a cross on one lapel and an American flag on the other as he emerged from the bedroom. "Doctor but never Professor Smith, came down with a nasty outbreak of conscience. Greed. Stupidity…or maybe all of the above," Pastor Professor Renkin said, from the trigger side of a revolver pointed at John and Erica.

"Why?" Erica inquired regarding the entire situation.

"To why L. Harvey Smith committed suicide? Like you will?" Renkin volleyed back with a calm demeanor and the most cordial of smiles. "After you push those coolers and backpacks you brought in towards me, please."

John and Erica looked at each other, had a silent conversation about everything they never talked about, then, in conclusion, with the advice of the third brain between them (which some called Spirit) picked up the coolers and backpacks, they stepped back two steps. After shaking their heads in a unanimous three-way vote, the duo looked straight at and into Jenkin's mind, and if he had one, soul.

"NOW GODDAMN YOU DELUDED BLEEDING HEART KEFFER LOVING MOTHER FUCKERS!" Renkin yelled back with a Capetown Afrikaner accent. He made his point known by a round of bullets that broke the handles on the coolers and straps on the backpacks, making them fall to the ground. Aiming at John's head, while looking at Erica, Renkin reached behind him and threw them two large sacs and a metal suitcase. "What's in those Walmart carrying cases you brought her, goes into these!" he commanded. "Please," the appended.

"So," Erica said while complying with the request, and realizing that it wasn't time for John to die yet. " Is there a special Nobel Prize for starting a disease that selectively targets colored or uncooperative populations?"

"Having a cure on hand just in time to save who you want to save, and giving vaccines to friends, family, and fellow countrymen," John added, assisting Erica in the request, sensing that if there wasn't an ace up her sleeve, there was an abundance of them in her cleavage, up her ass or in the face only women had.

"While making a killing on the stock market at just the right time, selling cures and vaccines, with..." Erica noted, looking at the label on the sac.

"….Manheim Pharmaceuticals?" John said, thinking and saying the same thing. "Who made a killing in the American Pharmaceutical market in 1946 with the help of the files from groundbreaking biomedical research studied from Concentrations Camps in Europe and China using inferior races as involuntary 'volunteer subjects'."

"Whose names you forgot of course to put on as authors or the acknowledgment sections of the research publications because…well, there were just too many of them," Erica put forth. "Or because their ethnic names were too hard to spell?"

Pastor-Professor Renkin took in a deep breath, recalling good days from the past and re-dedicating himself to the agenda for his Mission in the present. "Someone has to rid the world of its diseased…inferior and undesirable elements," he finally said by way of explanation to the dumb students or predestined for meat prey.   "As members of the intrinsically superior white race, you do understand."

"No, I, we…DON'T!" John blasted back, fueled with primal rage that had, up till this time in his life, been aimed at himself.   He threw down the sacs and suitcases, folding his arms in defiance. Erica did the same. Renkin answered with two bullets shot into John's leg. To John's amazement, he felt the sensation of the bullets as a primal pleasure, somehow.

"Can't kill a ghost," Erica noted with a snide smirk to a confounded Jenkins.

Renkin took two big steps toward John, then licked him in the leg, knocking out metal pads Erica had insisted as being part of his long underwear for a trip to hell when it froze over. Renkin fired again, this time causing John's leg to hurt, and bleed.

"Werk machen Sie Freiheit," Jenkins proclaimed with a German accent, pointing John's attention to the loading process. "That means…"

"Work makes you free," Erica said as she whipped off her scarf, using it to wrap John's wounds.   "Over that holiday camp, Manheim Pharmaceuticals got its first scientists from…Auschwitz was it?"

"Buchenwald," Renkin boasted. "And my father made something of Manheim Pharmaceuticals!   Created jobs for many Americans! Christian Americans and even some Jews. With miraculous medical marvels that saved many American soldiers in Korea and Vietnam. Who was fighting the Communist Cancer? My grandfather after he left Germany became a model American!"

"Like Werner von Brown," John pointed out. "Inventor of the V-2 rockets that bombed London did for NASA after he was made an American citizen."

"Hey…John!" Erica offered. "Pastor Professor Renkin does have a point here. With what's in these coolers and backpacks we brought, and the ones he has stored someplace 'safe' (material) he can make America pure, secure, moral, Christian, and….White."

"Along with the rest of the world," Renkin added. "Africa is a tribal mess.

That has to be managed. Just Like South America, India, and the most godless demons on earth, the Chinese."

"Ah yes, Erica," John proclaimed with a cordial tone. "I can't tell you how many made-in-China syringes I used in the clinic that had defective needles on them. Made by slave labor in Bejing," He then turned to the Pastor Professor who was not on his or Erica's original list of suspects, thinking that maybe it was on the Eagle's. "But I bet when you sell the vaccines and cures for Mad Indian Disease to the 'good' Chinese, it will teach them how to be loving and obedient Christians."

"Indeed," Erica exclaimed. "Yeah….Like Herr Professor Renkin's' friends and family…who well….if any cases of Mad Indian Disease, happen overseas, will find themselves so sick with the worse variant of MID that not even Jesus can save them. Since these antidotes and vaccines in these samples, we stole, and what was left in Smith's storehouse, and other places that even the too good to be maximally effective Doctor Baldino here doesn't know about, are as effective in curing and preventing MID as the last place New York Giants defensive line is effective in preventing a sac from the first place in their division Philadelphia Eagles."

"Or the third-place Dallas Cowboys," John added, playing along with Erica's game and, most probably, his own.

"Huh?" the learned always finding the right words to say at the pulpit or the lectern Professor Pastor let spew out of his dropped jaw.

"We sort of did a switcheroo with the samples from Smith's lab," Erica pointed out. She began walking circles around an even paler-faced Renkin whose legs froze into position as if nailed to a shaking floor. "And I found his supplier, made a special order of my own for the carcinogenic toxin. That was specially mailed to our friends who…"

With his oversized bearlike hands, Renkin grabbed hold of Erica's thin throat with his left hand, while holding his gun on John with his right.

"What friends!   What friends?   You bitch...!" Transposing his words into action, Renkin rammed Erica's head into the wall with a thud loud enough to break her thick skull and the wall.   All the while he kept his eyes and the business end of his pistol on John. Who knocked the gun out of Renkin's hand, and then gave him an undercut in the belly, causing him to fall to the floor.

The fistfight was fiercer than anything John had witnessed or Renkin had ever participated in. After doing severe damage to most of their vital organs, they both lay on the floor, out of breath with their faces and hands coated with each other's blood, and their own.

Meanwhile, Erica gathered the material she came with, as well as two 'Christmas sacs' from the bedroom that 'Santa Manhiem' was slated to deliver to good boys and girls and bad ones, which category they fit into depending on their political affiliations and ethnicity.

Just as both men were about to come out of their corners for a final round in the rink, Erica blew a whistle. She then fired Renkin's pistol within two inches of his crotch, then John's. "While I'd love to stick around and see two boys fight over Lille ol me," she said to both of them in a Dixie accent... "I...and we....have to go," she continued, looking at John.

Erica helped John up, then extended her not-shooting hand to Renkin. The Professor who was never heard to use any expletives gave her the finger. She shot it off, causing him extreme pain, voicing four-letter words that even George Carlin never used in his prime. John, out of pity or a healer's reflex, pulled off the bandana from his aching neck and wrapped it around the bleeding stump.   Erica placed his revolver under her belt, covering it with her coat.

"And...eh...Professor Renkin, or whatever your real name is," she said, after which she slapped him in the face, silencing his foul mouth and toxically pleasant tongue. "If one chink, spear chucker, redskin, or raghead gets even a mild case of Mad Indian Disease overseas, your son Klause, daughter Teresa and soon-to-be daughter Taylor gets a case of it that no one can cure."

"You wouldn't!" Renkin blasted back through gritted, bloody, and a few missing teeth.

"You'll do anything to serve, please, and save your family. Me and Doctor John here…" she shot back with as much compassion and sincerity as unbridled rage. "Will do a whole lot more for ours. That family being…anyone who's not yours. Selective compassion to the two hundredth power in the interest of humanity, right Doctor Baldino?"

"Yeah," John replied, putting aside his dedication to Universal Compassion for more practical considerations. Erica gave him two of the sacs and one of the coolers, pretending they were too heavy for a member of the 'fairer sex' to carry. Upon lifting them up with his hands, John surmised that they were.

"Doctor Baldino…John," Renkin pleaded "You walk out that door with her

and your life will be changed forever. And you'll be on everyone's shit list," his threat, and sincere warning.

John contemplated the matter. He stared into space, then through a narrow slit in the window through which a ray of sunshine penetrated into the room and his soul. "Life is…change," the more brains than balls scientist-physician and now, finally, superspy concluded. "And…a man is measured by the greatness of his enemies," he said looking downward at his one-time colleague, as well as the corpse of Smith, his once most trusted and liked friend. "Or how many people don't like him," he concluded, thinking about how his intense desire to serve humanity would displease most of the scientists he ever knew, or would know. Envisioning them all demoting him from Doctor to Mister, then Mister to Inmate.

"And if something happens to us," Erica added, bringing John forward to his new role in the world. "Something worse will happen to your family, Klause, Teresa, and Taylor."

"And you," John said, in the event that one of Renkin's other secrets was that he harbored as much indifference, or hatred, to his own biological family as the families of those belonging to 'inferior' races and dedicated to 'defective' ideologies.

With that John and Erica left the room, carting with them all of Santa Renkin's et al Christmas 'gifts', closing it behind them.

"We'll find you!" Renkin yelled out while stumbling to the door, and then opening it. While Erica and John calmly made their way to the elevator, he appended. "I'll find and vanquish you, your friends, and your families!"

"Too much Hoboken Halloween Koolaid mixed with Patterson peyote," Erica commented to a trio of innocent-looking and curious academics with "Annual Manhattan Psychiatric Meeting' name tags on their sports jackets emerging from the elevator who witnessed Renkin's rant.

"Hoboken and Patterson both being in New Jersey," John added, with the snobbery of a Manhattanite whose consciousness of the world goes as far West as the Hudson River.

It got a chuckle from the Dull Out Virus-infected shrinks who were licensed to contain creative madness but, apparently, had never enjoyed the experience of it.

Without further ado, John and Erica entered the elevator, the door to the microphone and camera lacking a private mobile chamber closing behind. Them. "You were bluffing about the if you throw a rock into my people's garden I'll toss an A-bomb into yours. Right?" John asked Erica.

She smiled, averting her eyes and thoughts, then pressed the bottom going down to the service entrance.

No one followed John and Erica as they carted the sacs and suitcases out of the lobby and onto the busy street, losing themselves in the crowd of NYC pedestrians. They were all walking at different speeds to avoid different demons and reach different destinies. The 'sojourn in the overpopulated concrete, hot dog and pretzel smelling wilderness' led them to the East Side of Central Park. John followed Erica, yet again, trusting her perhaps more than he should have. "So where to now?" he asked, finally halting in mid-step. "Not one more step, until you give me some explanations. Because…"

"Because you proved yourself worthy of knowing as much, or more than your Brother Vincent does? Or I do?...which you have." Erica answered.

"No," John replied, looking at and into her soul. It was Alive, hurting, scared and remorseful, all at once. "Because I love you."

"And I love you," she said. "Which is why I'll give you….this." Erica put down her bags, and kissed John, tenderly, on the lips. Saying with her touch and every Pacinian vibration/electric current fiber in her body that it was the truth. Her most important truth.

John felt the universe applauding the event, and not because a small crowd of tourists and hard-bitten New Yorkers clapped their hands, vicariously enjoying the kiss. Seeing them from the corner of his eye, John motioned for them to go away. As did Erica. They finally left the happy couple alone.

Upon seeing that no one was watching, Erica pulled away from John, then took her bags in hand, then the ones John had been carrying. "And now, it's time for you to go away, again, to disappear?" John said, recalling the moment near this very spot nearly three decades years ago when she became an officially dead scientist.

"For now," Erica replied. "I have to go, and you have to…get reacquainted with your family." She handed him a business card, containing no writing on it. "Put it under UV light, and you'll find your brother's whereabouts, and, maybe, your dead superspy parents. Both on THIS side of the dirt."

Such was what John always wanted from Erica, and demanded many times. But he wanted Erica more now. More than ever. This is why she smiled at him and said 'later' in German, Russian, French, and finally Apache. Then disappeared down into a subway station with a motherload of 'medications' that could save the world, or destroy it.

A crow landed on John's shoulder. "Yeah," he said to the bird, which screeched like an eagle to his inner and outer ears. "Yeah…I know…The greatest gift two loners give each other is the assurance that somewhere out there is another crazy sailor trying to cross the ocean in a rubber dingy," he said to the bird.

The avian companion cawed, looking at a vendor selling fresh hot pretzels. "Yeah, I know, we'll talk about it after lunch," he said as he walked over to the stand with the bird on his shoulder. "Unless you filled yourself up eating another Prometheus liver already last night?" he said regarding the Greek god who, being more human than his Olympian 'bosses', defied Zeus and gave humanity the gifts of fire and literacy, both of which were used for constructive and destructive purposes.

The crow said 'no' to John's inquiry about the defiant humanitarian whose punishment was to have his liver eaten by crows at night and grow back during the day, while tied to the ground with unbreakable chains.

"OK then," John said, walking towards the vendor, who upon closer examination, had a First Nations face. A kind one that he found himself trusting. "Lunch here for both of us, then a visit to my family who…well…will have to be ok with inter-species relationships," He continued, purchasing two pretzels. Smelling it and tasting it, of course before he gave one to the crow, now perched on his shoulder. "I have a feeling that this is the beginning of a beautiful…alliance," he said with a Bogartesce accent. "Tansi," he said to the part Apache, perhaps Mohawk or perhaps Commanche vendor.

"Later then," the reply, in Italian.

How and why the vendor addressed Baldino in his ancestral tongue…that would be determined in his next adventure, or Mission.

ABOUT THE AUTHOR

MJ Politis departed the womb in Hoboken, New Jersey, in 1951. To make good on what everyone who supported, taught and challenged him did, he obtained a Ph.D. in physiology in 1978 which was used to publish 46 research papers in medical journals in reconstructive neurology, toxicology and cancer treatment. He went on to obtain a veterinary degree to extend medical care to fur bearing souls in a wide variety of clinics and cultural settings across the US and Canada. In order to diagnose and cure numerous maladies of the human soul, he obtained an H.B.A.R.P. degree (human being, aspiring Renaissance person) as author of over 80 novels and novellas, as well as producer/director/writer on 27 comedo-dramatic films, which can be accessed through www.longriderpress.net. He has been owned by horses for the last 40 years, currently residing in Interior British Columbia, Canada as home base, regularly commuting to New York to maintain global perspective.